RUNNING FOREVER

C.A. SOLE

Helifish Books

Published in 2023 by Helifish Books

Copyright © 2023 CA Sole

ISBN: 978-0-9954809-8-8 (Paperback)
ISBN: 978-0-9954809-9-5 (ebook-ePub)
ISBN: 978-0-9161108-9-2 (PDF)

British Library Cataloguing in Publication Data
A CIP catalogue record for this book is available from the British Library

I am sincerely grateful to my wife and others who have provided invaluable input to make this a better book.

RUNNING FOREVER

1

SYBIL'S MURDER HAD an enormous impact on me. So much so that for seventy-five years I would scan the crowds for a likely culprit. Sometimes I even went out with the sole purpose of looking for men in the right age bracket. I'd follow them and watch them in cafés and bars, in hotel lobbies and lifts, on trains and, later in life, on planes, too.

I was ten, Sybil was in her early- to mid-twenties. I loved Sybil. She was good to me – better to me than my mum. It wasn't that Mum was nasty. On the contrary, she was really good, kind and as generous as it was possible to be in wartime. But Sybil was that little bit better.

Dad was incarcerated in a German prison camp for the last two years of the war, so Mum had to cope with me on her own, do her best at work, which I was told was important, and do everything she could to keep life as normal as possible. Naturally, she had ill-tempered moments, but Sybil was always cheery. Sybil gave me gifts, just little things, nothing important or expensive, just things like a slice of cake or a biscuit or a couple of sweets. Even then, I understood that it was the thought that counted. Mum, on the other hand, worked long hours and was often home late and too busy to cook niceties. She had to leave me to my own devices much of the time, whereas Sybil often had time for a chat.

Sybil treated me as an adult, equal in age and maturity to herself. To my mum I was a child, which of course I was, and I don't blame her now, but I did then, because Sybil was so much closer to me in my eyes. I think she saw me as a little brother as much as a friend, because she didn't seem to have many, in spite of all the visitors that knocked on her door. It was clear that she enjoyed my young company when I snuck out of our house to see her.

When it began, I knew she lived on the street, but I'd never had any contact with her. The first time we spoke was when I was being shoved around by two much bigger boys, White and another, who sneered that my dad was sitting out the war in a German hotel, not fighting like their fathers were.

'That's a lie. He fought and got captured. He's a prisoner of war.'

'Don't answer back, you little creep.' One of them shoved me. I fell on my bum. They stood over me, not actually kicking me, but nudging me with their feet, threatening.

Suddenly, from nowhere, the lady who lived opposite was there. '*Oy.* Leave him alone. What kind of cowards are you? Two to one, and bigger than him, too.'

'What's with you, Granny? It's just a bit of fun.'

Sybil slapped him across the ear. The smack echoed off the wall and must have left his head ringing. 'Beat it, you coward.' Then to me, 'You all right, love? I'll see you home.' Which she did, disappearing before Mum let me in.

Mum forbade me to see or even speak to Sybil. 'She's not our type of person, Andrew. You'll learn all sorts of awful things if you talk to her.'

'Like what?'

'Bad things that people like us don't do. You're too young to understand, but we don't mix with her sort. That's final.'

But it was too late when she laid down the law about Sybil; we were already good friends.

She lived across the road from us. I could see her front door from my bedroom window. It was brown, with a brass knocker, which she polished every week. If my window was open, the knocker's sharp rat-tat-tat would have me jumping across the room to see who was visiting my friend. What was interesting was matching the men to the way they knocked; whether a man walked with confident strides or short, hesitant steps; whether he looked around before turning to her door or apparently could not care less, or whether he walked past her door as if summoning the courage to go in. These signs let me predict whether he would rap with loud, bold strikes, or timidly, as if not wanting to draw attention to himself or have the neighbours see him. Today, I wonder whether the style of knocking was an indication of the way he behaved once inside.

Sybil worked at the ammunition factory, as did many women during the war. She worked a shift system, which allowed her to sometimes be at home during the day, and this was when I could visit her if I wasn't at school. My mum was usually dusting or cleaning or in the kitchen if she wasn't doing her bit for the war effort. I only found out later she worked in some intelligence unit in the manor about three miles away.

Mum being in the back of our house meant I could tell her I was going to play with friends and she wouldn't see me running to meet Sybil via my secret path. It wasn't secret at all, of course, but it was to me. It led from the lane behind Sybil's house to the road which ran between our homes. It was overgrown and covered in bushes, and I could disappear into it and not be found, I imagined.

I was sitting next to my pretty, fair-haired soul mate (yes, that's what she was, a soul mate) on her back steps looking out at her garden. Narrow, to match her two-up, two-down semi-detached house, it was surrounded by a low hedge. A short stretch of uncut grass and weeds led to a tiny, dilapidated shed with warped timbers and a broken window. The depressing nature of this view escaped me at that age. I didn't even compare it to our own garden which was many times the size; the lawn mowed, the borders sharp and the shed freshly painted with something my mum had got from work.

Sybil used a heavy perfume that had been on too long. I didn't have the experience then, but I guess it was cheap. It was certainly strong enough to smother the evidence of a day's work. We were both eating a cake Sybil had made. It wasn't very good, but it probably couldn't have been better given the food rationing in force. Cake was cake and not to be rejected. I was maudlin. I missed my dad and had these odd bouts of self-pity. On top of that, I'd twisted my ankle and it was sore.

'You miss him, don't you?' She put an arm round my shoulder and pulled me closer.

My mouth was full of cake. 'Mmm.'

'It'll be over soon, and he'll be home. You'll see. Do you want another slice? I haven't got anything else to give you, I'm afraid.'

'No thank you.'

'Take off your shoe and sock. I'll massage your ankle. We'll get the blood flowing into the muscle and it'll heal much quicker.'

I had just done that when there was a knock on the front door – a hard, impatient sound, probably from one of the bolder characters. I jumped. Sybil looked up and to her watch. 'Damn, I forgot. Quick, Andrew, take your shoe and go upstairs to my room. Hide under the bed until I tell you to come out. Don't make a sound, not a squeak. It might be a little while. *Quick, go.*'

I'd never been upstairs and had no idea which was the spare and which was her bedroom. The detail didn't come to mind then – only later when I relived what happened. To the left was a plum-coloured counterpane; a small dressing table with a hairbrush and some bottles and jars; a white painted wardrobe, a suitcase on top; net curtains and a worn rug on the floor. Was this where she meant? It had a herby smell, maybe lavender. I don't remember.

Uncertain and hoping not to let my friend down, my shoe in one hand, I tiptoed across the landing to the right. This room was spartan: a neatly made bed with no bedspread; no other furniture than a bedside table with nothing on it; the curtains closed, the room the darker for it; and bare floorboards.

The stairs creaked. No time to switch sides. I dived under the bed. Dust rose. A sneeze threatened. Somehow, I smothered it.

Voices on the landing. Small talk between strangers.

The valance over the bed left a three-inch gap to the floor, enough to see legs. I prayed they were going to the other room – in vain.

Sybil's high heels clicked across the floor. Squeaky rubber soles below grey trousers followed her, mud on the inside of his turn-ups.

Their feet were toe to toe for a moment.

'Put the cash on the table, dear.' Sybil's finger, with its blunt, unpolished nail levered off her shoes. Her skirt fell to a crumpled circle around her ankles. The seam on her right stocking wasn't straight. The man hadn't moved, his toes still pointed in her direction.

'Come on, dear,' she murmured. 'Let me help you.'

His trousers fell to the floor, white underpants followed. As if in a desperate hurry, his jacket and shirt were tossed a few steps away. His socks stayed on – charcoal with a vertical yellow stripe down the outside.

My breathing was louder than a locomotive venting steam. I raised my arm so my jersey covered my mouth. A piece of fluff settled in front of my eyes. A silent puff and it tumbled away.

Their feet were no longer in my vision. The bedsprings creaked above me. A short giggle from Sybil. I knew her giggles, and that one sounded false. A grunt from him. Confusing. What were they doing? The movement was first over my head then lower down, then one side, then the other, all over the place. It gave me no clue. The irregular, fumbling motions settled into a steady rhythm.

We boys had talked about sex at school – did the girls discuss it too? Stupid, uneducated talk with no idea what it was or how it worked. One kid said he'd seen his sister at it, and what happens is … We all laughed, some nervously. We made dirty, immature jokes with no clue whether what we described was even possible. We were ten years old or even younger, how would we know?

The man's efforts were audible – *ugh, ugh.* Sybil seemed to pick up on his grunts and cried out in time with the creaking of the bed. Was she in pain? How could I help her?

It didn't last long. The movement stopped and silence fell. Was my friend hurting?

'All right, dear?' So, Sybil herself must be, thank God.

The bed creaked, groaned, almost rocked. Violent motion – a struggle? What on earth?

A brief gasp, '*Mmmh.*'

Then a dulled repeat, '*Mmm-mmmh.*'

Feet pounded the mattress for a few seconds – *thump, thump, thump* – before slowing and finally stopping, leaving me with a massive question mark. And silence. A silence so deep he had to hear me breathing. A silence I would forever associate with death. Whatever had happened was something dreadful.

What could I do? Attack him with my little fists, with my shoe? Scream, shout for help? I had to do something. But I did nothing, and I've lived with the guilt ever since.

I bit into my jersey and tried to still my quivering. Eyes closed, but listening for some sound from Sybil. What had he done to my friend?

The man's feet landed on the floor six inches from my nose. His socks were still on but crumpled down, the yellow stripe twisted around. His right ankle had a large port-wine mark on the outside – kidney-shaped, with the oval side facing up. His hands reached down and pulled the socks straight, and the birthmark was hidden.

He took his time getting dressed. Took the steps to retrieve his shirt and put it on, doing up the buttons with no hurry. Well, I supposed that was what he was doing, because I couldn't see anything higher than his waist. His was the first adult penis I'd ever seen. It looked enormous to me, and later I wondered if mine would grow to that size. When he bent down to his trousers, his back was to me, his face hidden.

Was Sybil watching him? Why wasn't she dressing too? Why was she so quiet, so still? I couldn't answer these questions – but I knew.

Shoes on, the man stood and faced the bed, faced me. I almost lost control of my pee. But he turned and left. The stairs creaked and the front door slammed. I scrambled out and turned to Sybil. But for her stockings and suspenders she was naked. I'd never seen a woman totally nude before. Vague memories of my mother, her breasts, but nothing else. But I only thought about my friend being naked later. At that moment I just wanted to see her face, because something wasn't right. Why was it covered by a pillow?

I pulled the pillow down to cover her breasts. Why? I don't know, some inborn sense of modesty, perhaps. I didn't know what to do. I'd never seen a pulse taken or felt an artery for one. How could I know if she was all right? I took her limp hand. There was no response. How do you recognise an absence of life in the eyes if you've never seen a corpse before?

I cried. I darted out the back, across the unkempt lawn, past the derelict shed and onto the hidden path. I ran.

And I kept quiet, because I knew Mum was going through a bad patch with Dad a prisoner and good news so scarce. I didn't want to add to her troubles. She'd be upset and very cross with me for disobeying her.

DAYS PASSED AND nothing happened. I spent my time in my room staring across the road and harbouring my guilt – I should have done something to stop him. No matter how much I willed her to come to life and let me in for cake and a chat, nothing happened. Mum came home from work and tried her best to make us tasty meals. She listened to the radio hoping, I suppose, to hear of advances that would tell us Dad was coming home soon.

The police arrived two days later and broke into Sybil's house. I watched them from my window. How they knew about her, I never learned. When they knocked on our door, Mum was still at work. They asked me about Sybil, and I didn't lie, except to deny I'd seen her. I was really scared, lying to the police. Then Mum cycled in and they asked her the same questions. But she wasn't kind about Sybil, calling her a loose woman who didn't belong in the village, and a bad influence on me until she, Mum, had put a stop to it.

Whether the police continued their investigation elsewhere was a mystery. In any event they left the area and didn't quiz us anymore.

'Will the police come back, Mum? Will they find who killed her?'

'I don't know, darling. They do lots of things we don't see or hear about, and these days they've lots to attend to. I wouldn't worry about it. Women like her, leading the sort of life she did, attract the wrong sort. Their world is filled with drunks and robbers and generally nasty people.'

'But Sybil was different. She was nice, Mum, kind and friendly.'

'That's enough of that. If I'd let you see her, she would've drawn you into her criminal world. I don't want to hear another word about it – her.'

But I couldn't shut Sybil out of my thoughts. She had saved my reputation on another occasion. I was in the village shop. The place was crowded with plenty of kids jostling each other and larking about. White and his friend, along with a third boy and two girls, were there too. I was standing next to a box of boiled sweets and Liquorice Allsorts, counting out pennies from my pocket money. I was absorbed and never noticed what happened. I looked up to see the shopkeeper, a tubby little man called Mr Balls, old and normally friendly, pushing his way through the kids in my direction. Instead of his normal cheery expression, his face was flushed with a grim set to his mouth.

Close behind him was White, pointing. 'It was him.'

'Turn out your pockets, you.'

I didn't understand. 'Why?'

'Because I say so. You've been stealing. You were seen.'

'No I haven't.' But my hand came up full of boiled sweets. *What?* Then I saw that White was holding his hand to his mouth and trying not to laugh, and in the background his clan were giggling. A horrible feeling came to life in my stomach. Mr Balls thinks I'm a thief. What will Mum say? This isn't fair. I'm in trouble.

Mr Balls said, 'And your other pocket.'

That was empty, but he felt my shorts anyway. He grabbed me by the ear and pulled me to the door. Behind was hysterical laughter.

'Go home. I'll be round later to speak to your mother.'

Needless to say, Mum was furious with me, and ashamed. She couldn't believe I had done such a thing. I tried to explain that it wasn't true, that I had been set up, but Mr Balls's word was of greater import than mine, apparently.

Mr Balls left, saying he wouldn't go to the police this time, they had more important things to worry about, but if I did it again he wouldn't hesitate to take extreme action. 'We can't have young people getting away with shoplifting, they'll be hardened criminals next.'

Then Sybil knocked on the door. She had on a red coat and a green scarf. Her hair, normally down to its full length, was tied up in a bun as if she'd just come from work. A usually buoyant person, she had a ready smile for anyone; but now, for the first time in my experience, her face was grim. Mum answered the door. I wormed in beside her, worried that some further disaster was going to hit me, but gave Sybil a little smile, which she returned with a softening of features and a glimpse of teeth.

'Yes?' Mum was curt. Speaking to a prostitute was very uncomfortable for her.

'Mrs Duncan, I live opposite, so I know who you are and I know your lad – he's a good boy. I want to set the record straight. I were in the shop this afternoon, and I saw them boys what are always picking on your lad. There was lots of kids about, and with all the shoving around, he wouldn't have noticed, but the one bully put an 'andful of sweets in Andrew's pocket. The little sod then reported Andrew to the owner. Mr Balls then pulled your lad out of the shop by his ear. I told Mr Balls when he came back. I told him that it were the other boy, and he said all right. I don't know what he'll do about it, though.'

Mum nodded and said, 'Thank you for telling me.'

I thought at least she would ask Sybil in for a cup of tea, but the chasm between Mum and the likes of Sybil was too great. She would be different today, times have changed.

It was so unfair. Sybil was my best friend, and some killer had taken her from me. I swore I would look for him as long as I lived. On the train, perhaps: the man across the aisle with his trousers hitched up exposing his left ankle. Is his sock choice similar to the ones that had been inches from my nose while under the bed? The man changes legs, now right over left. That sock has fallen lower showing the bare white skin of his ankle – not him. In a restaurant, a man, suspicious in my eyes, is at the next table. I need to get lower to see. I drop my fork as an excuse to bend and study his exposed ankle – ridiculous, I know, but I was obsessed.

I would find him. I would see him hang. And, after they had abolished capital punishment in Britain, I renewed my vow. I would do it myself.

2

I WAS BORN in 1934. As I write this, on the twentieth of January 2020, I am eighty-six years old today.

Except that I'm not.

I'd better explain by way of an unforgettable experience. It was an experience that I've relived many, many times. With each recall another detail worms its way out of my subconscious and adds colour to my memory …

It's 1968. I am piloting an army helicopter over the mountainous and forested terrain of north Malaya. From the air the undulating green carpet stretches to the horizon. In a way, it's an illusion, for the ground itself is hidden far below what's visible. The trees reach sixty metres in height, desperate to outstretch each other, trying to grasp the sun. Their bushy tops form a dense canopy of foliage, below which is a freefall to solid earth.

Thailand is not far north of here. As a hangover from the Malayan Emergency, the army is engaged in an ongoing hunt for communist terrorists who hide in the jungle on both sides of the border. From their temporary and shifting camps they try to recruit from the indigenous population and harass the local authorities. British troops spy on them and engage them to disrupt their murderous activities.

On board the helicopter is a troop of four soldiers. Their commander sits up front, next to me. His mission is critical. Our destination is a tiny clearing, a helipad which we'll not be able to see in this dense jungle until we're almost over it. GPS has not been invented, so I have to navigate using time and distance and by reading my map. The commander too is monitoring the route on his map, making sure I stay on course and ready to bark a correction if necessary. To these men, detail is critical; mistakes cost lives.

'Contact,' the soldier snaps through the intercom.

'Got it,' I answer. I take the machine past the clearing and circle it once, looking for the best route in without hitting anything – it's very small. It's going to need a steep, almost vertical approach.

'What are you doing? We haven't got all day. The longer you stay up here, the less our chance of success.' The man glares, his eyes a cold grey. His microphone is loose, and he has to hold it up to his mouth.

'You have your job, and I have mine.' I turn away from him to look out my window and inspect the helipad, but I'm still talking. 'My responsibility is to get you safely on the ground. If I hit something, we'll crash and your mission will be stuffed. Better to waste thirty seconds making sure than to bugger it up.' Satisfied, I turned back and flicked a combative glance at the commander, before slowing for the final approach.

I have to concentrate, and now is not the time to argue. I should cut the man some slack. He's tense. He's going into action, he might be killed in the next two weeks before his team is extracted, and he's well aware of the dangers of this landing.

On the ground, the troops pile out and unload their kit: massive packs, weapons and a seemingly unlimited amount of ammunition – enough for at least two weeks patrol. The commander gives me a comradely nod of thanks and a thumbs-up. I return the gesture and apply power. The climb out is vertical and deliberately slow. Great care is needed. I have to watch the foliage through the upper windows. The rotor tries to suck branches into its orbit as if to self-destruct. Once clear of the canopy, I can breathe again and add more power to move forward. The engine roars.

Bang. A violent left yaw. The loud crack is smothered by a high-pitched screaming of components no longer functioning in harmony. The turbine winds down in a couple of seconds. A horn blares – low rotor speed. Warning lights flash on the panel. The aircraft drops.

The training kicks in. I stand the helicopter on its tail – put the tail into the trees first, they teach, it may cushion your fall. There is no other choice anyway – I'm too low over the treetops and too slow. The top of the canopy looms at me as the machine plunges into it, as if diving below the surface of a dark pool. Individual veins in a million leaves stand out in stark detail – funny how the mind registers minutiae sometimes. The rotor is still turning. It smashes into branches, twisting the machine this way and that. I am a rag doll. My helmet smacks into bits of the cabin that are not normally within reach. Then we, the machine and I, are through the canopy and falling clear, unhindered by vegetation. The aircraft tail hits the ground first and crumples, cushioning the impact. But I know nothing, feel nothing. I'm out cold.

The troop commander's face swims about in front of me. Sweat is beading on his forehead. He's doing something, but keeps glancing at me, checking on me. He's talking softly, his voice reassuring, but I can't take in what the man is saying. Pain creeps in, not suddenly, but little by little as my consciousness returns. With each short breath a knife twists in my chest.

Fire is the danger. My harness is released. The pressure on my torso subsides. The other men are there. Together they get me out of the wreck, carry me clear and lay me on the ground. I want to help, but can't. Two of them cut away my flying suit. Another man is talking on the radio, and snatches of transmission reach me between the sound of my own wheezing gasps: puncture, lung, bleeding heavily, helicopter *now*, doctor, plasma. The blood in my mouth tastes of iron. Something dribbles down my chin.

'You'll be all right, mate. There's another chopper coming, we'll have you out of here in a flash.' The troop commander was expelling air from a syringe. 'Something for the pain. Nighty, night. See you on the other side.'

JUMP FORWARD FIFTY-ONE years to October 2019.

My relationship with Detective Chief Inspector Payne was one of those odd situations where we both took an instant aversion to one another, and neither of us knew why. Like two dogs, lips curled, hackles raised, we circled each other purely because of some innate dislike and hoping our masters would call us off before blood flowed and pain followed.

Ever since Alex was so savagely murdered last August, the DCI had made it plain that even if he couldn't nail me for that murder, he didn't trust me and would find something to pin on me at some time in the future. I thought he was narrow-minded and undeserving of his rank.

A middle-aged man of medium height, balding, the remainder of his hair close cropped and with piercing blue eyes, he knocked on my door in mid-October. 'I'd like a word, Mr Duncan.'

Never drop good manners even if you're feeling grumpy after one too many beers the night before. 'By all means. Come in.'

His first steps were hesitant. 'Where's your dog?'

'He's in the garden. There's no need to worry, he won't go for you unless you attack me or I tell him to – which isn't likely. Coffee?'

DCI Payne looked up the stairs as if expecting to once again see Alex's corpse, her arm hanging over the top step, blood dripping off her fingers. He turned away and walked into the lounge. 'No. I'll come straight out with it. What were you doing on …' He fished his notebook from his pocket and flicked over the pages. '… July the ninth 1944? It was a Sunday.'

I managed to laugh, but the question shook me. Payne's stony face forced me to be serious. '*1944? Inspector*, I'm sorry, but that is a very stupid question. You know perfectly well that I wasn't even born until '85. How can you possibly ask that?'

'*Chief* Inspector,' he corrected me. 'Another team are investigating a number of cold cases and searched the data base for DNA matches. We have your DNA on file from the murder of Alexandra de Villiers in August. It is a perfect match to DNA taken from evidence gathered in 1944. What this says is that you were present in this woman's house at that time or close to it. To support this, your fingerprints were found to be a match to some found in several rooms in the building.'

'This is absolutely ridiculous. You can't seriously believe that I was there. If I was, I must have been a child, so the fingerprints will be useless. Plus, I'm pretty sure DNA wasn't even used until the '80s, was it?'

'1986 to be precise. But evidence gathered at the scene has been safely stored. A request from some powerful source to find the killer of several women around that time led the team to obtain DNA from this evidence. As for fingerprints, they stay the same throughout our lives, although the size will change, obviously.'

'You said, several women.'

'Yes, all prostitutes.'

I laughed again. 'First you implicate me in a murder forty years before I was born, then you imply that I, as a child, consorted with prostitutes. I'm beginning to see how a virgin birth might have happened.'

At that moment Lupus came in. He stood beside me and stared up at the DCI. Payne took a step back. He knew not to engage the dog's eyes to avoid being confrontational, so he tried to keep looking at me, but could not help glancing down at Lupus. Lupus stayed motionless, intent on the detective. It was amusing.

'This is no laughing matter, Mr Duncan.' Payne's face was a picture of frustration. He knew it was ridiculous, but he had a job to do and had to ask the questions. He probably took my seeing the funny side of the matter as me laughing at him personally. He took a deep breath. 'Look, I admit it seems impossible, but this is serious. DNA does not lie, so there's something going on, and people above my pay grade are going to have to find out what. It could change the way DNA is used in solving crimes, the guilty could be innocent and vice versa. Huge implications.'

I nodded.

'Two murders, and you're linked to both. Something's going on, and I intend to find out what. I'll be in touch. Don't go far.'

WHAT I HAD told the Chief Inspector about my date of birth was a lie. I was thirty-four in 1968 when I had my accident. It was the medical treatment and recovery afterwards that was responsible for my condition. I'm convinced of it. There is no other possible explanation for the impossible.

When my consciousness returned, I gradually became aware of more tangible things: my wrists were tied to the bed frame so I couldn't pull the endotracheal tube from my throat; clean sheets, white walls and machines that hummed and beeped. A figure in a white coat, a stethoscope round his neck and a clipboard in his hand filled my view.

He was cheery and spoke in terse sentences. 'You're a lucky fellow. Quick-thinking soldiers. Battle first aid. Another ten minutes and we couldn't have saved you. You almost died – exsanguination. Lost over four pints, old chap. You'll be weak as a kitten until you build it up again. You had internal injuries, broken ribs – one of them punctured your lung. We've got you intubated, but we should be able to take that tube out soon, now that you're conscious and breathing on your own. Good job you're fit. Don't try to talk. Best go back to sleep. See you later.'

I was thirty-four then and I'm thirty-four now, fifty-one years later. Of course, it was many of those years before I realised I wasn't ageing. Then it was time to think. Was it the massive blood transfusion? Was it the trauma itself – did the damage to my body change something within me? Or was I always programmed to stop ageing at thirty-four? So many questions, and more than a few impossible answers.

I was married to Saffron when I had that accident. Her support while I recovered was invaluable. Ten years later, she died of cancer. Through her pain she observed how I had not aged over that period. 'I'll be going soon, but something's different about you, Andrew. You'll not die of natural causes.'

Ten years ago I met Alexandra de Villiers, a woman who had not even been born when Saffron died. She thought I was thirty-four, because I told her I was, not my true seventy-six. Once again, I was utterly captivated.

Being forever young is not as advantageous as you might think. I have had to hide from society for a long time. Old friends, for example, have asked why I've not aged as they have. Doctors have commented, at which point I've switched to another. I have two false identities and multiple documents in different names. All because if the pharmaceutical giants get hold of me and find out why I don't age, and therefore cannot die in the natural course of events, they will develop treatments to be sold for enormous profits.

My view is that overpopulation is a root cause of the world's environmental problems and many of the issues that are detrimental to a civilised society. How I conduct my life is governed by two issues: my perennial lookout for Sybil's killer, and avoiding Big Pharma – my body must never be used to add to the earth's woes. I suppose most people would think I'm paranoid, and probably stupid. Fortunately they know nothing about it, and I could counter their argument by claiming, truthfully, that several eminent scientists and philosophers, both past and present, support my views on population.

In June 2019 I had the first open approach by one of the big pharmaceutical corporations for me to cooperate with them (I didn't know which one at the time, but Jakub Kowalski was their man). That was followed fairly soon afterwards by my battle with NiPetco, another giant. NiPetco actually abducted me and tried to gain my cooperation for medical experiments. I suspect a doctor who had known me for many years realised something was odd about me and sold his suspicions to at least two companies in the industry.

At the time, my Alex, a freelance reporter, was investigating a paedophile ring. Those perverts hired an assassin, and Alex was no more. As her partner, I was the police's prime suspect, not least because she had unwittingly given me a motive for killing her. I only found out after she died that she was extremely wealthy and, with no other relatives, had left her estate to me.

Fact: I have not aged since the accident. To the world, I'm thirty-four. I look it, I act it, I have the endurance of a thirty-four-year-old, and I'm as sharp as one, with the added benefit of eighty-five years of experience. To avoid drawing attention to my impossible condition, I currently claim to have been born in 1985, a claim that has to shift every few years.

DCI PAYNE'S VISIT was laughable, of course, but it was also worrying. Throughout my life so far, I'd managed to shut down any inquiry before investigators got too close to reality. But any probing into my past risked my true history being exposed. Surprisingly, though, the greatest effect of this new investigation was how it summoned memories of Sybil and how much she supported me.

I'd been moaning that Mum was sharp with me for no reason.

Sybil said, 'She don't mean to be like that, Andrew love. She's worried about you an' your future. She's unhappy 'cause your dad's a prisoner, and she works bloomin' hard in that big manor house up the road. Whatever they do there, it's top secret, and there'll be a weight on her shoulders. She works long hours and don't get the time off what I do. She's bound to get cross sometimes.' She shrugged. 'Me – me job's easy. Boring, working a machine to push bullets into casings all day – I do it 'cause it helps. I got regular shifts and no stress, so I can kick a ball with you and feed you cake easy. You need to get your mates to join us with the ball.'

'I don't have any mates that like to do that.'

Sybil had given me a long look and followed it with a hug. I loved Sybil, yet I hadn't defended her, I'd let her down.

But I needed to focus on the present. This fresh police activity needed attention. I slipped a harness on Lupus and we set off for the park as we often did at this time of day.

Lupus is a Malinois-cross failed police dog (he was said to be too friendly). Malinois are incredibly athletic and require a huge amount of exercise, and Lupus was no different. He was hard work, but a loyal friend and he'd saved me from crises several times. It looked like rain, but when you have a dog like Lupus, weather can never stop you from taking exercise.

The park was composed of two areas, separated by a line of trees and bushes. One part was simply grass, while the main feature of the other was a cricket field and clubhouse. Benches and tables outside this pavilion allowed spectators to watch and support the club bar in the shade of some large trees.

Other people out in the park at that time were a woman playing with a child, another with a tiny, excitable dog on a lead and a heavy-set man in a black coat leaning against a van on the road behind me. The smell of his cigarette wafted over to me from forty metres away. On one of the club benches was another man, with a pair of binoculars. He was staring up into the trees above him, presumably watching birds. Twitchers normally wear casual outdoor clothing in my experience. This one was dressed as if for a funeral, including shiny black shoes.

I was using a ball thrower for Lupus to make him run. After the umpteenth time looking down to gather up the ball, I raised my eyes and caught the binoculars switch from me back into the trees. The man behind me hadn't moved and must have lit another cigarette.

So, they're still at it.

KIRSTEN ANSWERED MY call on the third ring, the smile in her voice unmistakeable. '*Andrew*. This is nice.'

'Fancy a stroll with Lupus? I need to discuss something. We'll have a drink afterwards.'

'Where are you? Give me ten minutes to finish here.'

When DCI Payne tried to prove I murdered Alex back in August, Kirsten Pearman acted as my barrister. She refused to help me without knowing the truth, so I told her my true age. She took a fair bit of convincing, but came to believe me and understood why my condition had to be kept secret. If the police learned of Alex's investigation, they would learn about me, so we had to work on our own.

Along with a private detective, Mitch, we brought down a gang of paedophiles who were abusing young girls (one of those unsavoury individuals was a senior NiPetco executive). We found Alex's real killer and, with a little underhand threatening and a touch of black-mail, I managed to force NiPetco to give up their interest in me – I live in hope.

Kirsten would come from the adjoining field, so I moved in that direction and away from the man with the van. She appeared between the trees. Lupus saw her and raced over, knocking her flat and licking her face. Laughing, she struggled to her feet, wiped her cheek and came towards me. Lupus stuck close.

I turned around so we were heading back towards the pavilion. 'I'm going to have to leave for a while.'

'*No*. Why? Where?'

'See that man walking away from the clubhouse and towards that black van where another is smoking what must be his third cigarette since I've been here? Now I have company their plans will have to be scrapped, whatever they were.'

'What do you mean?'

'As before when NiPetco abducted me, I've had the feeling I'm being followed. The one walking was watching me through binoculars.'

'If they want to abduct you again, then why didn't they?'

'Lupus. They won't try while he's around, not with his reputation. I need to get out of sight. I've done it before using my Charlie Maxwell identity. There's always a job for me in Kenya on anti-poaching work, both flying and on foot.'

In single file with Kirsten leading, we took a footpath which led away from the park towards a farm. Away from the office, she had undone her 'barrister bun', as I called her work hairstyle. Its red cascade tumbled down her back, swinging unevenly to one side as she limped.

As a young girl, she'd once fought off her abusive stepfather and tumbled down the stairs, breaking one leg so badly that it was an inch shorter than the other. From being the mistrustful, remote and humourless woman she first appeared to be, Kirsten had become a really good friend who knew my impossible condition, believed me, and, I was sure, wanted more intimacy from our relationship than I could give her.

'Do you think it's NiPetco again?' she said over her shoulder.

'I can't rule them out, but it's more likely to be whoever Jakub Kowalski was working for. They, or another lot who know about me, aren't going to give up. I need to go and die somewhere to vanish from their radar.'

It began to drizzle, and Kirsten pulled the hood of her jacket over her head. 'Don't use language like that, Andrew. You're not going to die.'

I laughed. 'Figure of speech, but you never know. There's another reason I have to leave, though.'

We stopped to talk to two horses, one of which was chewing the wooden fence. I reached up to stroke its neck. It twisted round to nibble at my sleeve. 'Stop it, you.'

'I'm waiting.'

'Sorry. Exchanging thoughts with a horse keeps me sane.'

Kirsten rolled her eyes. I told her about Sybil's murder and of the police interest in the cold case. The horse had taken a fancy to the taste of my jacket. I offered it a handful of fresh grass instead. 'The problem lies in my name coming out in association with this. Imagine the headlines: *Unborn Man Accused of Murder*, subtitled: *Cold case DNA points to man as murderer before he was born*. NiPetco, or whoever, know my condition. They could force me to do what they want, or they'll explain to the police how I was alive back then and could well have been present at the killing. So, as soon as the police come to terms with the impossibility of my killing Sybil and give up questioning me, I shall leave.'

Kirsten nodded. 'You have no idea who the killer might have been?'

'If he was as old as thirty, he'd now be a hundred and five and should be dead. But he could have been as young as say, seventeen, in which case he'll be ninety-two and still with us.'

'I understand … I suppose it's best you go. Isn't there another way?'

Something in me wanted to allay her concern with closer contact, but I couldn't allow myself to even think of entering another relationship. There were a number of reasons not to get more deeply involved: it was only three months since Alex was hacked to death, and I had learned that when my partner aged and I didn't, matters could get very awkward. It wasn't fair to the woman, and I didn't want the pain of another loss. History has a way of repeating itself.

Kirsten brightened, though. 'I told you I would be your eyes and ears here in England if you need me. That promise still stands.'

'Thanks. There's only one thing I need you to do, if you will – look after my friend here.'

The drizzle turned to large drops. Lupus shook the water off his head. He was between us, enjoying a pet from both.

She laughed. 'That's the only good thing about your leaving. Lupus becomes mine, all mine.'

'On loan only. And it'll be a while before I can go. I need to renew Charlie Maxwell's passport and wait for the police to lose interest.'

3

AT ONE TIME I had three passports and three commercial pilot's licences. All so I could escape attention from those looking to learn why I was not ageing. There was my original and true identity, of course. Then there was that of Dan Peabody.

Dan was an American invention. I never knew for certain but he was probably brought to life by the Central Intelligence Agency in the guise of Air America. Soon after I'd left the army, I had a call from a man with a Southern States drawl. He offered me a salary beyond my dreams for clandestine flight operations in Southeast Asia. They wanted me and other nationalities precisely because we were not Americans, and we were to fly helicopters whose origins could not be traced. But that was decades ago, when I had been widowed and lacked some purpose in my life. Dan Peabody and his mercenary activities were just what I needed, a catharsis that would not bury my memories but put them in a different section of my mental library, available to be taken out and read when needed, but not sitting on the front desk dominating my thoughts on a daily basis.

But now, Dan's professionally produced passport had long since expired. Forty-plus years later, I would never be able to get that identity brought to life again, as any communication between the CIA and me was strictly one way, and Air America ceased operations in 1976. I had no clue how to contact them anyway.

So my favourite alter ego, Charlie Maxwell, would have to be brought to life again. Charlie's passport was out of date, but the shadowy little man who produced it was still forging out a livelihood in his cellar.

Charlie operated in Kenya. He first went there on contract to fly a helicopter on anti-poaching operations. Because he was an experienced soldier, he saw that improvements could be made as to how the rangers on the ground operated. With approval, he joined foot patrols and followed the trackers, gave enhanced firearms training and suggested changes, most of which increased the rangers' success in catching poachers. He became a trusted 'brother' in the group and was always welcome.

I contacted my Kenyan boss and told him I (Charlie) was available. With typical hyperbole, he said I was missed and should jump on the next plane. I wish it had been so simple. DCI Payne seemed determined to pin something on me and would not declare that I was no longer of interest. To avoid suspicion, I did not want to vanish until he had lost interest in me. To do so might invite a search for me, including border checks, thereby exposing my false identity.

Cyril, my forger, told me his business was booming and I would have to go to the back of the queue, which meant at least a two-week wait. Hopefully, Payne would have given up by then.

At least one pharmaceutical giant was getting closer, though. This weighed on me, because NiPetco had abducted me in August, when Alex was killed. To avoid a second attempt, I tried to conduct my life with some other person or Lupus beside me at all times. The dog's reputation alone was keeping me reasonably safe and was probably the reason why they had not tackled me while I was in my house and out of sight.

I was keen to leave and get rid of this threat, but with the police holding me back, as well as my wait for a passport, I was getting testy.

I had to deposit a foreign cheque. By closing so many of their small branches, the banks confined their activities to the main towns. Customers, especially those who did not work in the towns, had to take more time out of their day to do their banking. This meant I had to visit the branch in Newbury, which was inconvenient and didn't put me in the best of moods.

Newbury is a pretty town with plenty of old buildings and narrow alleyways off the main roads. Walking along some of them always makes me wonder what took place in them in previous centuries – so much history is embedded there. My bank was down an alley which is sided by the blank brick walls of tall buildings that shut out the sun. It leads off the main thoroughfare, which is restricted to traffic and so primarily carries pedestrians, although the odd vehicle navigates the crowd to deliver goods.

My cheque deposited, I walked out into the wide area in front of the bank. Two young girls were discussing an outfit in a shop window and giggling. A woman with a pushchair walked briskly past heading for the main street, her toddler wrapped in a red blanket and with an oversized red beanie on its head. Two men in black coats were looking in the window of the store opposite, apparently at female mannequins. One was a tall, heavy character, the other a shorter, lighter build – the same pair from the park. In the reflection, undistorted by the naked plastic torso behind, my eyes met theirs.

It was time to gain the cover of the crowds. Ahead of me in the alley less than a handful of people moved along, well wrapped against the chilly wind that funnelled its way between the walls, intent only on their destination.

The pace of meanderers who clog the pavements like refuse blocking a drain drives me nuts. It forces me to accelerate to get ahead of them all, even though I know that I'll never reach the end of them – for every one I pass, it seems two dawdle ahead. I also don't like being overtaken on foot, whether that's on a mountain, down a country lane or in a shopping mall. It's more a need to keep pushing myself ahead of others than a desire to beat this or that person.

With quick steps I made for the main street, overtaking the strollers. Heavy breaths laboured behind me, and hard shoes thumped the paving. That was the big one; I could outrun him. It was the quiet one with a lighter and more athletic gait who was the more sinister. To look back or to run was to surrender. How would they take me? Their choices were limited in a public place. A syringe of some sedative, perhaps? I lengthened my stride.

'Excuse, excuse.' His words echoed off the blank brickwork on either side. Not a British accent.

It was about thirty metres to the pedestrian way – thirty paces to the safety of sauntering shoppers.

'Excuse, sir. You drop cards.'

No I didn't. Twenty paces.

A hand plucked my sleeve. 'Please to stop, sir. Your money.'

No it isn't.

The woman with the pushchair was in the middle of the passage ahead of me, scolding her child. The red beanie decorated the cobbles two metres away. Three males charged down on her. Panicked, she shoved the chair to the side, but didn't make it. I went to the right. One goon followed, the other went left and almost knocked the pushchair over. The woman screamed some obscenity at him.

I was out on the main street. Many more people were about, and across the way were two black uniforms. It helps to have played rugby. I dodged through the throng of shoppers to the police. The goons stopped. Ten paces separated us.

'Officers.' I gave them my best grin. 'You chaps get so much blame and abuse these days. Few people seem to appreciate the good work you do and the courage so often required to do your job. I just want to say, thank you. I want you to know there are sensible members of the public out there who think you're doing a marvellous job in very difficult circumstances.'

Two previously grim expressions lightened up. One nodded, the other grinned. 'We do our best, sir.'

It was doubtful that the goons had heard what I said. They must have thought the worst, because I just caught a glimpse of two heads hurrying through the crowd.

They were safe, though, and there was no way I was going to draw attention to myself by encouraging questions from the police.

ANOTHER ALLEYWAY FURTHER down the main street led to the car park. There was no sign of the two goons; nevertheless I took an alternative, cheeky and crowded route through the front and out of the back entrance of a store to reach the parking area.

The car park was almost full. On the far side, at the exit was a ticket machine and a little cabin left over from days when a human sold you tickets. The big man was leaning against the booth. The smaller man was out of sight. My car, higher than most, stood out halfway down the row. I always reverse park so I can get out quickly and without any hassle.

Where was the little guy?

He wasn't crouched and hiding next to my car. He wasn't underneath it. While there, I knelt to look for any additions to the original construction: a tracking device or an explosive device. Nothing was obvious. Damp patches on my trouser knees were, though.

A click on the key fob released the door locks, but they immediately locked again. I tried again. The locks refused to stay open. Was this a fault or was someone messing around with my fob's signal? Thieves do this with a device that reads the frequency of the fob's transmission, and they can then steal the vehicle.

Someone in the car park was watching me unlock the doors and then immediately locking them. It must have been the little man, but where was he? I would have to use the manual key, but that might set off the alarm – too bad.

My phone rang. Not a known number.

'What?' I'd lost any desire for pleasantries at that moment.

'Andrew, you're not going to access your car until you've listened to what I have to say.' Something in the voice was familiar. The English was good, but a foreign accent was just discernible.

'What, Kowalski?'

Jakub Kowalski, the slick individual who had tried to get me to cooperate with his employer in June. He had failed but he didn't give up. In a distinctly amateurish fashion, he had followed me. I had been aware of a presence on a number of occasions, and it was most likely his.

'Andrew, I know you have been interviewed by the police about a cold case. The murder of a prostitute in 1944. Whilst the inspector accepts that you cannot have been there as you weren't yet born, you and I both know that's not true. Thanks to your unique condition, you do not age and were present at the scene when you were ten.'

'I haven't time to listen to your rubbish. Let me into my car.'

'I have a proposition for you. You agree to join our company investigation into how your condition is possible to see if we can replicate it. You will be a partner in the venture and will be substantially rewarded.'

'Kowalski, you don't give up, do you? I told you before, I'm not interested and will not participate. I will not provide you with samples or be experimented on. Now, let me open the car and leave me alone. Which company are you working for? After all this time invading my privacy, you should at least tell me who you represent.'

He ignored that. 'Andrew, it's quite simple really. Either you cooperate or we will go to the police and explain that certain aspects of your identity are false, your condition is real and that therefore the DNA they found is definitely yours. You could then be found guilty of murder.'

'At the age of ten? There are a number of reasons why your argument doesn't hold water, Jakub. I'm not going to get into them now, though, I have to go.' I opened the fob and pulled out the metal key. If I remembered correctly, there was only a fifteen second interval after opening the door to start the engine or the alarm would sound, drawing large amounts of attention. That would not be good.

As I passed through the exit, I gave the big goon a good natured wave. But the seriousness of Kowalski's threat immediately settled on me. If his company managed to convince the police that my condition was real and that I was actually eighty-five, then not only would I be questioned again about the murder, but my secret, the one I had spent decades protecting, would be public knowledge – an absolute disaster in my view. And why wouldn't the police believe a pharmaceutical giant? Such a company was not going to waste time and money on researching an impossibility, therefore they must believe it to be possible.

How the hell had Kowalski's company found out about the cold case and my involvement? There had to have been a leak from within the police. Surely they were the only ones who would have information on a seventy-five year old crime. Could Kirsten, as someone with connections within the police, find out?

Who else would the sneak have told? He, or she, would be well rewarded if they kept the papers informed. It would be a front-page story for a while, and my life would become hell: exposure, publicity, medical freak – everything contrary to my nature, everything I've fought to avoid for decades.

To drop out of sight, to leave the UK, had become a matter of urgency.

4

A STEADY DRIZZLE marked a dank day, and low dark cloud stole the light. Frustrated by my inability to leave the country quickly, I spent many hours giving my energetic friend as much exercise as I could. Lupus didn't care how wet he became. All he was interested in was the endless high-speed pursuit of his ball. I tired of it first and took him home to dry him off.

The post had arrived. The usual wasteful leaflets and an A5 envelope with my name and address typed on a label. I turned it over; there was no sender's address, and something soft was inside.

Odd. A pair of women's knickers fell out. What on earth? Held up to the light, they were mostly composed of crimson lace. Pretty; they deserved a shrug and a wee dram.

My phone whined and showed Kirsten's number. What the hell was she thinking, sending me a pair of her knickers? No, this was not something she would do, far from it. 'Hello,' I said, trying to disguise my suspicion.

But it was not her voice that replied. It was most probably a man, but was scrambled through a voice-changer. 'You have your mail?'

'Yes.' It would be absurd to ask who it was as they do in the movies when he had taken the trouble to change his voice.

'What do you think?'

What the hell was going on? 'They're too small for me.'

'Do not joke. You don't recognise them?'

'No. Why should I? What the hell do you want?'

'The owner is your friend. She is with us. For now she is safe.'

Jesus. Kirsten. They had Kirsten. Who were they? The message of her knickers was ominous and ugly. Was she all right, unharmed? A shiver went through me. I'd had months of experience in avoiding my pursuers and fighting off these vultures on my own and I now took it in my stride. But just twelve weeks previously, Alex had been slaughtered by a frenzied assassin. The whole ghastly vision of that savage attack hit me like a sledge-hammer: her mutilated flesh, so many stabs to her abdomen and a half-severed arm – so much blood. Kirsten was not as close to me as Alex was, but she was now a … a what? A hostage?

I had to keep the tremor out of my words. 'What do you want?'

The voice-changer rasped. It made his message much more sinister. 'An exchange. You come to us. No dog, understand? No dog. We let go your friend without harm.'

'And if I don't?'

'We are not bad people, we are not killers. She will live, but maybe not want to look in mirror when she go home.'

Not bad men, eh? They won't kill her, they will simply disfigure her. They will deliberately cut into that porcelain complexion or pour acid over her face simply to get hold of me. Her prospects of finding a husband or life partner will be severely reduced, her confidence crushed, her self-worth battered, at least for a time, if not forever.

'You think about this. We will call tomorrow and give instruction how you surrender to us. When you have do that, she will be free.' The line went dead.

I had taken extreme steps to avoid being discovered as a freak of nature, because I believed it was vital for humanity that my condition was not replicated. Would I throw all that effort away to save anyone, perhaps a stranger, from a ghastly future? No, I'd already determined that person would have to be sacrificed for the greater cause.

I was close to panic, because this wasn't some stranger, this was Kirsten, for whom I suddenly realised I cared a great deal. Should I hand myself over to these people to save her from a life of misery? Should I give up on my cause, something that had consumed my attention and my will for decades?

I'd told Kirsten there was no future for us as a couple, and she'd acknowledged that, being willing to live life with me for the moment. We'd taken it no further, and I'd suppressed any feelings I had, for I believed it was the right thing to do – keep my distance. But now?

I was miles away with these thoughts. The phone's whine startled me. A hidden number. I snapped at it. 'What?'

'DCI Payne here. There's a lot of questions going around about your DNA. They've tasked a few specialists to look at what might be going on. They want a fresh sample from you, witnessed in case there was a mix up last time – which there wasn't, it was on my watch. Can you come to the station tomorrow morning first thing so we can take one?'

'Please' would have been nice, but this was Payne, so I wasn't surprised. 'Certainly. I'll be there about eight.'

'Bring your passport and proof of residency – a utility bill, say.'

AT SIX THE next morning I was halfway through my second cup of coffee when my phone rang. The same distorted voice said, 'Are you ready to come to us?'

I wanted to know if Kirsten was all right, but he wouldn't tell me if she wasn't and I didn't want to appear too concerned, so I just said, 'Yes.'

'Write down.' He read out a postcode. 'Be there at ten hours. It is space next to old factory, open space. Stop car at end where you come in and walk to other end. You will get more instruction when there.'

It was raining hard when I got to the police station. A few cars were parked outside, only two of which were unmarked, but there was no way of telling if they belonged to the specialists. There was no point in getting soaked to save a minute or two, so I petted and talked to Lupus for a short while before making a dash for the entrance. Payne gave me a nod in greeting. 'They haven't arrived yet. You want a coffee?' He left me, told a junior to get the drink and buried himself in a computer.

Time marched on and nothing happened. Half past eight and the promised team had not appeared. Payne was concentrating on something else and didn't seem to notice. Seconds became minutes, and they passed. Available time was running out. I was on the point of making a scene when a frumpy woman and two male equivalents came in and made for the coffee machine. Payne got up and joined them. Pleasantries and a joke were shared.

All those witnesses for me. It was laughable, really, because there was nothing wrong with their first DNA result at all. It was all due to my not telling them when I was born.

But it wasn't a laughing matter at all. This performance of theirs, added to the time taken to obtain a result and tell me what I already knew, just delayed my leaving the country and changing my identity again. Even less a laughing matter was the need to make sure Kirsten would be safe and sound, and time for that was getting shorter. If they stuck to their word, giving up my freedom would see her safe, but then somehow I would have to escape their clutches.

I marched over to them. 'Are you the team taking my DNA?'

'Yes,' the woman replied. 'We'll be with you shortly. Just finishing the coffee.'

Blood threatened to burst from every vein in my head. 'We had an appointment at eight o'clock. It is now ten to nine and I have something else to attend to, something which is not going to wait. You either get this process started right now or I'm leaving.'

One of the men did not like being spoken to like that. 'As my colleague said, we'll be with you shortly. There's no need to be difficult.'

'Difficult? You are forty-five minutes late for an appointment and you don't even apologise. You just stand here, chat and drink coffee. I see that as unacceptably rude. I am doing you a favour, I am not a suspect here and I don't appreciate being treated as one. Now, let's get on with it.' I held out my documents for inspection.

As the man said, it did not take long. The woman said, 'Thank you.' The men said nothing. One of them was examining my documents. He shrugged, shuffled them together and made a note on a form.

Payne had kept quiet throughout the process, but as I left he said, 'Sorry about that. Timekeeping's important.'

I wasn't surprised he agreed with me, but it was interesting that he voiced his opinion. Perhaps he was warming to me – fat chance. He went on to say that the observers were satisfied that they had the correct person and that the sample would be analysed. He'd let me know how it went. He didn't have to, I knew the result.

There were fifty minutes left to reach the place where I was supposed to give up my life. Maybe an hour before Kirsten was freed.

I GOT THERE with eight minutes to spare, with Lupus's head hanging over my shoulder as he scanned the world ahead.

An old factory building with bare concrete walls was the destination according to the Satnav. A glimpse through open doors at the end showed steel girders supporting a rusting iron roof and idle machinery in precise rows on a floor strewn with rubbish. The road into the site had once been tarred, but over the years heavy wheels had carved deep, unavoidable potholes in the crumbling surface, potholes which were now puddles of unknown depth. The car shuddered when a wheel dropped into one. At the back of the building was what used to be a truck park with the width to turn a semitrailer, but was now a mix of gravel, puddles and mud, with litter everywhere. The rain was too hard for the wipers to clear it enough to see any detail, but a dark blue van faced me some fifty metres away.

The voice had instructed that my car be left at the end and not to proceed into the parking area. I turned the

Volvo around so it faced back the way I'd come in. My phone rang. 'Leave car there. Get out. Walk to end of truck park. Keep phone on.'

'I'm not doing anything until I know you have Ms Pearman and that she's unharmed.'

'You do what I order, or she will get a wide mouth, from one ear to the other.'

'That's not going to get me to cooperate. I have a better plan. You let her go and she walks towards my car, and I will walk to you at the same time. We will cross in the middle. I will reach you, and she will reach my car at the same time.'

Silence.

'All right. You make trick, she will be shot.'

So, he had a gun and a knife. But did he have the will to use them?

It was still raining hard, but we couldn't wait for it to stop. The sooner this was over, the better. It might actually work to our advantage to have reduced visibility.

'I want to see her ready to walk before I move.' I stepped out of the car and was met with a whiff of burned plastic and human excrement.

There was no answer, but the van's side door made its distinctive sound as it slid open. Kirsten stepped out. She saw me and gave a little wave. I gave one back.

'I'm starting to walk. Tell her to move now.'

'She come. I have rifle point at her. No trick.'

'There'll be no tricks.'

Kirsten walked towards me. Was her limp more pronounced? I tried to match her pace. It was important that she reached the car before I got to the van. Her hair no longer bounced; soaked and bedraggled, it clung to her head in straight lengths. I grinned at her from a distance. She smiled back bravely. I stopped, and she stopped next to me.

I moved to put myself between her and the van, where the rifle was. It was safe enough; they wanted me alive. 'Are you all right? Sorry about this.'

'Walk. No talk.' The shout from the van echoed off the factory wall.

Kirsten smiled and nodded. 'I'm fine. They haven't hurt me.'

'Lupus is in the car. Let him out and lock yourself in. Does he have a rifle?'

A smack to the side of the van got our attention. 'No talk or I shoot.'

She stared at me, ignoring the command. 'There's a handgun in his right jacket pocket. Are you sure about Lupus? You insisted that he stay leashed last time, because he might have been killed.'

'And you released him and saved me. Let him out of the car.'

She nodded and walked on to the Volvo.

I watched her go and once again wondered how un-comfortable it must be for her to have a limp. Maybe she didn't notice it anymore. She had almost reached the car.

'Walk, Andrew Duncan, or I shoot her.'

A piercing scream came from behind me. Another thug had her by the arm, pulling her away from the car. She raked a hard shoe down his shin. He lost his grip. She stretched for the car. The goon got another grip and tried to drag her away. I couldn't see the detail, but she must have got one finger at least round the door handle.

The dog was out. Kirsten was in his way. He twisted and leapt past her, jumped and landed high up the thug's chest. The man staggered back. Lupus, snarling, had his arm, worrying it, pulling, ripping at jacket and flesh. The man screamed. Kirsten was at the tailgate, a jack handle in her hand. Her blow to the man's head made me wince. He went still.

I whistled, turned my back on the scene and walked on to the van, taking my time. Five metres to go. My captor was shifting about, left and right, trying to watch both me and the action at my car. He had to stay where he was, his priority was me, but he needed his mate. This one was the chain-smoker from the park. No rifle was visible. His right hand was in his jacket pocket, though.

To me, the sound of an express train would have been less evident than that of Lupus's galloping paws. But the man's attention was now solely on me, mistrustful and focused. He didn't hear, and he stood no chance. When he did see the dog he started to pull his hand from his pocket. Lupus got there first. Pure fury. Pointed teeth sank in. The gun was flung to the side as Lupus shook the arm, ripping it to shreds. Blood spurted from the side of the dog's mouth – a punctured vein.

I picked up the gun and called Lupus off. He stood there panting, blood round his mouth and looking pleased with himself.

The Volvo stopped beside us. 'Nicely handled, Kirsten. Are you all right? Please give Lupus some water, his bowl's in the back, and bring the first aid kit before this clown floods this area of outstanding natural beauty with his blood. I'm going to have little chat with him.'

The smoker's sleeve was ripped to shreds. Blood dripped from the fabric. I found a dressing and put it over his wrist. 'Press down on that hard, while I sort a bandage.'

He was trembling and breathing with audible gasps. '*Shit, shit, shit.* This hurt … That fucking dog dangerous … Fucking dogs like that must be shot … I report this.'

'Another word out of you and I'll walk away and leave you to die. This is how people commit suicide, you know. They slit their wrists in the same place and bleed to death. Who are you working for?'

'No one.'

'How much is no one paying you? Hold your arm out so I can put this bandage on.'

No answer from a sullen face, but the arm was extended.

'I suggest you go to hospital and get this sorted properly. My dog has a very dirty mouth. I've seen what he licks, and you are now carrying a stack of diseases in your bloodstream, so you need a tetanus jab. Same with your friend over there.

'What are you going to tell your boss when he finds out you've failed to catch me again? That you two professional heavies were outwitted by a woman and a dog? You're pathetic, aren't you? You can tell him from me that if he doesn't leave me alone, I'll not bother with little men like you next time, I'll come after him.'

A CYCLIST SHOT out of a side street in front of us. His black lycra-clad backside with hi-vis yellow stripes almost met the dirt, saved only by my violent swerve and harsh braking.

'*Bloody idiot,*' I yelled across Kirsten and blasted him with the horn.

He stabbed his middle finger at me. If she hadn't been there, I'd have been tempted to take it further. Instead, I said to her, 'Sorry, but some of these people …'

She smiled. 'You need Boudicca-type scythes on the wheels to cut them to shreds. What now?'

'I'm taking you home.'

'Don't evade the question. You know what I mean.'

'Right now the police are flummoxed by the confusion over my DNA, and I can't blame them. Eventually, though, they'll join the dots themselves, or some pharma giant will give them the clues to do so. As long as they fail to reach a conclusion I have to be around, no matter how long it takes, because to leave before their process has finished will look suspicious and attract closer investigation.' I had run through this argument many times in my own head. It was exasperating and always caused a sigh. 'The trouble is, every moment I stay here, the risk of discovery gets greater.'

'Do you have to go as far as Kenya to hide? Surely you could find somewhere closer?'

'Kenya is where, as Charlie Maxwell, I am known and have rewarding work. Everywhere else I would have to start again, possibly learn a language and be under the watchful eye of the local constabulary until I'm accepted in that community.'

'How long is this going to be for?'

'Depends. I've some ideas on how to end it and return, but can only do so when these companies no longer see me as a lab animal. We'll have to see how it plays out.'

'Are you talking weeks, months or years? Will there …? Never mind.'

'Will there what?'

'Will there … will there be an opportunity to visit you? To see what you're doing? I'd love to go there and see the elephants and rhinos and honey badgers and snakes and zebras, every wild animal on its home turf. And what better way to do it than with a friend?'

I withheld my reply for a moment. I see what you're doing, Kirsten. Don't go down this road. Please don't try to get any closer, you know it can't work. It'll be harder for both of us if we allow this relationship to develop in a normal fashion. You're only hurting yourself by nurturing affection.

But … That phone call telling me she was a captive had forced me to face the truth. That she was more than just my barrister, more than just a friend – much more. But I couldn't tell her that. There was no safety-chain on the door to my feelings. If I as much as cracked the door, those emotions would mass and storm the exit. A full-blown love affair would result, and I wasn't ready for that; it was too soon – wasn't it, Alex? And, having her involved while I was doing illegal things like using a false identity would be a dangerous complication for her.

My eventual reply was abrupt, and I hated my tone. 'I don't know. It depends on the circumstances at the time.'

Kirsten turned away from me, apparently watching the passing scenery, but I don't think she saw any of it.

5

IT WAS A surprise when, three days later, DCI Payne rang and said there was no further need for me to be available. The boffins had their evidence and were working on it, and wanted nothing else from me. A day after that, I collected my renewed false passport. I was set to go.

Saying goodbye to Kirsten was difficult. We were on the brink of something special. We both knew it, but I couldn't admit it to her. One sign of weakness from me and the way I'd planned to conduct my life would be wrecked. I could cope with that, though. What was more important was what it would do to Kirsten as she grew old and I didn't.

It was as hard leaving Lupus. I'd left him before, of course, but that had been for little more than a month at a time. This trip had no foreseeable end, which opened the question of whether I would ever see my dog again. At least I knew Kirsten would look after him.

My genuine passport, as Andrew Duncan, saw me onto the flight to Nairobi and entry into Kenya. There are no Border Force passport checks leaving the UK. Only the airline takes passport details, and they don't share them unless Border Force asks for them. On my return, I would use the same genuine Andrew Duncan passport to book the flight and enter the UK. Meanwhile, once in Kenya, I would adopt my Charlie Maxwell identity, complete with authentic-looking documents, including a Kenyan visa. If some official was nosy and diligent, he would find the discrepancies and I, in whatever identity, would be arrested. But I wasn't planning on doing anything to cause such an investigation, so why should he?

I, as Charlie, had been working for three weeks flying a contracted helicopter on anti-poaching operations. A further week was spent on a ground patrol with the rangers, tracking and hunting the poachers themselves. It was stimulating and rewarding work, especially when the rangers caught their quarry.

I had some time off and was relaxing over my second bottle of Tusker in the Serova Stanley Hotel's Thorn Tree café. The place had changed enormously over the years. From a genuine open-air cafe bordering the street, with its signature acacia, the thorn tree itself, in the middle, it had been modernised. The tree was once used as a noticeboard, with messages stuck on its thorns: *'Jim and Mary, we're at the Waterbuck guesthouse. Catch us there until the 20th, Clare and Sally.'* or *'Couple in 4x4 looking for travelling companions to Lake Rudolf. Leaving on 16th.'* That tree had died, as had its successor. It was replaced by yet another, which had been protected by erecting proper noticeboards carrying similar messages. It served the same purpose, but the atmosphere of the place had been lost.

In this very position, back in 1982, I was approached by a woman, an ex-army wife I'd known in 1970. She had greeted me using my true name, Andrew. Because I was trying to hide that identity behind Charlie's, I had denied that I knew her. It was too long ago to matter, but I haven't forgotten it because it reminded me that old acquaintances could pop up anywhere and compromise my identity. Of course, anyone who thought they knew me would expect to see an eighty-five-year-old, not a man of thirty-four. Hopefully that would prevent a difficult conversation.

Unfortunately, it wasn't one of the attractive women in the café who stood at my table this time, it was young man in an ill-fitting shiny suit.

'Mr Maxwell, sir, my name is Paul Mbabazi. How do you do?'

'Fine.' What the hell did he want? And how did he know my name? My beer was slipping down very nicely in my own company, and I didn't need an interruption. He probably wanted to sell me something, or be a game guide, or guide me through some bizarre and unrealistic offer to make a fortune.

'Sir, I would like you to meet someone. It would be most advantageous for you to do so. Would you accompany me, please?'

His choice of words was odd, as if he had stepped out of the past or been educated by an octogenarian gentleman or missionary. But it was more his accent than his language which was a surprise – cultured English with barely a trace of his African heritage, which was most unusual in that part of the world.

After too much of it, the persistent pressure of hawkers and odd-job men and beggars makes one irritable. 'You're going to have to give me a good reason to leave my beer, which I was enjoying in peace until you invaded my privacy.'

He let that slide off him like water off his glossy plastic suit. 'My apologies, Mr Maxwell, sir. The gentleman who wishes to speak to you was insistent that I come immediately, so please don't shoot the messenger, as it were.'

'Who is this man?'

'He prefers to introduce himself, sir. He is a very rich and powerful person, and I believe you will benefit greatly by listening to what he has to say.'

I don't know why I agreed to go once I'd finished my beer, but I regret that I did.

MBABAZI USHERED ME into the hotel's Presidential Suite, a set of rooms with a distinctly colonial feel to them: a red carpet with a pattern of white motifs, green walls, dark stained wooden door frames and arches, sumptuous chairs and old prints lit by individual picture lights. Two table lamps were there but, along with the main lights, had not been switched on. Thick curtains were closed but for a narrow gap which allowed a thin shaft of sunlight to penetrate the darkness. A stench of prolonged human occupation overcame the air conditioning, contributing to a thick, stifling atmosphere. It required an effort to take the first breath.

'Welcome, Mr Charlie Maxwell. Thank you for coming to meet me.'

It took me a second or two to find the source of those words. An extremely obese man had spread himself across the couch, motionless. He was dressed in black trousers and a black smock, and was almost invisible in the gloom, in spite of his bulk. He held out his hand but made no effort to get up. Unnecessary movement was probably difficult for him. Mr Creosote from The Meaning of Life came to mind.

His voice was quiet, but authoritative. 'My name is Idi. Not Amin. No, no, not the famous Idi Amin.' His pudgy face exploded into laughter, exposing a row of brilliant white teeth. Wheezing, he added, 'Many people think I must be that terrible man, but he is dead many years now.'

After shaking his fleshy hand, I said nothing. He would tell me what he wanted in due course. His breath came in short, laboured gasps, as if the mountain of his body constricted his lungs.

'*Paul*, get Charlie a drink. What you like, Charlie? Everything is here: Scotch, cognac, beer, gin, champagne … I have everything.' Half a tankard of beer was within his reach. A packet of potato crisps had spilt over the table and onto the floor. Another waited to be burst apart.

'I'll have a beer please, Paul. How can I help you, Idi?' My vision had adjusted to the dimness, and details of the room and the mountain I was talking to were more apparent.

'You are expert in aeroplanes and all things about flying: how they work, about the petrol, about the drivers – the pilots and the mechanics.'

'I'm a helicopter pilot, I don't claim to know much about fixed-wing aeroplanes nor about the maintenance side and the engineers. I certainly wouldn't call myself an expert.'

Idi's toad-like eyes vanished behind his lids as he grinned at the exchange. But those lids did not entirely close, and he was watching me through the slits.

'You are a modest man, Charlie. The little you know, it is many times more than anyone else here.'

I shrugged and waited.

'I am a successful man. I am a rich man. My trucks carry many things, including the kitchen sink, as you say.' His laughter boomed into the room. 'All over East Africa, from Goma in the Democratic Republic of Congo to Mombasa on the sea; from Juba in Sudan to Zambia, Malawi and Mozambique. All goods, all over. But like all clever businessmen, I am not satisfied. There is more to be done, and some things to be done better – in other ways, new ways, by Ajok Transport.'

This man sought praise. 'You have a powerful business. I've seen plenty of your trucks on the roads. So many that I never notice other companies.'

'Thank you. I am growing all the time. I take over the little guys, give them some money and tell them to go away. Mostly they do. Some, they don't like it, but I don't give them the choice. But now I want to try something new, and that is where you can help me.

'There are goods in Goma which are very, very valuable. The best way to move them is by aeroplane. I don't know about airlines. It is very technical. There is a company in Goma that does these things, and I want them to fly my goods for me. But I want to be sure they will move my stuff safely. I want to know they won't damage it, and they won't crash and I'll lose everything. I want you to inspect this company for me and tell me if it's efficient and safe or a bad investment.'

Plenty of companies flew into and out of Goma but only a few were based there. None of them were large – the biggest had five aircraft. It would take two days to inspect the company properly and another to write a report for Idi.

I could do this; I wasn't needed for over a week.

Then a problem sprang to mind: I had a ninety-day tourist visa for travel to Kenya, Uganda and Rwanda, but I didn't have a visa for the DRC.

'Paul will take care of that in a few hours. Give him your passport.'

'I'll think about it, Idi. If I accept, it'll cost you three thousand dollars including my written report.'

'*Eesh.*'

'That is a reasonable rate for work like this. I'll be taking a lot of responsibility in saying certain things, things I could be sued over. So you're paying for professional training, experience and knowledge, and you aren't having to pay for me to fly from the UK to do the job.'

We bargained for five minutes, but I refused to give in and eventually Idi, his whole massive body shaking and wobbling, laughed. The experience left him breathless, but when he recovered he agreed to my price.

'Idi, I'm going back to the Thorn Tree. I'll think seriously about this over another beer, but I do have other commitments and I will not jeopardise those. I'll let you know in an hour.'

BEING BACK IN the almost open air of the Thorn Tree was a release from the unpleasant environment of Idi's dark, claustrophobic den. I found a corner table, ordered myself a beer and breathed in the petrichor which wafted in from the rain-soaked street outside.

Idi Ajok's proposal was like a piece of fish that may have been left out too long. You're not quite sure if it's gone off, no matter how much you sniff at it. But there was a whiff of something dishonest, even criminal, about the man.

Many of the customers in the café had not moved since I'd gone to see Idi. A few suited businessmen had arrived for an after-work drink, but most people were casually dressed. One odd couple, past middle age, harked back to the early 20th century by dressing in Out of Africa khaki safari suits. An elderly woman in a flowered dress looked remarkably like the army wife who had collared me in 1982. I tried to shrink from her view; recognition was the last thing I needed. An attractive young woman in jeans, a loose top and a leather waistcoat sat alone two tables away from me. Her most distinctive feature was a pixie cut of almost white hair. She wasn't sitting facing me, but had to turn her head, which meant it was obvious when she was looking in my direction.

She took what looked like a postcard out of a suede satchel and studied it. I waved at a waitress, holding up my bottle of Tusker and a single finger. This was going to be my fifth bottle this afternoon. Was I drinking too much? Undoubtedly, but given my condition, I had a rather cavalier attitude to my health.

As I looked back, the pale head dropped from me back to the postcard. Or was it a photograph?

For far too long I had been avoiding attention. After NiPetco's attempted abduction of me back in August, my antennae had worked overtime. Some would say I had become paranoid. If so, I couldn't deny it, but being so had kept me safe ever since. If what the pale pixie was holding was a photograph of me, I needed to get out of Nairobi, and the opportunity had just been offered to me.

I hadn't noticed a camera above Idi's door, but it opened unassisted at my ring. Paul stood facing me about two metres away, out of reach. 'Come in, Charlie.'

Idi was still sprawled across the couch, a whale of a man. His expression was bland. He said nothing as he waited for my answer.

'All right, I'll do it. What happens next?'

Paul said, 'Give me your passport. I will get you a visa for the DRC. You can travel to Goma tomorrow morning. I will meet you at Wilson Airport and give you your passport back.'

'Surely it's too late to get a visa at this time of the evening.'

'Idi——'

The man himself stirred. His jowls wobbled. 'If I say I need a visa in one hour at midnight, they will do it.'

I raised an eyebrow at that and held my passport out to Paul. He said, 'I'll meet you in the terminal at Wilson at eleven thirty. Our flight leaves at twelve fifteen.'

He must have booked my seat on the off chance that I would accept the job. 'Idi, I'd better warn you: the standard of aviation in the DRC is appalling, so do not expect this company to be any different. What's its name?'

'It is named after the active volcano north of Goma: Nyiragongo Air. It is owned by a Frenchman, Jacques Mertens. I expect because he is French the company will be better than its rivals, even if it is small.'

'Not necessarily,' I said.

'I shall send Paul with you. He can translate if there are difficulties, and I want him to observe and learn from you, so we will know how to handle this Mertens in the future.'

6

I'VE ALWAYS HAD a soft spot for Wilson Airport, primarily because of the Aero Club, which, for members, had a homely feel to it, with old and bold pilots, icons of East African aviation, propping up the bar in the evening and telling unlikely adventure tales to anyone who would believe them. Now, it's become more commercialised, with modern rooms and all the amenities such an establishment can offer. Even so, I like it and Charlie Maxwell has been a club member for a long time and hence can make use of the member facilities. In fact, bored with a hotel in the town centre, I determined to stay at the club for my next time off.

Paul Mbabazi had reaffirmed Idi's promise that there was no problem in obtaining a DRC visa for me the previous evening. What was the source of the man's influence: money, drugs, violence? Or all of the above?

The next morning I was having an early lunch outside at the club while waiting for my transport to Goma. My coffee was almost finished when a Cessna 208 Caravan taxied in. There are plenty of Caravans in East Africa – it's a popular and reliable workhorse – but I knew this was my lift because Nyiragongo was painted on the tail, with the outline of a volcano behind the lettering.

I drained my cup and went to the fence to watch. The pilot opened the doors and let the passengers out. They trooped off to immigration under the supervision of the ground staff while their bags were loaded onto a trolley and followed them. The pilot ignored them and supervised the refuelling.

Paul met me in the terminal and handed over my passport. He had abandoned his shiny synthetic suit for jeans, a T-shirt and hi-vis orange trainers.

The pilot was filling in paperwork when I greeted him. I told him who I was and that I would be inspecting his company by mutual agreement. He was a little shorter than me, maybe five foot ten, and muscular, with pale hair and pale eyebrows. Washed-out blue eyes regarded me with a cold, blank expression.

'Mertens,' he said as he pushed the documents across the desk to a clerk.

He had to be the owner's son; he was too young at about thirty-five to be the founder. His white shirt had four-bar epaulettes. This was interesting: in commercial airlines where there is a definite rank structure based on experience and qualifications, four bars indicates a captain or aircraft commander. Three bars designates a first officer. But in general aviation, rank is less well defined, and some inexperienced pilots will wear four bars simply because they have command of an aircraft, however small. Such a presumptive attitude might impress a few passengers, but will be frowned on by those who have spent many years getting to captain level. Which was this younger Mertens, experienced pilot or arrogant novice?

There were five other passengers for the nine-seat Caravan: two nuns, an African couple, and Paul. Along with their bags was a cat in a crate and a goat in a cage. I carried only a small backpack with my laptop and a change of clothing. I asked Mertens if I could sit up front with him – I wanted to observe his cockpit procedures as part of the safety inspection – but he said, 'It's not permitted.'

Strange, that, when one of the incoming passengers had been sitting in front.

'Are you going to restrain that cargo?' I asked him, as it was piled into the rear of the cabin and could shift in turbulence – I had visions of a caged goat decapitating a nun as it flew forward.

'Not necessary.' He was certainly arrogant.

The flight was uneventful, Mertens's procedures appeared to be sound as far as I could tell from the front row of seats behind him, and his landing was smooth.

At Goma, Mertens got out and walked away, leaving the ground staff to see to the passengers and the baggage. He got into a black Mercedes with heavily tinted windows and drove off.

Paul said, 'I have my own accommodation here. I will see you tomorrow. Beware, Charlie, Goma can be a very dangerous town and you should not go out alone. At this time riots and protests are rife because UN troops are failing to protect the public from the rebels and guerrillas. Also, the DRC army is thoroughly disorganised – they are useless, in fact.' He ushered a scruffy little man forward. 'I have hired Claude here to take you to your accommodation. I think you will find it more homely than a hotel.'

Paul vanished, and the driver gave me a broad grin. He beckoned and led me to a rusty jalopy of a vintage that used window winding handles and swivelling quarter-lights. The interior stank and the plastic seats were sticky and split. The car started with difficulty, but eventually burst into life before the battery gave up.

Leaving the airport, we headed south, parallel to and in sight of the runway, with an industrial area to our left. Sheds and warehouses were interspersed with shacks and tiny dilapidated houses crammed together as if space was a premium in that vast country. A cemetery followed, and after that, more housing for the masses. People swarmed, going about the very business of living: shopping, eating, drinking, talking, laughing, jay-walking and interrupting the traffic. Chukudus, heavy cargo scooters with wooden wheels, propelled and ridden by youths and older children, transported massive loads of bananas, cabbages, sugar cane, wood and any variety of goods to market. Women, great loads balanced on their heads, somehow managed to keep their goods from falling in spite of the jostling mob, and bare-ribbed, mangy dogs trotted about searching for scraps.

Before we reached the main road, we passed through a MONUSCO checkpoint, MONUSCO being the French acronym for the UN Organisation Stabilisation Mission in the Congo. The troops manning the checkpoint regarded us and every other vehicle with a disinterested glance and did nothing.

There was something wrong with the gearbox as Claude struggled to get the car into third. It backfired a few times, but we made it through the town in spite of the minibus taxis that honked and barged their way through the throng. Once across the main road, we passed increasingly opulent houses before reaching a villa on the shore of Lake Kivu.

A long life's experience has taught me to notice details that a younger person might have to make a conscious effort to see. Off the road, a driveway sloped down towards the lake. A high wall, topped by four strands of electric fence, surrounded the property. Thick vegetation outside the wall was separated from it by about two metres of clear space, robbing intruders of cover, possibly.

Claude drew up to the gates and stopped. Nothing happened. The gates themselves consisted of long, vertical bars with spearhead finials and a horizontal bar halfway up with shorter spears reaching just above it – Victorian-style. The driver pushed the large button in the centre of his steering wheel, which produced a sort of strangled duck's quack that immediately died. Further thumping on his horn did nothing. There must have been a guard watching somewhere, though, because the gates swung open on their own. Was there CCTV, or was there a guardhouse behind the two-metre wall?

I thanked the driver, hoped fervently never to travel in his jalopy again, slung my backpack over one shoulder and made my way across the brick paving to the front door. This wasn't a hotel; where had I been delivered? A clue was the black Mercedes with tinted windows standing on the forecourt.

A SERIES OF solid clicks came from the front door before it swung open. Six heavy deadbolts, at least two inches thick, had retracted into their housings. Interesting – it was like the door to a vault. It would take explosives to knock the thing out and suggested that the owner felt threatened.

A servant dressed in white welcomed me with a smile and a faint bow of his head. He ushered me through the hall. Wide, sliding glass doors on the far side of the living room led out onto a verandah. Beyond that was a tiled patio and a swimming pool surrounded by lawn.

Two men were outside. One sat with his arm resting on the table next to his glass. The other was Mertens the pilot, standing with his back to the pool and thus facing me as I stepped out of the house.

Two German shepherd dogs, one black, were lying beside the seated man. As one, they sprang to their feet. I hesitated. The man did not get up, but gave the dogs some calm command. They sat, but watched my every move.

'Ah, M'sieur Maxwell. Welcome. Do not mind my boys. They are really *minou*, pussycats. This is Caesar; this black one is Brutus.' He was certainly in his high eighties, possibly over ninety. Paper-thin skin stretched over his skull-like head, wrinkled and sunken into every cavity. He was bald bar closely cropped white hair at the sides. His narrow face with high cheek bones and a pointed chin housed pale blue eyes and white eyebrows – undoubtedly pilot Mertens's father. Thin lips smiled without warmth. 'Would you like a drink? I thought it would be more, er, 'ospitable to have you stay with us. Better than a 'otel, *n'est ce pas*?

Once again, his son's expression was blank and un-welcoming. He remained silent. Beyond him and the pool, the grass stretched to the edge of a lava field, the remnant of an old eruption, which descended in a steep slope of almost impassable jumbled rock to the waters of Lake Kivu.

I moved to sit next to Jacques, close to the dogs, and let my hand dangle down to their level. A cold nose damped my fingers, then another. Although maybe not; it could have been the same one. I wasn't going to look and make eye contact.

'Your house appears to be built on the lava.'

'No. You cannot see it, but the ground under the 'ouse was 'igher. In 2002 the lava came in two rivers, one to this side and one the other side of us.' He spread his arms indicating both directions. 'We were cut off. We were an island. It was not nice, the children were frightened. Naturally, we saw it was coming and escaped. The rivers came together after the pool and went into the lake.'

'Not good to see your home about to be buried. What about next time?'

Mertens ignored that. 'So, you have come to inspect my company?' His pale eyes glinted above steepled fingers. 'Tell me again exactly who hired you.'

'As I mentioned on the phone, my client wishes to remain anonymous for reasons I don't understand. However, his business is transacting in certain valuable items. He wishes to ensure that his goods will be carried safely and securely in your hands. I promise you I will not be intrusive, and everything will be strictly confidential. I could not survive in this business if I divulged other people's secrets.'

Mertens shrugged. 'Nothing is wrong. Everything is done by the book. The Legion taught me that the only way to do things is the correct way. Eric 'ere was also in the Legion. The same discipline was taught to 'im, and 'e is in control of the company, day to day.'

'You're talking about the French Foreign Legion?'

Jacques sipped at his drink, put it down and challenged me with his look. 'Naturally.'

'Then we have an understanding. I was also in the army.'

The old man gave another thin smile. 'There are soldiers and soldiers, of course. Some are better than others.'

It was a provocation I couldn't ignore and came from misplaced pride and arrogance. The Legion was renowned for its discipline and achievements, but they were no better than any other crack unit. 'And some have failed to beat the others since the 11th century.'

His glass rattled as he put it down, and this was not an old man who normally had a tremor. Eric made no attempt to hide his anger, but anything he might have said was forestalled by a slim, graceful woman stepping through the glass doors. There was something attractive about her, in spite of a thin, pinched mouth and dark circles under haunted brown eyes. She gave me a polite smile and held out her hand. 'Céleste.'

CÉLESTE ANNOUNCED THAT dinner was ready and beckoned for me to follow her. Jacques put his hands on the chair arms and pulled himself forward to the seat's edge. Using his stick he stood upright without a hint of a shake. Initially, he had the stoop of an old man, but immediately corrected it by forcing his shoulders back and straightening his torso.

The yelling of a drill sergeant came to mind: 'Shoulders *back*, chest *out*, stomach *in*.'

Jacques's knees had an old man's bend to them. As if by way of afterthought, he jerked them straight and strutted through the door. His pride as an old soldier would not be relinquished.

Eric said nothing; he neither replied to me nor to his father nor to Céleste all night. She, who was Eric's wife, tried to keep an amicable and harmless conversation going, but Jacques would override her and switch it to aviation, apparently seeking every opportunity to be confrontational. Not the best way to make a good impression before an inspection. All it did was make me curious as to what might be the cause of this apparent tension.

Dinner was excellent, and Mertens was generous with the wine – whether out of manners or because he thought my tongue would loosen, I didn't know. It certainly wasn't because he liked me. If I hadn't been so wary and defensive in this company, I'd have made a larger dent in his cellar.

Generally, dogs like me. I've only once been bitten, and that could have been an accident. However, I'm well aware that not all dogs can be trusted. That Brutus and Caesar would not stand for any nonsense or anyone harming those they knew, I had no doubt, but I could not resist trying to make friends with them. After some initially tentative stroking, the dogs ignored the hostile human atmosphere and enjoyed my attention.

Jacques was keeping an eye on me and how the dogs responded. '*Minou.* They are friends, because I am 'ere with them. You should not think they are 'armless.'

I went to my room early and made sure the door was locked. Burglar bars on the window, which are normal in most of Africa, made my world a little more secure. For the first time that evening I could relax.

The next morning I went in search of breakfast. Aromas of freshly baked bread and coffee wafted through the house. The only person in the dining room was Céleste, who was tending to some plates on the sideboard and had her back to me. She straightened up with an awkward movement which looked painful.

'Good morning,' I said from the doorway.

'*Bonjour,* Mister Maxwell.' She gave me a pleasant smile. 'Did you sleep well? Please help yourself.' She waved a hand at the sideboard. The movement made her wince, a reaction she quickly stifled. 'There are croissants, pain au raisin, pain au chocolat and, of course, coffee.'

As I finished eating, Paul appeared in jeans and a bright green T-shirt with the inscription 'I love Goma' backed by the outline of a volcano. His red baseball cap was on back to front. 'The car is ready when you are, Charlie.'

Fortunately, the car was not Claude's, but a clean, modern Renault Mégane. The drive to the airport took us away from the affluent lakeside properties, through comfortable suburbs and the town centre to past the end of the runway. This seemed to mark where the standard of living deteriorated sharply. As I'd seen the day before, the housing was more closely packed, extending even to squatter-type shacks clumped around industrial units, workshops and stores.

Nyiragongo's office was in a warehouse in this area. All that was at the airport were the aircraft themselves and a check-in kiosk. I was allocated a desk, and Paul found a chair and came to sit beside me. I asked him to move to the other side; he was crowding me. Before he moved, he whispered, 'You must be careful what you say here or anywhere in this town. Mertens is a powerful man. He has massive influence and does not like to be contradicted or opposed.'

'I've noticed that. Thanks.'

A secretary said in good English, 'What would you like to see? I can help you with whatever you need.'

I settled down to work, explaining to Paul what I was looking at: the operations manual, the pilots' and the engineers' records – what experience they had and whether they were properly licensed. I showed him errors and omissions, and he was attentive at first, but after an hour he lost interest. What he learned or didn't learn wasn't my concern, and his presence was distracting, so I was glad he left. When I asked for the maintenance records, they were brought in by the chief engineer, Etienne. The documentation had been meticulously completed in black ink, which was an increasingly rare practice in this digital age. The reason probably lay with Etienne, who was a middle-aged – and, I suspected, very conservative – Belgian.

'Why don't you computerise your records? Most operators do, these days. It saves time and is less prone to error.'

He shrugged. 'I know my way, and I don't make mistakes.'

I laughed; it always pays to keep relationships friendly: you get more out of people. 'Nothing to do with being an old man, then?'

He gave me a genuine smile, nodding. 'Old is experience. One day you will see.'

Since, in reality, I was almost twice his age at eighty-five, I could only give him my best grin and change the subject. 'Etienne, I can't see a paper trail for this entry in the log-book and a booking by a client.'

The chief engineer looked at the documents, shook his head, opened a filing cabinet and shuffled meaninglessly through papers. Playing for time while thinking up an excuse?

Whatever he pretended to find in the files wasn't there. He sat again, embarrassed. 'There must be some mistake – sorry. In time I will find the reason and correct the fault. This is not normal. The documentation must be lost.'

'It was only yesterday,' I said. 'Never mind, let's take a break from this paperwork and go and see the aircraft.'

Etienne gave me a friendly pat on the shoulder and issued a volume of orders in French. He pointed out of the window at the darkening sky. '*D'accord*. The rain is coming.'

Paul popped up again as if he had been waiting for just that moment. We were issued passes and, accompanied by Etienne, drove to the airport gate. From there we walked over to a Twin Otter which was parked on the far side of the apron. This aircraft is a robust icon of a plane, with two engines and seating for nineteen passengers. It's tough, has a short take-off and landing capability and is truly at home in the bush environment, making it very popular in Africa.

I walked around the outside to begin with, followed closely by Etienne. Paul perked up and asked plenty of questions. I climbed into the cockpit and he jumped in the other side. Etienne stayed on the ground at my open door, looking up.

Paul looked at the array of dials and switches, clearly baffled. 'What do you see?'

'Nothing out of the ordinary. Could do with a clean, though.'

Etienne shrugged. 'It will be done. It is not important.'

'No, but it is an indication of standards.'

He laughed and slapped me on the knee. 'Of course, you are right.'

Walking slowly through the cabin, I checked scores of items for safety issues and could find nothing to report on.

'What about this?' Paul held up a seat belt which had frayed very slightly on one edge.

'It's fine for a while.'

Etienne grinned his agreement. '*Oui*. Is okay, but I change if you want.'

The two rear rows of seats had been removed, presumably to fit in cargo that was too big for the separate baggage compartment. Like any similar sized aircraft, the seats fit into rails and lock into position. Similarly, tie-down fastenings can be locked into the rails to restrain cargo. The rails are often left uncovered and so accumulate dirt. The one I was looking at had something odd lying in it. I dug out a clump of silky blackish hair with my pen. Etienne was watching; his eyes had narrowed and his mouth had set in a thin line. Paul had stopped asking questions and poking around the aircraft and was now peering over my shoulder. His almost inaudible whistle told me he knew exactly what the clump was. But it was what conclusions he drew from the find that interested me, especially since it was this aircraft whose flight records for the previous day were 'missing'.

I put the hair down next to the rail and took a photo of it with my phone. I would have preferred not to have Etienne witnessing my pocketing of the find, but there was no way to avoid it.

The chief engineer's good-natured cooperation had evaporated. Paul was staring at him, but I had no idea what was going through his mind. My own look must have shown suspicion, though. Etienne turned away and muttered about time being short, it was about to rain and we should get back to the office. He fell back and pulled out his phone.

SOME YEARS PREVIOUSLY, I was being driven through the back streets of Kinshasa, the capital of the DRC. It was hot outside, the kind of heat that leaves one breathless, as the dust and stench of garbage seemingly robbed the air of oxygen. Near the station, the traffic's slow crawl came to a halt. The car's air conditioner fought the temperature with an icy, but welcome, blast. Roadside stalls sold all manner of cheap goods, from colourful plastic buckets, fly-swats and gadgets from China to local, more traditional things, alongside food stalls and stands selling little plastic bags of drinking water. Plastic bags that would be discarded in the street when empty, because there was no rubbish disposal system.

These were conditions to be expected in a city like this. Not so the next stall we passed. The street temperature was some thirty degrees, but that was not the problem for the turtles, though, it was the midday sun.

Pulled from their home in the Congo River, the poor creatures hung upside down by one or maybe two legs from a line. Unable to drink, they twitched and baked to death in their shells. The individuals who were selling them must have been devoid of feelings. The turtles were the most obvious victims of these disgusting humans, because they were hung there, dying in full view at eye level. But, looking down at what else was for sale, I gained another goal in life.

Pangolin skins, small antelope horns and long curved teeth from a big cat were in the front row of the display. Behind them lay eight severed hands in a neat row, with four gorilla heads, the lips curled back, exposing the teeth in a hideous deathly grin.

What makes an innocent animal any less valuable than a human? We know the difference between right and wrong, an animal doesn't. That doesn't make the animal less worthy; on the contrary it gives us the responsibility to care for the rest of nature, just as we expect our more fortunate brothers and sisters to care for us.

Four great apes' lives taken for these inhuman traffickers to profit. I've had a need to kill a man for good reason three times in my life, and I've restrained myself on each occasion. No one would describe me as sensitive, but at that moment the urge to be sick was only quashed by the compulsion to eliminate the despicable creatures that caught, killed, butchered and sold these body parts.

Of course, I did nothing. But in doing nothing then, I found myself about to do something now. The long, thick hair in my pocket meant that a mountain gorilla had been transported in that aircraft. I knew it, Etienne surely suspected that I knew it – and Paul? What role was he playing in this?

7

THE FAMILY WERE gathered on the verandah watching the tropical downpour when I went to join them in search of a drink. Heavy drops created a mini storm in the swimming pool and smashed noisily on the roof and the tiled patio beyond.

'Was your work satisfactory?' Jacques Mertens was nursing a pastis. Its anise odour hung in the air around him.

'Yes, thank you. Your staff were most cooperative, and Etienne was an excellent host.'

'Did you find any problems?' His intense look was challenging me to say something about the gorilla hair. He could think what he liked, I wasn't going to admit that I knew what it was.

'No, nothing serious. I'd rather give you a full description tomorrow before I leave than half the story now.'

Eric spoke for the first time since I'd been there. He refused to speak in English which, as a pilot, he had to know. It was a deliberate insult to me. My knowledge of his language was adequate for following a simple conversation, but not speaking it. 'Céleste, get me a drink,' he said. No *s'il te plait,* no please, simply an order.

Without acknowledging him, Céleste left her chair, went to the drinks table, poured a pastis and added a little water. She put it down with unnecessary firmness on Eric's side table and turned to me, her face taut. 'Can I get you something?'

Before I could reply, Eric snapped, 'There is too much water in this. What are you thinking of?'

Her eyes narrowing for a fraction of a second, Céleste continued to look at me, waiting for an answer.

'A beer,' I said, and smiled at her. '*Please.*'

Her mouth twitched before she turned back to her husband and picked up his glass.

Throughout the evening the Mertens clan tried to be polite. Jacques conducted most of the conversation, which almost entirely revolved around living in the DRC and the current crisis.

'Some people were killed by the Allied Democratic Forces in Beni on Sunday,' Jacques said. 'Then the guys rioted, because the MONUSCO does nothing. They want the UN to go away, because they're corrupt and, er, are supposed to protect the people, but they don't. Also, the Congolese army are pathetic and disorganised, the people say. It's true. A single company from the Legion would sort this out in one day.'

'Four protesters were killed in Beni when they attacked MONUSCO buildings. It is a worry.' It was the first time Céleste had said anything beyond offering drinks.

'You worry about everything. Get some backbone,' Eric snapped in French. Why was this man so ridden with anger?

Céleste looked away, but her jaw tightened for second.

Jacques continued. 'Yesterday another protester was killed in Butembo. That's about fifty kilometres this side of Beni. And today, 'ere in Goma, they have blocked the road to Beni.'

'Does this concern you?' I asked.

''Ere is normal. It comes up and it dies. The same for years. There are many minerals and precious stones in east Congo – diamonds; and columbite and tantalite, or coltan. It's complicated; there is the ADF – they say they are loyal to Islamic State – there are the M23 guerillas and a militia called CODECO. They are all trying to be top dog to win the riches. They terrorise the locals for food, money, phones, everything. The people are right about the MONUSCO and the army. You cannot blame them, but all riots can be dangerous. The police like to shoot, and there may be arms in the crowd. We stay at home, no problem.'

'Would you like another beer?' Céleste asked.

Yes, I would. In fact you can bring the whole case. I bit my tongue on that, though. Something said I should keep my wits about me that night. 'No thanks; perhaps some water.'

She smiled and went to get a glass.

After some excellent food, our bad tempered and disparate company went back out onto the verandah. The rain had stopped and the temperature had cooled. I sat and looked up as Jacques lowered himself into his chair, taking the weight on his arms as an old man would. He paused halfway down and hitched up his trousers.

Jacques Mertens's right ankle was scarred by a vivid, kidney-shaped port-wine birthmark.

IN MY ROOM I struggled to come to terms with the fact that after seventy-five years I had chanced on Sybil's killer. Through all that time the image of the bare legs, the grey socks with a yellow stripe and the port-wine birthmark had never changed and never left me. It was all I had had to find the murderer, and I had clung to the details and kept them fresh in my mind in case I ever came across him. But the chance of finding him became less and less, as he was getting closer to death with each passing year. It was an incredible coincidence, almost unbelievable – but it was possible. What were the chances of there being another white male in the world with a port-wine birthmark on his right ankle? What were the chances of that birthmark being the shape it was, the oval side facing up?

There could be little doubt.

There must have been something I could have done to stop Sybil's murder, even if I was only ten years old. Merely scrambling out from under the bed would have put him off. My shoe could have been a weapon. I could have done something. But I didn't. I did nothing. Being a child at the time was not an excuse.

The murderer could have been any age over, say, sixteen. I, Andrew Duncan, was now eighty-five, so the killer would be ninety-one. Mertens could be that age or even a few years older. It was easy to believe that Jacques was a murderer: there was something hard and criminal about both him and his son.

Kirsten, in England, was two hours behind me. She had said she would help if anything arose and I was out of the country. It was time to respond to that offer.

'*Andrew*. This is nice. How are you?'

'Charlie when I'm here, please, Kirsten.'

'Oops, of course, sorry.'

I gave her a brief rundown of what was happening. 'I've been accommodated in the company owner's house rather than a hotel. I thought they were being hospitable, but now I realise it's because they want to keep an eye on me and be able to deal with any problems I find. They know I've seen the gorilla hair, and I've no doubt they'll do whatever it takes to stop me reporting it.

'But that's not why I've called. You remember how I witnessed Sybil's murder? I've found her killer.'

There was silence for a moment and I thought the connection had dropped.

'Are you sure? He must be ninety at least.'

'He is. He has the exact same birthmark on his ankle that I remember. The chance of that being duplicated is next to zero. Please do something for me.'

Kirsten's tone changed from chatty to professional. 'Of course, anything.'

'I told you before I left that the police are researching cold cases. Please do your own investigation and research missing women and unsolved murder cases, probably of prostitutes, in 1944 and maybe later. This man, Mertens, killed Sybil for no apparent reason. He didn't know her, and there'd been no argument. If it was a random murder, then maybe this man was a serial killer who preyed on prostitutes. If he wasn't, then why was Sybil a one-off? I have to know before I take action on it.' I gave her as much information about Mertens as I could.

'Okay. I've a friendly contact in the police. He's the complete opposite of our friend Payne. He'll help, plus I get on well with one of the office staff who has access to the records.'

Before I could reply, a slight metallic sound came from the door.

'Kirsten, my bedroom door has just been locked from outside. They're planning something. I've got to get out of here tonight; it's too risky to stay. I'll call you when I can. One last thing: how's Lupus?'

'Your dog is fine. He's healthy, hard work to entertain, and he misses you.' She paused, and in a softer tone, said, 'Take care of yourself, Andr— Charlie.'

Don't, Kirsten. Please don't try to get closer.

8

LIKE ALMOST EVERY house in Africa, the windows of Mertens's home were barred. The joke was that it was as much to keep the residents confined as to keep intruders out. In my case, with the locked door, it wasn't a joke.

The bars were formed as an iron frame screwed into the outside wall at the four corners. They stood away from the wall to allow the window to be opened, but by less than a foot. This meant I could not get at the screws, because I couldn't stretch around the partially opened window – unless there was no glass, of course.

The lights of the verandah shone out across the lawn and the pool, but not round to my window. Shadows flitted on the grass as someone moved, but I never saw an actual person. Their conversation was unclear and in such rapid French that I couldn't understand it anyway. They were there, not thirty metres away. They were within earshot and would see me if they took a couple of steps away from the house. I had to be extremely careful. One of the dogs appeared, stretched, and went back out of sight.

My exit had to be quick and would best be left to when they packed up for the night. But what if they came for me before going to bed? They surely weren't going to leave me alone all night. The best time would be when they left the verandah. They would be as distant as they would ever be and facing where they were going, into the house.

In preparation, I stuffed everything I had into my backpack and found my pocket-knife, which had a screwdriver on it. With my hand wrapped in a towel it was easy and quiet to smash the window. The glass fell onto the lawn outside with the only sound being the chink of one shard hitting another. I stopped and listened. The old man wheezed a laugh, but there were no signs that they'd heard me.

Eric stepped off the verandah, walked a few paces to the side and took a piss. The light flickered in the stream. Why didn't he go inside to the toilet? He turned and looked in my direction, holding his stare for several seconds. Could he see me? I was in the shadows, but I froze. Any movement would be spotted. He turned away and strolled back to the verandah, zipping up his fly. I breathed out.

With the window glass cleared, I could reach the screws holding the bars in place. They were stiff but they yielded, and it was easy to bend the frame enough to open the window fully.

The next stage was not so simple. There was a lawn to cross, dogs to avoid and an electric fence to deal with. And only God knew what was going on in the town beyond, because the sounds of yelling and anger and scattered gunshots did not bode well.

My best way off the property was going to be the gate. It was scalable and there was no electric fence. The problem was going to be getting to it without alerting the dogs, which may have warmed to me, but I couldn't trust them.

Beyond the gate? Hopefully the rioters would have dispersed before I got outside.

Once I'd escaped the property, what was I going to do? I had to get out of Goma, where Mertens had a huge amount of influence. Leaving by road would involve some Congolese, and how many of them would tell Mertens? I couldn't trust anyone.

The quickest way would be to fly. I could steal an aeroplane, but I only flew helicopters. Sixty years ago, I had first learned to fly on a tiny, fixed-wing plane, and I'd dabbled in it a couple of times since. That hardly made me competent. But I knew all the principles, and I could steal one of Mertens's Cessna Caravans. Although my fixed-wing aeroplane experience was severely limited, I had spent enough time as a front-seat passenger in Caravans to be familiar with the cockpit and controls, and I knew the engine – it was essentially the same as in several helicopters in which I had thousands of hours. It was worth a shot – a bloody risky shot.

Where to go? That depended on how much fuel was in the Caravan. If it was full, it would make Nairobi, but I didn't have the documentation for an international flight, so wherever I went it would have to be a country airstrip where I wouldn't be noticed. There was an Aero Club strip in Kampala in Uganda that I knew, but even better was the airstrip on Mount Kenya, near Nanyuki where I had worked as a helicopter pilot. I couldn't actually hide there, but the familiarity of the place would be more welcoming.

What about Paul? I was contracted to Idi Ajok, and it was not my choice to have Paul along. He wasn't my responsibility, I didn't trust him and I didn't know where he was anyway. He could fend for himself. After all, he hadn't been watching my back.

A BRIEF SHOWER passed. As if it was a signal, the conversation from the verandah changed tone. Chairs scraped on the tiled surface. Caesar and Brutus bounded onto the lawn and sniffed around. Those two were going to be a problem.

The Mertenses were calling it a night. They could be at my bedroom door in a couple of minutes. There was nothing for it, I'd have to brave the dogs.

It was a squeeze, but I got out of the window and under the bars. Next, the gate. The way to get to it was around the end of the house, which meant going left from my window, away from the verandah and along the back of the building. If the dogs stayed close to the house, they wouldn't see me – if they stayed there.

The verandah was clear, although a shadow was moving about – Céleste, putting things away. Ten more steps and I checked again. She was watching me, her figure in silhouette and the light shining through her diaphanous skirt. Caesar was held back by her right hand, Brutus by her left. She was fighting to control them, her body being jerked back and forth, left and right as they lunged towards me. Those were strong dogs; she would not be able to hold on for long. But I seemed to have an ally –

what was she risking in helping me? The best I could do in return was to give her a wave as I ran.

Next obstacle: the gate guard. His little booth, its door latched open, was behind and back from the wall, with a view of the entrance. The man was slumped over the desk, his head on his arms, his beret beside him. Was he actually asleep or just resting? To immobilise him or to let him be, hoping he wouldn't wake up, that was the question. Speed was essential, Céleste would not be able to restrain the dogs for much longer.

I snuck into the booth, ready to deal with the guard if he woke. His uniform shirt had a stain on the back and his boots lay in the corner. He was snoring. I crept out again.

The gate was easy to scale and I managed to do it without waking the guard. In the car, we had turned left into the house, so I turned right leaving it. There was a danger of getting lost in this unfamiliar place, so I wanted to follow the vehicle route as closely as possible.

Mertens's opulent district of luxury mansions on the lake shore gave way to less expensive, but still large, homes, all surrounded by solid walls with electric fences and steel gates. Further on, houses filled their properties from wall to boundary wall. It seemed more important to have the largest house possible than for the kids to be able to run around it. Still further on my way to the main road, the buildings became smaller and more numerous, with corrugated iron shacks erected in the garden for more space. The streets were strewn with litter. Pools of black, oily water lay in potholes and the stench of garbage polluted the air.

I followed the *Avenue de la Paix,* knowing it would eventually angle in to meet the main road. After fifty minutes, midnight traffic could be heard honking and roaring a couple of blocks away. This road, the N2, which runs along the west side of Lake Kivu and then on to the north via Goma and Beni, was where trouble might occur. Barriers of rocks and rubbish, burning tyres, old furniture and wood, the standard African road-block, were not my concern. It was the mood of the young people rioting that worried me. As a white man, I stood out and could be taken as someone from MO-NUSCO. Even in more peaceful times, walking the roads in this violent region at night was not recommen-ded, so I tried to keep the N2 in sight and stay on the side streets.

Around one corner a group of youths were chanting and brandishing sticks in some kind of war dance. Four spectators were singing and clapping with them, but the only people being stirred by their demonstration were themselves. I deviated.

The N2 branched north to Beni. There was another mile to walk to get round the end of the runway and reach the far side of the airport. More small groups of dancers firing their own enthusiasm stopped or slowed the traffic. It was amazing how many people were out this late at night.

The rain had passed and much of the cloud with it. Some stars were visible. The heavens were on my side so far – between Goma and Nanyuki in Kenya were some high mountains and the last thing I needed was bad weather at night in an aeroplane I didn't even know how to fly. That would be insane – the situation was insane anyway.

THE AIRPORT GATE was manned by a lone Bangladeshi UN soldier, whose pale blue helmet clashed with his green camouflage uniform and brown skin. Mind you, that blue helmet would clash with anything. There would have been more troops readily available somewhere behind him, but they were probably sleeping and would hopefully stay that way. It would be best for me to talk to this little fellow on his own. His pacing up and down in front of the gate could have been something to do, but it could also have been helping to calm his nerves, for the occasional rattle of automatic fire came from the direction of the town. From nearby, though, came the sound of chanting, a rhythmic repetition of male voices. It conjured images of men stamping out the beat and brandishing knobkerries and pangas – whipping themselves up in a war dance.

'Good morning,' I said cheerily in English. 'How are you this morning? Lovely, this time of day, isn't it. But I bet you've had enough and want to get some sleep.'

The soldier's round face lit up at the sound of a language he understood. His smile was broad, but only lasted a few seconds. He glanced at the street behind me.

'How has your watch been, quiet so far? What's your name?'

He nodded and grinned. 'All quiet this night. My name is Mohammed Khondakar.'

'It's not good, all this violence is it, Mohammed?' I delved into my backpack and handed him the airport pass I had been issued the previous morning, as it was still valid.

He studied it carefully, his fingers trembling. He kept looking up from the paper and into the darkness behind me. 'Why you want to come in at this time? No one comes in this gate at this time.'

I didn't answer, but listened. The chanting was getting closer. He searched my eyes for a few seconds as he too listened – I think for reassurance.

'I've got a very early take-off, Mohammed, and I've got a lot of preparation to do. I've got to be in Nairobi by six.'

'Where is your car? How did you get here?'

'I got a taxi. You think I walked – me, a white man? They would think I was part of your lot, UN. I don't want to think of what might happen then. These guys scare me. What do you think?'

Another burst of gunfire, probably just someone showing off, erupted not far away. The chanting was coming from the airport road. In a few minutes they would be at the gate.

Maybe because I was a foreigner and talking English, he was reassured and handed my pass back. 'Yes, I am scared, but I will do my duty. I think I must wake the guard. One man cannot stop these people.'

'Will you let me in, please, Mohammed? I don't want to be out here alone facing them.'

'Yes, sorry.' He opened the gate enough for us to get through, and ran to the guardhouse.

THE AIRPORT WAS dead. Security lighting reflected off shallow puddles in the apron tarmac. Except for a bit of shouting, probably from my friend Mohammed rousing his mates in the guardhouse, not a sound came from within the perimeter. Outside, the war chanting was getting closer. That militant mob would be at the gate within minutes and would keep the UN troops occupied for a while. Suppressing the urge to run, I walked to the aircraft as if I belonged there.

Two Nyiragongo Caravans were parked amongst other similar-sized machines. My first task was to open the doors, which were certain to be locked. Fortunately, eighty-five years of various activities, some of which I won't admit to, had taught me how to pick simple locks, and aircraft doors are not difficult.

If you travel around Africa, you learn that having a torch to hand is a good idea, because wherever you go you'll suffer a power cut at some stage. Mine's an adjustable LED head torch. I selected the minimum brightness and worked on the locks.

In the first machine, the fuel gauge read half. If there wasn't a Caravan with full or nearly full tanks, this plan was dead and I'd have to try my luck on the road.

Time was slipping by. It took too many precious minutes to pick the lock of the second aircraft, but at least this one had full tanks. Fuel quality is another hazard. It's essential to drain a small amount of fuel from each tank to ensure there's no water present. Water contaminates fuel naturally through condensation inside the tank, but it's not uncommon for thieves to steal fuel and top up the tank with water. It took time, but better that than having the engine fail on me after take-off.

While walking through the town over the last hours, I had tried to visualise the route and where the high mountains were. Most days in November are cloudy; as a consequence the month sees the highest rainfall in the region. Anything other than clear weather en route could see the end of me. But I was in luck: after the earlier rain, the sky had cleared. I willed it to stay that way.

Many modern pilots would think nothing of totally relying on the GPS, or Satnav, to navigate. But being 'old-school' I was taught to use a map, and when GPS came along it was welcomed as an aid, but the map was primary. If there wasn't one in the Caravan, I would be totally reliant on the GPS, which has been known to fail. I also spent the time thinking through technical aspects of flying an aircraft like the Caravan: the aerodynamics of it, what steps to take if the engine failed, what its landing speed was and at what speed would it stall and fall out of the sky? The answers to these questions were in the flight manual, but the minutes were slipping by and I needed to get airborne and out of Goma. Once clear and having gained altitude, the aircraft could be put on autopilot, and I could dive into the books. This was not the way to handle an aircraft conversion, but needs must.

I had to spend a few moments familiarising myself with the cockpit, to make sure I knew the position of every gauge and that every switch was correctly positioned. If something went wrong, seconds lost searching for a critical item could prove devastating.

Two soldiers, their blue helmets standing out under the hangar security lights, marched towards me. No time to follow the checklist now: Battery –– ON, Fuel – ON, Boost pump ––ON – Starter – Engage. Thank goodness I knew this engine.

I took my eye off the rising gauges for a second. The soldiers hesitated as the turbine lit with a muffled pop and the whine increased. But they found courage and advanced, splashing their way through puddles of rainwater. Getting away from there was suddenly more important than following the checklist. I released the brakes. The Caravan began to move. The soldiers were in its path. They split and ran, one to each side. I half expected to get a bullet or two from behind.

The take-off checklist told me what to do. I managed to complete it before turning from the taxiway onto the runway. As far as my limited knowledge could tell me, everything was set.

The one thing that would normally be on was the transponder. This unassuming little box responds to Air Traffic Control radar with a code that tells them who you are and where you are. I made sure it was off. There wasn't a squeak from the control tower even though the airport was open. It was probable that, with no expected traffic, the controller was asleep.

'Here we go.' I advanced the power lever.

This was exciting: charging down a runway at night in an aircraft I'd never flown before and desperate for it to reach seventy-five knots so I could get airborne. Why was it taking so long – was something wrong? No, it was just my nerves.

After an agonising wait, although a good bit less than a minute, the Caravan left the ground. I was off. With a bit of height below me, I pulled out the checklist and readied the machine for its flight. The most important thing was to set up the GPS. Without it and no map, I only had a broad idea of what compass heading to set and was quite likely to run into a mountain if I got it wrong. In the way was Mount Karisimbi, at fourteen thousand, seven hundred and eighty-seven feet to the south of my track, and, once in Kenya, Mount Satima at over thirteen thousand feet, to the north. Although, by the time I got there, dawn's first light would be showing.

There are few worse feelings than being in nominal control of some thing or situation over which you actually have no control and lack the skills to manage. It was a long time before I had everything sorted and my nerves had settled. I had two great worries: colliding with a mountain and having to ditch in Lake Victoria during the one hundred and sixty mile crossing – there were no life jackets in the aircraft, I don't like swimming, and there were bound to be crocodiles near the shore.

Thought: if I crashed would they trace alcohol in my blood? I'd had one beer hours ago and walked it off over nine kilometres, so probably not. It shouldn't have an influence on my flying, not that anyone could tell as I couldn't fly the thing properly anyway.

Fortunately it was a clear night. Looking out the left side window, away from the instrument lights, uncountable stars littered the sky, and the moon, a sliver of silver, enhanced the beauty of the scene. Aside from the engine's drone, it was so peaceful that all the accumulated tension from Mertens, the gangs of rioters and my stealing a plane fell away. For a while I was at peace with the world and could have stayed that way all night.

Although the moon was visible, it was past the last quarter and was not likely to show me a lump of solid rock right in front of me. I climbed to fifteen thousand feet to make sure I was above the mountains, if not by much. Legally, you're not supposed to fly above ten thousand feet without oxygen, but I wasn't legal anyway and, from experience, I knew that fifteen thousand was not going to affect me much. I hadn't counted on my lack of sleep, though. God, I was tired. It was almost twenty-four hours since I'd slept, and the reduced oxygen at that altitude was having its effect. That awful semi-conscious, zombie-like state where you drift off, the fall of your head jerks you awake, and ten seconds later it's falling again was on me. I *had* to stay awake. If I could avoid hitting anything, after an hour I'd be over the western shore of Lake Victoria.

To keep myself awake I reminisced about Sybil. I needed to reinforce my ten-year-old's promise to find and deal with her killer. Sybil had protected me, stood up for me and supported me, never mind treating me to cake and other goodies. When I wasn't busy, I used to wonder when we could next meet. Her visitors annoyed me, purely because they were meeting her, whereas I wasn't. I had loved her in my childish way, but when she most needed me to help, I had done nothing. Even though I now knew there was little I could have done at that age, my shame would not leave me. But now, the opportunity to right that wrong had arisen, and I was going to take it.

That led me to trying to make sense of the situation in the Mertens house. That the old man had killed Sybil, I had no doubt. I had been there. I had seen his birthmark. Once again the memory reminded me I'd done nothing to protect my friend, and again that revived my remorse. I would avenge her soon, though. But did he kill others, was he a serial killer, and why was his son so angry and bad tempered, and where did Céleste stand in all this? She had let me escape – me, a complete stranger, and obviously someone who was a threat to the family business because of what I knew.

The instrument panel lights held my focus as I monitored the state of the aircraft. Outside, slivers of reflected moonlight shimmering on the lake could be seen through the side window. I have to say it again, it was so peaceful and beautiful up there. I pushed my fear of ditching from my mind and let the autopilot take the aircraft into Kenya. High ground up to ten thousand feet and Mount Satima still lay ahead. Only after that could I descend for my airstrip at the foot of Mount Kenya by which time it would be light enough to see clearly.

The eastern horizon grew brighter. Below, the surface was still dark, but gradually I could make out the Mau Escarpment and beyond that the Aberdares. Being able to see what was below was a huge relief and I felt more confident as I prepared myself and the Caravan for landing. Back to the checklist.

I touched down at six o'clock with an enormous sense of relief (and a touch of pride). After sixty years, I had mastered a flight in a fixed-wing aeroplane and ended it with a pretty good landing.

Now to invent a plausible explanation of what I was doing back at the game lodge where I worked, when I was supposed to be on leave. I anticipated the questions. Why had I flown a Congolese aircraft there? Had I stolen it? What was I going to do next?

9

IT MUST HAVE rained the day before, because the ground did not release its usual cloud of dust with every step. An early sun sucked moisture from the soil, making it humid and hot walking from the landing strip to the lodge. My sweat-damped shirt dragged on my skin, resisting movement.

The smell of bacon wafting out of the kitchen told me I was ravenous. To eat or sleep? It was a tough decision, and the fact that I couldn't decide told me sleep was more necessary. I showered and slept till lunchtime.

I woke angry, a product of a racing mind while I was unconscious. I was suddenly sick of running from a range of people: Big Pharma in the form of Nipetco, who had abducted me; Mohammed Baqri, the assassin who had killed Alex; Don Cripps, the paedophile who had hired Baqri; the police – DCI Payne, who tried to pin Alex's murder on me. That was all behind me, with the exception of the pharmaceutical giants. I had spent too much time avoiding and hiding from these people in the last few months. I had only won battles with them when I'd gone on the offensive. So now I was going to do it again.

Mertens, quite possibly a serial killer, was smuggling great apes and other animals for massive profits. Dealing in wildlife is a cruel and barbaric crime. It gave me another reason to go after the man. His operation had to be shut down and he had to be punished by the law. My dilemma was that he had murdered Sybil, and I would personally see that he paid for that too. But which took priority?

'Charlie, what are you doing here? It's your time off, what you doing?' Robert Mwangi was Deputy Head Ranger. We had worked together for a long time and been on several patrols when we'd fought and captured poachers. It was always my intention to confide in him later and seek advice on what to do next.

'Hello, Robert, killed any baddies without my help while I've been away?'

'Two hundred of the bastards.' He laughed at his own joke. 'Why you here, Charlie? I thought you were making the ladies happy in Nairobi. Did they exhaust you?' He slapped me on the arm. 'You're getting old, my friend.'

If only he knew how old I really was. 'Ha, ha. I need to talk to you. Have you eaten? I'm starving.'

Over lunch I briefed Robert on what I'd been doing in my time off. I mentioned Idi Ajok, and he made a face but didn't comment. He had not heard of Mertens, but knew the wildlife trade had a hub in Goma.

'Robert, to stop Mertens and have him arrested I need your help. I'm not sure what you can do. What do you know about this business? Any suggestions? Who is Idi Ajok?'

'I don't know. That is a name from Uganda, but what his business is in Nairobi, I don't know. But,' Robert said, reaching across the table to slap my arm, 'there is a man in Goma who owes me a big favour. He's a small-time criminal. He used to be poacher. I saved him from a leopard many years ago, before you came here. It was a very close thing, and after I saved him, I arrested him. He was shaking with fear and was so grateful it was stupid. He promised me he would never poach again and swore to help me if I needed it.'

'And you think he'll have valuable information?'

'He knows what is going on in the whole DRC, Uganda, Rwanda region. Maybe his knowledge will not be accurate, but it will be better than nothing at all.'

THE CEILING FAN was out of balance. Its eccentric rotation produced a regular whoosh, whoosh sound, but it still produced a welcome draught. Beyond the verandah wall the cicadas were tuning their timbals for their evening chorus, and the dying sun cast an orange light on the acacia trees. It was peaceful.

I swatted at a mosquito, missed, and returned to stroking the condensation off my glass of Tusker. 'Any news from your man in Goma?'

Robert took a gulp of beer. '*Ndio*. He knows your friend Mertens. Actually, he works for him. I don't think it's an important job. *Jimiyu* – call him Jimmy – is too stupid for that. He is a messenger, a cleaner, a lookout, that sort of thing. He will talk about Mertens, but he is frightened. He says the Frenchman will kill him if he is caught talking to me. It has happened to other men.'

'Robert, I'm going back to Goma. I've got to sort this out. You introduce me to Jimmy and I'll take it from there.'

Robert shook his head. 'He won't talk to you. I must be there.'

'This could be dangerous and it's not your fight.'

'It is my fight as much as your fight, Charlie. This is a battle to protect the wildlife, so we are both involved. It is our job. If it is dangerous, then two of us will make it safer. As a black man I am not in so much danger as you. I can melt into the background – you cannot. You need me, I have the time, I will come.'

I couldn't tell him that saving wildlife was not my only reason for tackling Mertens. That would demand an explanation I was not prepared to give. 'Okay. I think we should go by air with me flying again.'

'Oh my God! This is more dangerous than Mertens.'

'Very funny. You will have entered the DRC illegally, I won't have, because they don't know I've left. On the other hand, when Mertens finds out his aircraft is back in Goma, he'll know I'm in town and will be hunting me. The aircraft needs fuel, and I don't know how to get any without alerting someone to this Congolese machine in Kenya.'

'How much do you need?' Robert was a natural fixer, the sort of man who would find anything you wanted in the most unlikely places: eggs for everyone when there wasn't a hen in sight, blankets when the supplies didn't arrive, chickens when the food was rotten (leaving enough to lay more eggs). Things fell off the back of trucks to satisfy Robert – but that implies he was dishonest, which was certainly not the case. He just had a magic touch for acquiring whatever he needed.

'A drum will do it.'

'It is too late tonight, I will get one from Nanyuki Airport first thing in the morning. The manager there owes me a favour. We'll sort out the payment later.'

'You're amazing. With a pump, we'll need a pump.'

Robert's look told me I had taken him for an idiot. 'Amazing. Were you going to suck and spit the fuel into the aeroplane?'

'Seriously, we need to get some kit and tools together so we can break into Mertens's office and store to find evidence.'

'I have a pen, tell me what you want.'

'In a moment … I'm wondering whether to contact Idi Ajok. When he hired me in Nairobi he told me he wants to expand and is looking at getting into bed with Mertens to add an airborne arm to his transport business. But is that the truth? He could be a rival and want to destroy Mertens. He might actually be working for the WWF or some such organisation and want to convict Mertens. Is he a criminal or is he genuine? If genuine, I owe it to him to report what I found.

'Then there's his man Paul Mbabazi. He was supposed to be watching me and learning, but he had another mission. He saw the gorilla hair, he knew what it was, but he avoided discussing it when I asked. I certainly don't trust him.'

'I think you must not contact this Idi. Let me make some inquiries, see if anyone knows who he is or what he does. The trouble is, out here, Nairobi is a long way away, and we don't know what goes on there, and mostly we don't care unless it affects us. I will make some enquiries first.'

10

THE LIGHTS OF Goma drew closer. We had descended to twelve thousand from sixteen thousand feet as soon as we were clear of the high mountains. To the north and slightly below us lay Mount Nyiragongo, easily identified at night by its huge molten lava lake, one of the greatest in the world, and by the fiery glow of its plume of smoke.

'Robert, read out the descent checklist, please.' I needed all the help I could get to fly this aircraft safely and had involved Robert from the start, getting him to read out the checks for me and keep a good lookout for other aircraft, clouds and high volcanos.

To avoid detection as long as possible, I held the altitude and descended quickly and steeply once over Goma itself. To the east, the orange of the advancing sun was giving way to a pale blue, and then, as we turned north and west, to the black of the night sky punctuated by the pinpricks of stars. Below, the runway lights and the black scar of the Nyiragongo lava flow that had cut the runway length by two thousand feet during its 2002 eruption could be made out. No communication broke through our headsets on the airport frequency. Was the control tower even awake? If I kept the aircraft lights off and made no radio calls, would the controller even notice?

To claim we touched down implies it was a gentle landing. Not so, with the landing lights on for only a brief period at the last moment to see the runway surface, I misjudged it and we fell out of the air about ten feet too high. The Caravan bounced and shuddered. I over-controlled, and we porpoised down the tarmac.

'*My God.*' Robert clutched at the shield over the instrument panel.

The aircraft settled. I gave him a false grin, my own heart racing. 'Sorry about that. Relax, we're still rolling, so we haven't burst a tyre, and we'll make it off the runway.'

It was best to leave the Caravan amongst the wrecks and discarded aircraft that had been dumped at the beginning of the parking area. Hopefully, it would not be noticed for a while and Mertens would not realise I was back. We took the taxiway and turned right towards the junkyard long before reaching the control tower. It would have been cruel to deprive the controller of his beauty sleep.

I squeezed into a gap between an Antonov 24 and a Let 410 and shut down. Some of the wrecks had been there so long they were covered in thick coating of grey dust and algae which the rain had streaked down each fuselage. In this depressing graveyard, the Caravan stood out more because it was clean than because of the logo on its tail.

The less time we spent in the airport, the better, but I couldn't resist writing a short note to clip to the controls: *Sorry, engine temperature limits exceeded. Best inspect for a hard landing.* If Mertens had a shred of professionalism, he would now have the aircraft and its engine inspected, costing him time and money.

'Let's go, Robert.' We'd planned this carefully. As soon as possible after landing we'd run for the airfield boundary, keeping away from the lights. Robert had a pair of short bolt cutters with him. If we didn't find a hole in the fence – all fences in Africa have holes in them somewhere – we'd make one.

We were heading for Nyiragongo's offices and warehouse, and the way there was across the main road and into the slum and factory area. We reached the fence. Across the road was an early queue waiting for the next bus or one of the scores of minibus taxis that plied the route.

'Come on, we'll go further along to the cemetery. There shouldn't be a crowd there.'

Five minutes later we were well south of our goal. There had been no holes in the fence, so Robert had made one with a few quick clips of his cutters. We clambered through to reach the main road, waited for a gap in the traffic and ran into the cemetery.

'You are too easy to see, Charlie. You need camouflage.'

Robert was right. A white man in Goma was not unusual, but a white man in this slum area was dangerously obvious. In the middle of the track through the cemetery was a puddle. I stirred it up and slapped mud on my face, neck and hands. It stank of rotting garbage and oil and probably contained mosquito larvae and human excrement. I almost threw up.

Robert started laughing. '*Eeh*. You now a blackface. That is not PC in UK is it? They will call you a racist.'

Robert led. I followed him leaving just a pace between us. He would attract attention as the first of the pair, with less chance of me being recognised as a white man.

'Robert, we want to head north and parallel to the main road, keeping about a hundred metres from it.'

He giggled. 'Okay, racist.'

Picking our way between unmarked mounds of earth, sometimes with makeshift crosses and the occasional gravestone, we came to a dirt track that headed north into the slum. This was where I needed to be invisible. I pulled my hat lower.

Alleyways of dirt eroded into rivulets that harboured fetid pools of black water. They weaved their crooked way between shacks of corrugated iron, panels from bigger houses and sheets of peeling plywood. Overhead, a spaghetti of telephone wires was embroiled with power lines on top of leaning poles.

People were starting to move, emerging from dark recesses into the growing light on their way to work. Now and then the smell of freshly baked baguettes relieved us of the overriding stench of drains and stagnant water.

We had half a kilometre of this, with the increasing danger of my being spotted as more and more residents poured from their meagre homes to join the commuters on the main road. Robert kept up a strong pace. I found it difficult to stay with him when the crowds hemmed us in.

A man caught my arm and shouted something. I shook him off. 'Robert don't lose me. Slow down when the crowd thickens.'

'*Sawa.* Okay. It cannot be far now.'

'Agreed. Head more towards the main road so we don't pass it.'

'*Sawa.*'

'Where's your man Jimmy?'

'Somewhere in this stink. I'll find him, don't worry.'

More workers thronged the alleys. Everyone was moving to the road. We were being carried sideways as we tried to cross the main direction of travel. A man beside me had been there for a while. I prayed he wouldn't look at me, but he seemed focused on moving, unaware of others around him.

What would a place such as this be like if another thousand people were added, people who never aged, just bred and bred? Humanitarian disaster.

The blue roof of Nyiragongo's warehouse appeared at the end of the alley ahead of us. Before that was a scrapyard for vehicle parts, advertised with a column of rusting silencers welded together. A man stood beneath it. He stared at me, took some steps and grabbed my sleeve, pulling me back.

'*Robert.*'

Robert turned and raised his fist. I smacked the man's hand down. He backed off.

Nyiragongo's main office door was protected by a lock that was beyond my basic skill. The warehouse, which backed the office, had a wide roller door for loading, with a wicket gate. This was padlocked.

'Cutters, Robert.'

'No, that lock is too wide for these cutters, but I can try this bit.' He pointed to the staple and sliced through it with a single snip. Another one opened a gap to release the padlock, which dropped to the ground.

'You stay here and keep a watch. Close the door behind me and if anyone comes, try to warn me. I'll check with you before coming out.'

'Okay, racist.'

'Oh, shut up.'

He laughed, and I stepped inside, to be met with a warm and humid atmosphere, as if a rainy day's heat had been trapped in there. Was the muck I'd plastered on my face coming to the fore in the confined space? – because the place had an odd smell to it. Or was it just packing material?

A weak light on the end wall of the warehouse beckoned. A passage wide enough for a forklift separated cardboard boxes and wooden crates of all sizes that stretched the full length of the building. The forklift sat at the far end. To the left was an open space with a door that probably led to the offices. On the right and opposite was a wide, curtained-off area.

The smell was stronger. I couldn't identify it, yet it was familiar.

Behind the curtain, someone gave a brief grunt, and moved.

STEPPING BACK, I looked for a gap in the fabric, found it, and inserted a finger. Was this a security guard sleeping on the job, perhaps? Maybe he wasn't asleep but was reading or studying. If I widened the gap in the curtain, the stronger light streaming through from the warehouse would wake or alert him.

Using a finger of each hand I spread the gap just enough to see in with one eye. It was dim, and the figures were more shadows than real beings. Shadows that repeated themselves on the wall behind. Six dark eyes met mine.

Four large cages stood on a platform about half a metre off the ground. A young gorilla sat in the end one. He – I assumed he was male – was separated by an empty cage from two chimpanzees, each in his or her own cage. One of the chimps saw me as the curtain parted and backed away. With hardly any space to move, he bounced from side to side, smacking at the bars. The other was calm, but he watched my every move. The gorilla looked menacing, but I knew nothing of apes' moods or mannerisms.

'Hello boys, you're just who I wanted to see.' I took photos and let the curtain slip back. Head down to my phone, I checked the pictures. They were satisfactory, but I needed to put them in context, to show they were undoubtedly in the Mertens warehouse.

I looked up with a start. Jacques Mertens stood in the doorway to the offices, leaning on his stick, watching me. He said nothing, but his stare held my attention.

A sound – clothing rustled behind me. I ducked and spun around, but staggered under the blow. Pain shot through my upper arm. Ducking had saved my head, but my left arm died, numb and useless with pain coursing in. I clutched at it and looked round.

Eric Mertens had a pick helve in his hand. It would have split my head in two had it landed. Jacques still leant against the doorframe. His expression had not changed. I suspected it would not have changed had my skull burst open across his warehouse floor.

'Give me your phone,' Eric said in French, even though he knew mine was limited. He was two paces away, holding out his hand.

With pins and needles, the feeling was returning to my arm. I could flex those fingers. A little more time and I could retaliate. The passage to the roller door was clear. If I could dodge Eric and his pick handle, escape would be simple, for Jacques was too old and would be easy to bowl over. Then the mountainous bulk of a security man came out from between the crates and cut off my freedom.

I held out the phone. As Eric took it, I grabbed his wrist and pulled. He was off balance and a kick to his stomach put him on the floor. The guard was on me. He was too big. I landed a couple of blows but he shrugged them off. A punch in my face, another to my ribs and I was down. Eric was up. His kicks hurt. I curled up, but he stepped over and half killed me with a blow to my back.

'Enough.' Jacques's voice was sharp. 'He must talk before we finish him.'

The pain in my back was debilitating. I could do nothing. Eric and the guard picked me up and forced me into the empty cage. The guard clipped the padlock. The curtain fell back in place and the light dimmed.

They left. But they'd be back, and fairly soon. Sweat trickled down my forehead. I wiped it. The movement caused a stab of pain in my back, although overall it was easing. There was room to sit or be on hands and knees in the cage, but not to stand. I sat and looked at my companions. Chimps can be vicious, but the one on my

left was staring into space. He must have been traumat-
ised, they all must. He had moved to the far side of his
cage from me. I couldn't see the one beyond him, but
the gorilla on my right was staring at me.

I didn't know much about gorillas, but I did know that
to look them in the eye is confrontational. I caught his
attention, then dropped my eyes, trying to show him I
wasn't a threat.

What did he think of me? Did he view me as just
another example of the species that had captured him,
and therefore an enemy? What would he do if I were in
his cage? Gorillas are not stupid. Would he recognise
that I too was a prisoner and in the same boat as him?
He knew nothing of quantum physics (neither do I), but
I'll bet he instinctively understood more about emotions
than we have done since we left our caves.

I put my hand flat to the bars of his cage to see what
he would do. Nothing. His eyes flicked to my hand for a
second, then returned to staring at the curtain.

Poor animals, what was their future to be? Pets –
curiosities for oligarchs in Russia and Central Asia –
something to have in their mansions to show how
wealthy and powerful they were? Or in a private zoo,
perhaps.

God, we are an appalling species. Well, some of us
are.

Where was Robert? He'd be wondering what I was doing. Would he come in to find out? Yes, he would, and he'd walk straight into the mess just as I had.

Voices again and the curtains parted. Father and son stood there, the old man leaning on his stick. The guard was not evident.

'You are the kind of man who will refuse to talk – at first. But, M'sieur Maxwell, everyone talks in time, even the toughest. *Alors*, save yourself pain and tell me what you are doing 'ere. If you don't then we will put you with the gorilla. He is not 'appy. To 'im, the men that caught 'im and the ones who put 'im in the cage and the one who feeds 'im are the same. So are you, and every-one is 'is enemy. He is very strong. He can pull your arm from the socket, he can rip your head off your neck. If you do not tell me what I want to know, we will put you in 'is cage.'

'What do you want to know?' Pretending to cooperate would waste time and maybe allow an opportunity to present itself. 'I told you already why I'm here.'

Eric stepped forward. He held up a taser. It scared me. The pain would be disabling and extreme, though soon over. But in my period of incapacitation, they could do with me whatever they liked. But was the taser for me or the gorilla?

One of the chimps, sensing the rising tension, began whining. The other, as before, bounced around its cage.

'That is not the truth, Charlie. Who are you working for, who sent you 'ere?'

'I am here purely to assess whether your standards as an aircraft operator meet international requirements.'

Eric raised the taser.

I couldn't let them disable me, and searched desperately for a believable response.

A man came through the office door and called. Something was said. The pair hurried out, but not before Jacques turned to me. 'Think carefully how to answer, Charlie.'

They had been gone about five minutes when another guard came in with a large can of water for the apes. A long baton and a bunch of keys hung from his belt. He filled the animals' bowls and made a show of offering me some, laughing in my face. He put the can down and drew the baton. Pushing the thing through the bars, he poked the chimp in the belly. The animal screeched and backed away, but couldn't get far enough. It batted the stick to the side, but the guard fenced with it, laughing and poking the poor creature. The chimp screamed, his mouth wide, his canines bared, long and sharp.

Behind me came a deep rumbling roar. The gorilla was disturbed and angry. On the far side the other chimp gave agitated screams.

The guard had his back to me, but he was bent forward and out of reach. If he stood upright … He did. I gripped his collar and pulled him back with one hand then snatched the keys off his belt with the other.

The shock on his face was a picture. He didn't know what to do. He couldn't get the keys off me. If he left, I'd unlock the cage and get out and away. He was going to be in trouble whatever happened. He ran.

There were at least six keys on the ring. One after another failed to fit the padlock. Sweat ran down my cheek. The Mertens would be back in seconds if the guard found them. Two more keys left, or had I missed one? Was my key even in this set? I was fumbling in desperation. The last key fitted.

I looked at the gorilla. He looked at me. Imagination can run riot in some situations. Did something pass between us? More than likely not. 'I'll be back for you,' I said out loud.

OUTSIDE THE WAREHOUSE full daylight revealed a dirty, litter-strewn street wide enough for a single truck. The front and sides of the building had alleyways along them. The back butted up to a two-metre-high wall.

The opposite sides of the alleys to Nyiragongo's office and store were crowded with shacks: rusting corrugated iron roofs and iron or planked walls, with soiled fabric or plastic curtains serving as doors. Some of these were shops, and a couple were shebeens, outside which an overhang of sparse thatch provided shelter for cheap tables and chairs. Beer bottles, amassed on one table, told of heavy drinking the night before, and stale alcohol added its heavy odour to that of dirty drains.

When I emerged, Robert wasn't at the door as we'd agreed. There were no signs of him either. Where the hell had he got to? The alleyway was deserted. Either the people had already left for work, the stall-owners had not arrived, or the drunks were sleeping off their excesses.

Further in, at the second shebeen, lay a drunk. But it wasn't. Robert was sprawled across the street, his face bloodied and covered in dust. His right hand lay in a rivulet of foul water, his left beneath him. He had a pulse: strong and steady, he'd be all right. I took him by the shoulders and dragged him under a stall canopy. He groaned.

Who did this? It must have been one of Mertens's guards; so they knew he was there and backing me up. They would come back for him to find out what was going on.

Voices came from the entrance to the alley: African and French – Eric, who would be able to see Robert's legs stretched out into the alley. The body would hold Mertens's attention for a moment.

I needed a weapon. Behind the bar in the shebeen, a wooden club like a baseball bat lay on a shelf below the counter. However many heads it had cracked in its life was about to be increased. I squeezed myself into the shadow beside the bar's entrance.

The guard was beside me, a metre away. His attention was on the body, which he kicked. He said something. Eric answered. I couldn't see him, but he was right next to me, half a pace back. He stepped forward, his right hand visible.

I swung the club at head height round to my left as hard as I could. Eric's nose crunched as it broke. Blood spattered on the stick and the shack wall. A stab of vengeful satisfaction ran through me. The guard spun round at the sound and leapt at me. A jab to his belly and he doubled over. After that, it was simple to put him out of action.

Robert was stirring, trying to sit up. 'Rest for a while,' I said.

Mertens was unrecognisable. Blood covered his face. Diluted with saliva, it dribbled from his mouth, but couldn't hide the broken teeth. I fought down the urge to kick him as he had me. Instead, I rolled him onto his side to stop him choking on his own blood. 'You walked into that one, M'sieur Pilot, Legionnaire and Arrogant Bastard.'

I helped Robert onto a chair. 'You okay? Stay here, I'm going inside. I still need to get evidence.'

'No, Charlie, I'm okay, I'll come.'

Robert was strong enough to walk, but not to fight, if it came to that. He might be more of a liability coming with me but being unable to help. But time was of the essence, and we couldn't spend it arguing. I gave in.

The sound of a powerful engine approaching made us run to get inside the warehouse and close the door. Inside, nothing had changed. I drew back the curtains. Fresh growls and high-pitched screams greeted us. The apes were clearly agitated by the human violence they'd witnessed. Were they going to see more?

Robert took photos, plenty of photos, many more than I had. 'These poor guys. From peace in the forest to a prison. And they have done nothing, no crime.'

'Come on, Robert, we can't spend time in here.' Eric had to be dealt with. I wasn't sure what to do with him, but leaving him free to go back to his father was not an option.

I ran round the front of the building and back into the alley. Robert followed at a walk. A Toyota Land Cruiser blocked the way. I squeezed around it. Twenty metres in, Céleste stood, one hand up to her mouth, the other hanging loosely to her side. She was staring at Eric, who hadn't moved since he'd fallen. She turned at my cough, but didn't say anything, just pointed.

A yellow knife handle protruded from his chest.

11

HAD CÉLESTE DONE this, stabbed her husband? Or was it the security guard I'd clobbered? He wasn't there any longer, and who knew what motive he may have had.

I bent down to Eric with Robert standing over me. Mertens had no pulse. He was dead all right, not that there was much doubt with the knife buried to the hilt in his heart. We both looked at Céleste. It was difficult to see in the poor light, but no blood was obvious on her navy top.

Her eyes flicked from one of us to the other and read too much into my expression. 'I did not do this.'

'I don't care if you did or didn't. Where's the security guard who was with him?'

She answered a little too quickly for my suspicious mind. 'I don't know if it was the same man, but one ran past me as I turned in here. I was looking for Eric.' She bent over her husband and rifled through his pockets. Wallet, three phones, bank cards and change; she took it all. She saw me watching her. 'Because he is dead, these belong to me. If I leave them here, some local will steal them. Normally, he has two phones, but not this one.'

'That's mine.' I reached across her husband's body and took the phone from her. 'I think it's best if we get out of here right now. This place will be crowded soon. Take us somewhere we can talk. Not your house.'

'Naturally. I will not go there.'

Céleste rammed the Land Cruiser into reverse and stamped on the throttle without a glance behind. She tore out of the industrial sector, hand on the horn, braking sharply as the odd idiot dared to be in the way, and powering on again. I clung to the support, half expecting the airbag to slam me back in my seat at any moment, and listened to her swearing profusely in French. There was an awful lot of pent-up aggression in that lady.

We'd almost reached the main road when a man in jeans, a bright green T-shirt and a red baseball cap ducked out of the way. Was that Paul Mbabazi?

Céleste drove as fast as was possible through the morning traffic, using the bulk of the car to force her way between and around the minibus taxis, jalopies and motorbikes that crowded the streets. She headed for the lake, slowing only when we reached an empty stretch of road on the otherwise heavily populated shoreline, where there was no more competition.

'Where does this go?'

'This road and others go all around the edge of the lake. There are four or five marinas round the next corner.'

Up to that point I had not made up my mind how we were going to leave Goma. Now, with the baggage I intended to take with me, it was even more difficult to reach a decision. I hadn't considered taking a boat, though.

Robert was lying on the back seat with his eyes closed. 'Stay there and get your head right. I'm going to take Céleste down to the shore to talk.'

A weak hand flapped his acknowledgement.

We found a spot on a shelf of rock and sat a metre apart. A light warm breeze touched our backs before ruffling the water some distance out. In the lee of the land, the surface was undisturbed.

'Thank you for letting me escape your house.'

'It was nothing. The old man is evil. I know what he does, and I am ashamed that my husband was a partner with him in the crimes. They would not have let you go away alive. I am sure of it. I saw a chance to do something good instead of benefitting from their evil, as I have done. I think I have been looking for a reason to rebel for a long time now, but the opportunity has not come my way.'

'What do you know of the business?'

'Everything – I think. Of course, I do not know what I do not know. They are dealing in wildlife. They transport live animals and also body parts, which are much in demand by the Chinese and others. They make a lot of money. Normally, in this business there are different dealers. Some deal with the poachers, who are only paid peanuts. Others organise the transportation by land and air, and others deal with the end user, the customer. These men are usually in Kinshasa, and of course everyone adds their bit to the price. Jacques has cut out these middle-men. He does everything between the poachers and the customer, so he makes more profit. All the information is in the office.'

'What about conflict resources: coltan, gold?'

'Of course. They will deal in anything that brings money. It is not important to them what it costs in life and misery, and many people die in the mines.'

'I really don't care, but did you kill him?'

She looked at me for the first time since we had sat down. Her stare was steady, with no hint of guilt. Either she was telling me the truth or she was a very accomplished liar which, with a husband like Eric, she might well have become. 'No. I already told you that. I want to see this business stopped – it is evil, but I would not kill for it.'

'You're not sorry he's dead, though. Aren't you pleased he can't bully you anymore?'

'You have no idea. *Regardez.*' Staring me straight in the eye, she raised her top and turned her naked torso to me. Her rib cage was a camouflage pattern of blue and yellow bruises. An ugly discoloured area on her pert right breast matched the brown of the areola. It was no wonder she had moved so awkwardly during that first breakfast. 'I had every reason to kill him, and I am glad he is out of my life at last.' She spat towards the lake and pulled her blouse down to hide the painful evidence. *'Rot in hell, you bastard.'*

'That has happened more than once. Well, you're free now – what will you do?'

'I must leave immediately. The old man will suspect me and will kill me, even if he cannot prove it. I know him. I think he enjoys killing, or having people killed. What will you do?'

'Catching the little people, the poachers, the dealers, is simple. But hidden behind them are major criminals, some of whom are unknown. It's information on those people I need. When I have it, and maybe it's in the documentary evidence you say is in the office, then Robert and I will go back to Kenya where I'll report these crimes to someone who can bring a prosecution.'

She stared at me for a few uncomfortable seconds. Something had occurred to her, and it wasn't insignificant. 'Jacques has many men he can call. We must go before he makes it impossible. I will help you with the papers, and I can give you names, but you must take me with you.'

Did this woman mean everything she said? 'What car will we use, your Land Cruiser? Robert must come back with me. It could be an extremely dangerous trip. You should go to Kinshasa.'

'No, not Kinshasa. Jacques has too many connections there. I cannot go home, I cannot go anywhere else in this country. His connections are all French-speaking, I'm sure, so I *must* get out to Uganda or Kenya where they speak English.' Her tone was desperate, but her look was defiant. 'I don't think my car is suitable. There is a safe, not so big, but too big for my car. I do not have the keys to it. They are in the house, so we must take the whole thing and open it later, somewhere else. There are some trucks at the office. One of them will be better.'

'What's in the safe?'

'Money, of course.' She hesitated and looked away. 'It is very important. The money is for me, but also there is a book of contacts which you will want. I can use that as an aide-memoire and add some details for you to have a full picture.'

That sounded good, but was she being completely honest? Was there something she wasn't telling me?

On the surface my scheme was simple. Get incriminating evidence from the safe and drive away in the middle of the night to a sanctuary out of the DRC. After that, there would be one last thing before returning to life in Kenya. But, as she pointed out, unforeseen complications, like the lack of safe keys, were already affecting my plan – plus the other unknown. 'Céleste, who is Idi Ajok?'

She gave me a sharp glance. 'Why do you ask about him?'

'He is the man who hired me to inspect your company. He sent Paul Mbabazi along for the ride – to learn from me, he said.'

She went back to staring out at the lake as if it held all the answers. 'He is bad. He owns a big trucking company already, but he wants more and more. We knew he had eyes on Nyiragongo months ago, but air transport is new to him and will be difficult. He will get his fingers burned if he doesn't get expert advice. But more than that he is a gangster, a crime boss, a mafia boss. Nothing will stop him once he sees something he wants.' She sighed and looked up at me. 'He is no different to Jacques and Eric. They are all evil.'

'So you think he sent Paul with me as a spy? I was just a cover to get Paul in there?'

She shrugged. 'Knowing what I know, that is likely. What I'm sure of now is that with Eric dead, Ajok is not going to waste time in coming to take over the company. He will do it by force, and he will do it soon.'

'Did you see Paul this morning? He was on the corner as we left the industrial area. It's possible it was him that murdered Eric.'

'Maybe; it would suit his purpose. He may be recruiting local men to invade the office, to seize the trucks and property. It would be foolish for Ajok to use men from Uganda, where he lives. The Congolese would resent it.'

'We can do nothing in daylight. We'll have to use today to plan, and tonight we'll take the safe. It's a pity you don't have the keys.'

Céleste was still staring at the water. She shook her head. 'It is not important now. The safe is in a back room next to the warehouse, out of sight of the office. It is maybe too heavy to lift, but there is a forklift to load it onto a truck. There will also be a filing cabinet, I think. I need to check.'

'Robert and I can travel in the truck. You can bring your Land Cruiser and follow us.'

'I want to be with you, I will feel safer. If necessary, your Robert can get home on his own without suspicion – he's black.'

'Robert is my friend. He stays with me.'

She shrugged. 'It may not be necessary. Two of the trucks have double cabs with five seats.'

12

THE NIGHT WAS black at two thirty on Sunday. An absence of stars probably meant that rain was on the way, it being the season. Here and there we passed small groups of drinkers, some slumped over their table, one flat out on the ground and most well past comprehension. Tables crowded with bottles, the ground littered with cans, pools of spilt alcohol soaking into the shirts of the supine. Music thumped out of ghetto-blasters, and a drunk was dancing, though unable to control his limbs. The odd light from a shack glimmered from the darkness to show that there were others, more responsible, who focused on scratching out a living for themselves and their families.

Nyiragongo's store was in darkness. Céleste parked her Land Cruiser and opened the office door. She cancelled the alarm, chose two sets of keys for the trucks, tossed them to me and went directly to unlock the warehouse door. I gave the keys to Robert. 'They should all be big enough, so choose the one with the most fuel.'

'*Ndio, Bwana* racist. Yes, Boss.' He laughed, loving his own joke. I was getting tired of it, but at least he was feeling better.

The safe was out of sight in a small room which was separated from the warehouse by a drywall partition. The clunky cast iron object was too heavy for one man to lift and even Robert and I would struggle. We certainly wouldn't be able to lift it high enough to get it onto the back of a truck.

Enter the forklift. Using a tape measure Céleste found for me, I marked the position of the safe on the other side of the drywall where it faced the animal cages. The forklift punctured the walling with ease and further attacks created a massive hole with the safe in the middle.

The crashing sounds disturbed the apes. Behind their curtain and unable to see, the gorilla growled unhappily and the chimps squealed. These were foreign noises, harsh and violent and unheard in their forest home. What did they mean? What further terrors were in store?

There was nothing we could do for them at that stage. The best course was to get them out of Mertens's clutches as quickly as possible, but it couldn't be done immediately. Robert had found a vehicle. He parked it outside the wide loading-bay door, which he slid open, letting the cool night air mitigate the hot, humid interior. Céleste had been in the office; she came out to watch us, with a document still clutched in her hand. Whatever she was doing appeared to be less important than her viewing of the safe.

'Robert, can you tilt the thing so I can get the forks under it?'

With the forks under the safe, Robert let it fall upright and helped wiggle it into a more secure position. He went in search of tie-down straps as I tilted the forks back to stop the load falling off the front. 'This is fun. Stealing safes could become a new profession.'

Robert had chosen a Mercedes-Benz Unimog. This is an extremely capable four-wheel drive vehicle with a high ground clearance. They come in various forms, but this one was a long-wheelbase model with a double cab, a truck back, a six-litre engine and weighed some seven tonnes – it was an imposing animal. If we went off-road anywhere, we could not ask for a better thing to do it in.

The apes would surely enjoy the cool night air which could not reach them behind the curtain. Once I'd finished loading, I meant to open it. I turned my new toy to face down the aisle to the exit and the Unimog – and stopped.

Four men blocked the doorway. One was armed with a panga, the others with iron bars. Were these Jacques's men? If not, then whose? Idi's?

I put the safe down again and reversed the forklift. '*Robert.* We've a problem. Where's Céleste?'

He came out from behind the gorilla's cage with a cargo strap in his hand, the metal tensioner dragging on the ground. He looked down the aisle. '*Eesh.* She went back in the office, looking for something.'

'Use the forklift as protection. Stay with me.'

I drove at a snail's pace towards the entrance. Robert followed, one hand on the engine cover. The men filled the doorway. Behind them was the truck and beyond it, the street. The thug with the panga, the greatest threat, was second from the left. He and the end one were shoulder to shoulder, too close to swing their weapons effectively – idiots. Panga-man was dancing from one foot to the other. His mate was slapping the bar into his hand. Then he too began to stamp – spoiling for a fight.

A familiar voice came from the shadows inside. 'Charlie, you're outnumbered. Stop what you're doing and walk away. This is not your battle. Idi did not pay you to do this. I promise you will not be hurt if you go away now.'

'And what will you do, Paul? What are you going to do with these animals? Are you going to take Mertens's company by force?'

'This is business between Idi and Mertens. It has nothing to do with you. It is not your problem. Go away.'

He was right; it was nothing to do with me. So why had I agreed to help that great blob of an individual in Nairobi? It was that blonde pixie at the Thorn Tree. If she hadn't appeared to recognise me with the aid of a photograph, I wouldn't have realised Big Pharma had tracked me down again. Idi gave me an opportunity to run and I took it. In doing so, I had avoided being caught, but had now been landed with some vicious opposition. But, the future of the apes and many more animals after them was worth a fight.

I raised the forks – too high … Down a bit, to thigh height. 'I have a duty to stop the trade in these animals, and I'm going to do it.'

The two men in front of me were still performing a makeshift war dance. The beat of their feet and the slapping of the bar had fallen into time. Were they building their own morale or trying to frighten us? Probably a bit of both.

I put my foot down. The forklift jumped forward, charging at the pair. Clowns – the end one turned to his left and the panga one turned right – straight into his mate. That cost them vital seconds. The forks bore down either side of the pair, forcing them together. Their backs rammed into the edge of the Unimog's load bed. With empty space under the vehicle, they both doubled over and disappeared.

One of the best characteristics of a forklift is that it is rear-wheel steering, which means it can spin on the spot. The first man on my right leapt forward, his iron bar high over his head. I spun the steering wheel and caught him with the side of the right fork. He was down, hurt, but alive. The two under the truck hadn't surfaced – likely out of action. The last thug was flat out and not moving. Robert was standing over him with the buckle end of the cargo strap swinging beneath his hand.

'You have escaped this time, Charlie. Next time will not be so easy.'

Wherever Paul was, he was never anything but a voice in the shadows that night.

This episode brought back a question that had been niggling me: was Paul really acting on Idi's behalf? I couldn't put my finger on it, but something made me suspect that he was seizing this opportunity to carve out his own kingdom. If that was true, then where was Idi's gang? – because he would not take Paul's treachery lying down. Did it mean there were three parties battling for control of Jacques Mertens's wildlife trade? Mertens himself was certainly not going to give up his empire without a fight. If and when we met opposition, which of these disparate groups would they be?

Robert looked up at me. 'I'm going to find Jimmy. They say there has been rioting and protests against MONUSCO in Beni, to the north, and the road to Beni was blocked three days ago. Men have been killed. It will not be wise to go too far north. Jimmy can lead us out to Uganda using back roads before we do that.'

'Excellent, but hurry, it won't be long before Mertens gets here. And he won't be a happy man.'

'CÉLESTE, COME AND help me, please. We need to get this safe loaded.'

'First you must put the apes on.'

'What are you talking about? We can't take them.'

'Of course we are taking them. We have to.'

'No——'

'We *must*,' she shrieked, thrusting both hands out at me. 'I have to sell them to help fund my future. Without them I have nothing. Jacques has everything.'

'We cannot take them. They'll be extremely stressed by the journey. They might even die. We have no food for them, and it will be at least twelve hours before we reach Kampala. And when we get there, what are you going to do with them?'

'I have a tranquilliser to give them. That will calm them and relieve the stress. Don't worry.'

'That won't last for a fraction of the journey. We would need to keep stopping to check on them, and you cannot administer the drug over and over again, you'll kill them. You can ask Robert, he's a game ranger, and they do this all the time. The apes are not coming. It's too cruel.'

She had tears in her eyes. '*Bastard.* What will I do? I will have nothing.'

'You said there's cash in the safe, you have that. And until we open it I'll pay for you. Now, please help me with it.'

She flapped her arms up and down, her fists clenched. Her weak attempt to tilt the safe failed. She stamped her foot '*Aaagh.*'

I climbed down from the forklift to help her. Close up, her pursed lips were quivering and the wet on her cheeks glistened in the warehouse lights.

I tilted the safe. 'Okay, just hold it there while I get the forks under it.'

She sniffed and nodded.

Robert had parked the truck side-on to the loading bay door. I put the safe on board, hard up against the back of the cab, then added the filing cabinet she wanted. We draped the tarpaulin over everything and tied it down. We were ready to go, although Robert had not returned with Jimmy.

'What's really in the safe, Céleste? You haven't taken your eyes off it, like a mother with her child.'

Her hysteria had evaporated, and she had herself under control again. It was amazing how quickly her mood could change. Had a new plan occurred to her? She wiped her cheeks dry with the back of her hand, sniffed again and eyed me with caution. 'I told you, normally there is a lot of cash – for paying off poachers and other scum; also, important information: contacts, clients, dealers, etcetera. The information you want.'

'And the filing cabinet?'

'More of the same, and the accounts. What are you going to do about the apes?'

'We'll call in to the National Park office in Rumangabo on our way to Uganda before they start work. They'll know how to look after them. And from there we are not far from the border.'

Furious arguments lay in her eyes. She opened her mouth to speak but shut it when Robert appeared with a little man in a soiled blue shirt with a hole in one sleeve and torn black trousers. No hair bordered the deep scar that ran down one side of his head and disappeared below his collar. Was that thanks to the leopard Robert had saved him from?

'This is Jimmy,' Robert announced.

Jimmy showed us half a mouthful of teeth. Who had knocked the others out?

A DARK BLANKET of low cloud hung over the country, swallowing distant high ground, delaying the first light of day and threatening rain.

I drove. Céleste was beside me in the front, and from the rear seat came an unceasing stream of words. If they weren't between Robert and Jimmy, they were between Jimmy and someone on a phone somewhere.

We left the industrial-cum-slum area and turned right onto the main road. To the left was the airport, but on both sides of the road after that the shacks continued. Gradually they gave way to small, economical, more permanent buildings until, after some six kilometres, rough, manually tilled fields could be made out, with stretches of grass, bushes and low trees beyond them.

Nyiragongo, the active volcano that was responsible for so many deaths in recent times, was close, a real and massive threat hidden in the cloud. At a village in its shadow, the two in the back began to argue.

'What's going on, Robert?'

'Jimmy wants to get out. He wants to go back to Goma. He'll get a taxi.'

'But he agreed to help us after Rumangabo, to find our way on the back roads all the way to the border.'

'I know. I told him that, but he said the road is easy to follow all the way to Rumangabo, which is where we turn off.'

'We know that. It's *after* Rumangabo that we need his help.'

This was a worry. With the fighting between the M23 and the Islamist ADF rebels, the situation was in a constant state of flux. It was impossible to know who controlled what area. If we got lost or took a wrong turn we could end up in rebel hands … The consequences didn't bear thinking about. But we couldn't force the man. I stopped the truck and Jimmy was quickly out of the cab.

Robert slammed the door after him. 'He made excuses, something about family and that he had to go back, but I know he is frightened. He said that from here on we can expect roadblocks by any of the rebel groups, who want money, phones and expensive things. There will also be MONUSCO checkpoints. He says if we are stopped by any of these, there will be big trouble. He's frightened, he doesn't want to go to jail again, and he doesn't want to be killed by the rebels.'

'I don't blame him.'

'He also said that Paul is very angry that we defeated his men and escaped. He is now busy finding more men to catch us.'

'He may do that. This is not the fastest of vehicles and we have a long way to go – another three hours to the border, probably.'

Céleste had not uttered a word since leaving Goma. Now she coughed and said, 'Jacques will also be looking for us. He will be furious about Eric's death and us stealing from him. I worry, because he has many contacts, and I'm sure he will be organising an attack ahead of us.'

'That's not good … You were talking faster than a group of women in the market, Robert. What else did Jimmy have to say for himself?'

'He confirmed what Céleste says is true. Jacques is planning to stop us. I asked him if Idi Ajok still employed Paul, but he doesn't know.'

'Seems like we'll have some opposition.'

13

THE GRAVEL ROAD, which wasn't in too bad a condition considering its length and the cost of continual maintenance, was peppered with potholes large and small. They didn't worry the Unimog, but in some places rain had cut deep ruts through the surface, forcing me to slow. Raindrops dotted the windscreen; the wipers cleared them with a single stroke. But soon the potholes became puddles, which the vehicle's big tyres would empty with a splash, and the wipers had to work on high speed. The drive was nominally about an hour fifteen, but the sometimes slippery conditions forced me into a slower pace.

Half an hour out of Rumangabo we drove out ahead of the rain and saw a white, tracked, armoured vehicle parked off the road, its 30mm cannon pointing in our direction. I hesitated for a moment, but the barrel didn't track us, it was just resting in the last position selected. Bold, black lettering declared it as UN. On the opposite side was an armoured personnel carrier with six soldiers in their distinctive blue helmets, probably wishing they were somewhere else.

A blue flak jacket waved us down. All of us got out, taking the opportunity to stretch our legs. Two soldiers, Bangladeshi at a guess, nosed around the Unimog. The sergeant, who appeared to be the senior member of the squad, pointed up at the tarpaulin covering the load. 'What you got here, then?'

'We are moving some filing cabinets and other furniture to our office in the national park. You want to see? Your English is very good, is that from school?'

His face lit up as he realised he could have a conversation in a language he was familiar with. 'Oh, thank you, sir. I did learn in school, yes, but I also had practice in UK. My uncle has a small business there, and I worked for him for a while.'

'Marvellous. Whereabouts?'

'Bristol.'

'Bristol, eh. Nice place but terrible traffic.'

'Terrible, sir. Almost as bad as Dhaka.' He laughed. 'You go on your way, sir. Have a good day.'

I gave him a friendly pat on the shoulder, and we climbed back into the truck.

We found the national park headquarters easily. Robert and I went in to request that the apes be rescued from Mertens's warehouse. This was not something they did, the woman said, but she knew how to organise a team to collect the animals.

'The cages are in a warehouse that may be protected by armed guards. Your people should be prepared for that.'

She looked at me as if I was an imbecile. 'Our rangers are used to fighting. Many have been killed by the rebels, and some have been wounded fighting poachers.'

The grind of a starter motor was followed by the roar of a diesel engine running immediately to full speed. Who the hell drives like that? Robert looked out the window. '*She's taking the truck.*'

We scrambled for the door. Robert was quickest. He leaped up onto the right side of the cab. I jumped up to the driver's side, got a foot on the step and grabbed the door handle – locked, but the window was open. Céleste was leaning across to lock the passenger door. She couldn't reach it. I reached across her and snatched the keys from the ignition. She grabbed my arm and bit it. I dropped the keys on the floor somewhere. After a few revolutions of the dead engine, the Unimog stopped.

Céleste gave a single piercing cry and burst into tears. She smacked the steering wheel with both hands and doubled over it, oblivious to the horn blaring. I pulled her back and helped her out and down from the cab. She sank to the dirt, her back against the muddy front wheel, a picture of misery.

'You can't look after the apes, Céleste. It is cruel to keep them, worse to sell them. They must go back to the wild and the rangers here will help them and look after them properly. How much would you make from the apes?'

She sniffed and swallowed. 'For a live gorilla: a hundred and fifty thousand, but shipping must be paid from that. For a chimp: maybe seventy thousand.'

'Dollars?'

'Yes. Local prices are much less.'

'I understand you wanting to keep them, but you can't treat animals like that. How many gangs are dealing in wildlife in this region?'

She didn't answer, just sat there on the warming surface of the car park, a steady trickle of tears down her cheeks. We helped her inside and the receptionist made her some tea. 'You can get breakfast at the lodge here,' she said.

'Good idea. Let's do that and calm down. We need to eat anyway.'

With the opportunity to relax for a short while, I went outside and called Kirsten back home in England.

'*Andrew*. Oh, sorry – *Charlie*. I get so mixed up with all my boyfriends.' She laughed at her own silliness. 'How are you? What's happening? Do you need help?'

Unmistakeable pleasure resonated in her voice. A term of endearment was struggling to break loose amongst those questions, but she knew I avoided relationships, and why. She was patient, though, prepared to wait until I came around. 'I'm fine,' I said. 'How are you doing? How's Lupus?'

'Your dog is wonderful, but he misses you.' By which she meant they both did.

I brought her up to date with what had been happening, omitting the fight in the warehouse. 'We've got a bit less than two hours to go to reach the Uganda border. Then we'll be in much safer territory, as Jacques Mertens at least will not have any influence over there.'

'I'll keep my fingers crossed. You could be right about a serial killer. The police have identified eight other women, all prostitutes, who were murdered in 1944 and early '45. The reason this was not picked up previously was because the killings were spread around the country in the big cities – London, Birmingham, Manchester, Coventry and Glasgow – and the police did not have anything like a central database in those days; plus, there was a war on, of course.'

'You mean he deliberately travelled to distant towns to disguise the connection between the crimes?'

'It would seem so. He would kill a girl in London, then go to Glasgow and Coventry, before going back to London. The murders were spread over the full six weeks you mentioned. This was far too long for a British serviceman on leave, so it had to be someone stationed in Britain, or a non-combatant.'

'Or a Frenchman who wasn't serving, a man with a port-wine birthmark on his ankle.'

'Before you can use that evidence, you'll have to bring him to trial. Can you do that?'

'I may not even try to do it.'

'I don't like the sound of that. Don't do anything illegal, Charlie.'

I ignored that. 'Any similarities in the murders?'

'All through some form of asphyxiation. A pillow, airway blocked, strangulation ...'

We chatted a bit longer before saying goodbye, which ended with, 'Take good care of yourself, Charlie.'

'You too.'

'Including Lupus, you mean.' She laughed.

'Kirsten,' I added, 'sorry, but please don't call me unless it's critical. If my phone rings at the wrong moment it could put me in a risky position. I'll call you when it's safe.'

WE LEFT RUMANGABO in better physical shape than when we arrived. With a tattered map that Céleste found in the cab and following directions from curious locals, we took side roads to the Ugandan border on tracks so narrow and winding that we sometimes brushed the vegetation on both sides. Elsewhere the road widened enough for trucks to pass. But no broken vehicles blocked our progress, nor were there any collapses of the surface that we couldn't surmount. Two stretches of the road, both about a hundred metres long, had been churned into heavy, sticky mud-baths by large trucks. Ordinary cars waited on both sides of these wallows, waiting for someone in a big vehicle or a tractor to tow them, almost floating in the mud, through to firmer ground. I didn't stop, and the looks I got were not com-plimentary. Sorry chaps, and I hope we won't have to call on you for help at any stage.

I had known the slippery surface and deep mud would involve much low-gear work and make for slow going. The big engine would guzzle fuel for little forward progress, so, not far out of Rumangabo we diverted to Kabaya to find some fuel.

A lone woman on a corner sheltered under a huge umbrella, selling snacks, Coca-Cola and Mirinda. In return for her directions to the service station, Robert gave her extra for some drinks. I gave Céleste some cash so she could buy some food in a mini-market, while I supervised the fuelling.

She came back and watched the pump figures spinning up. 'This diesel may not be clean. It is normal to find dirt and water outside the main cities.'

'We've no option. We'll be in a worse situation if we run out before the border.'

After filling the tanks my supply of local cash was alarmingly low. In Uganda I could use a credit card, but not in a remote area of the DRC. I was the only one able to be the banker.

At around the halfway point, the road took a hairpin bend, almost doubling back on itself. Within the loop was a narrow, sheer-sided gully. On the outside of the bend, the hill climbed steeply and was dense with trees. Above and on either side of the gully were tiny cultivated patches of ground, too small to be called fields. The forested slope commanded the bend. A rare sign warned of the sharp turn. Taking my foot off the throttle, I let the Unimog slow itself; the less I braked on this surface, the more likely I was to maintain control.

Roadblock. A makeshift barricade was stretched across the apex of the bend, invisible until the last moment. To turn was impossible, to reverse too slow. There was no option. I stopped but left the engine running.

Three scruffy men in green camouflage appeared. What they were was anyone's guess: rebels, bandits or simple thugs. Two had AK47 assault rifles and wore military style caps; the other carried a general-purpose machine gun with a long belt of its ammunition draped over his shoulder, wrap-around dark glasses, and a beret pulled down over his head so it looked like a Yorkshire pudding. They were not an impressive fighting force, but they were scary.

One of the AK wielders came up to my door. His bloodshot eyes told of drugs and cheap alcohol. He yelled something at me, his words slurred, but he wanted us to get out, that was obvious. Drunk, ill-disciplined soldiers are unpredictable – a dangerous breed to be treated with great caution.

'Stay where you are, don't get out,' I called to the others, and climbed down, leaving the engine running.

He shoved me up against the cab. His breath stinking of booze, he mouthed some unintelligible words. Flecks of spittle hit my face.

'*Charlie.*' Paul's voice. How the hell did he know where to find us?

'Paul. Tell this clown to shut up. I can't talk while he's yelling at me.'

The bandit backed away, but levelled his AK at my stomach. Where was Paul? I couldn't see him, but his voice was coming from the higher ground to our left.

'What do you want, Paul?'

'You and Robert can go, but you leave the truck and everything on it, as well as Céleste.'

Céleste leaned down from the window above me and shook her head, panic in her eyes.

'Or what?'

'These guys enjoy killing. They think it makes them powerful, taking on the power of their victims, as they see it.'

'You can take the truck and everything on it, but not Céleste.'

Céleste slapped my shoulder. '*Non*. Not the safe. You must not give them the safe.'

'She has information I need. If she gives it to me freely, then she will not be harmed.'

Our situation deserved scrutiny. The Unimog was emitting the comforting, throbbing sound of an idling diesel just five metres from the barricade. This was a strip of light branches stretched from the right side of the road to about two thirds of the way across, leaving enough room to drive a vehicle round the end. A second, similar strip, some six or seven metres further on, began on the left side. A car could get through the block, but would have to snake at low speed round the end of one strip then the other. And Paul, where the hell was he? Wherever he was, my effort to see him was futile, and there was nothing I could do about it if I did spot him.

'Are you doing this for Idi, Paul, or is this your leap from lackey to crime boss?'

'Idi is old, a has-been. He is not effective anymore. It's time for someone strong to take over. You are wasting time. Give up now, or in one minute these guys will shoot.'

I called up to the cab, 'Did you hear all that?'

'*Oui*. Are you going to leave me to these men, Charlie?'

'Paul, give me one extra minute. I have to talk to the others, to Céleste.'

'Okay, one more, then they shoot.'

I climbed up into the cab. 'We've one chance. Get on the floor.'

My AK thug was standing with his back to the earth bank to the left of the Unimog, and it was a certainty that he did not understand my conversation with Paul, so he didn't know what was planned. The other two were in front of it. Could Paul see me? If he couldn't and the gun wielders did not know what had transpired between us, then precious seconds could be won.

The world erupted. Gunfire crackled. *What? Who?* The mini supersonic crack of bullets. At first the shots went wild, or we weren't the target. But some hit the truck, others ricocheted, zinging their way into the bush. The AKs on the road were slow to react, slow to work out which way to turn. Slow to take cover.

I slipped the truck into gear and charged. One man ahead leapt clear. The other didn't, and his thump was felt through the cab. In the wing mirror, one man was waving his weapon around, looking uphill for someone to shoot. Then his rifle fell and he followed. Bullets shattered the windows and ripped through the bodywork. A loud clang from the back said the safe had stopped a round.

The Unimog thought nothing of the feeble barrier ahead and smashed through with no more of a bump than that of the body we left behind.

Round the hairpin. Now all the shots were aimed at us. Two more hit the cab, and another clanged into the safe behind us.

'Stay down.'

A straight stretch lay ahead and I was able to accelerate to an unsafe speed. 'Everyone okay?'

'I'm good,' said Robert. 'That was lucky. No one hit and we got away.'

'Céleste?'

She cleared her throat. 'I … I'm all right. Who … who … was that shooting?'

'Anyone's guess. They could have been a group of rebels, they might have been Idi's men if he knows of Paul's treachery, or they could even have been Jacques's people. One thing's for sure, they wanted to get rid of Paul's men before dealing with us, so it was probably Jacques's boys. How does everyone know where we are?'

14

WE TRUNDLED ALONG the back road to the Uganda border, passing two-room houses, tiny plots of maize, cassava or other crops and the occasional abandoned, corroded wreck. Our progress was slow, interrupted by the condition of the surface. No one felt like making conversation. Céleste was downcast. Her head was turned away, gazing out of her window at the passing forest. Whether she saw anything was doubtful, because her troubled thoughts caused her to frequently wipe her eyes and sniff.

'Any idea how people know where we are, Céleste?'

'I was thinking of that: it is possible that Jacques has put a tracker on each of his vehicles. He is paranoid about control of his company. He has to know everything that is going on to make sure no one is cheating him. Maybe that is how he knows where we are.'

'Then we must find the thing and get rid of it before we stop. Robert, search in the back there for anything that looks odd. It might be magnetic. You too, Céleste, please. Look in every possible hiding place.' I drove on while they scrabbled around. Céleste had her fingers under the dash and amongst the wiring. She even felt in front of my knees and feet, pushing my leg to the side with an impersonal shove.

The comforting, reliable roar of the engine faltered. It died, stuttered, died again, then came back to life. Céleste's eyes went wide. In the back, Robert muttered something obscene, which was not like him.

'That's dirty fuel. We'll have to stop and clean out the system.'

In front of us was a split in the road; the main part continued straight ahead, and a minor track led up the hill to the left. On the right was a steep drop down into a ravine. I took the main road for about a hundred metres then parked. 'If there's a tracker it must be outside the cab somewhere. Let's find it first. Then we can hide and take our time while they can't trace us to clean the fuel system.'

Céleste searched the truck bed and areas of the cab she hadn't covered before. I examined the engine and front suspension, and Robert spent his time grovelling around under the vehicle. After ten minutes, he held a small black box in the palm of his hand. 'Is this a tracker? It was stuck to the chassis on the inside. There's no connection to anything else.'

'Well done. Chuck it away.'

Robert hurled the device into the defile. 'They will think we have crashed down there, maybe.'

'Maybe,' I said, and briefly considered leaving tyre tracks up to the edge of the drop, but it wouldn't fool them for long. 'Let's go back and up that other track and see if there's a place we can stop. If we make it that far.'

THE TRACK LEFT the main road and immediately climbed a steep, rutted path between giant trees. The engine didn't pack up, but it certainly wasn't happy, hesitating and stuttering while belching black smoke from the exhaust. We had to fix this urgently, but dense forest enveloped the track, leaving no way to get off it.

Céleste gave an excited shout. 'There's a house.'

A sliver of dirty white, the corner of a building, an unnatural object, projected out of the vegetation ahead.

'Stop here.' Robert opened his door. 'I'll go and take a look.' He melted into the trees with the practiced art of a ranger.

'Charlie, I've been thinking. I'm sorry for my attitude and greed and putting stress on you because I wanted to keep the apes, and for trying to steal the truck, which would have left you stranded. I'm sorry.' Céleste reached across the cab and touched my arm, letting her fingers linger for a while.

I didn't respond until she dropped her hand. 'It's all right; understandable and forgotten.' Which was a lie.

Robert appeared at the side window. 'There is no one here. The place is empty. I think there has been fighting and the people have fled. We can hide here.'

I coaxed the reluctant Unimog up the track and parked it between two ruined huts. Other buildings, square, plastered and mostly about two rooms in size, had been white with red iron roofs once upon a time. Now, years of mud and dust and tropical rain had stained the walls from the ground up. There was nothing abnormal about that, but the walls were also pockmarked from bullets. Daggers of shattered glass were all that remained of every window. Doors hung off broken hinges, and the whole centre of one had been shot out. The pale skeleton of a dog lay dismembered on the track. Not a scrap of flesh had escaped the scavengers.

Céleste took a deep breath, her hand to her mouth.

Whatever had driven these people away had been horrific, but it was to our advantage. 'This is ideal,' I said. 'No one's coming back here in a hurry.'

Robert and I raided the truck's toolbox and got to work. Céleste looked around the hamlet. After a few minutes she came back with a dented bucket. 'You want to use this to catch the diesel?'

The Unimog had two tanks, each with a filter, which were both half clogged with dirt and a fair amount of water, although how much of that was from the last refuelling was anyone's guess. We let fuel out of the tanks into the bucket and examined it. There was a lot of water. We kept draining until it ran pure diesel. At the bottom of the bucket was at least two litres of water and other muck. How this engine had kept running, heaven only knew.

Robert tightened a connection. 'Do we have enough after wasting all that?'

'Don't throw it away,' I said. 'Let it settle in the bucket then we can cream the good stuff off the top and pour it back in the tank. That should give us another five litres or so.'

'Time for a test, Robert. You ready?'

The starter turned. The engine ground over but would not catch. Again, and again. 'We'll flatten the battery, and then we'll be stuffed.'

Hell. What more could we do to get this thing going? Robert was scratching his head, his mechanical knowledge was thin. Céleste was nibbling her fingers. Being unable to get out of the country with the safe and the information I needed would be to lose everything we'd fought for, Céleste would be penniless, and we'd be in a very dangerous situation.

'We shouldn't need to bleed air out of the system, we haven't let any in. Let's try once more.' I turned the key. Again it ground slowly over, then sped up as a cylinder caught, then died. I switched it off to give the starter a break.

Robert banged on the door, grinning. 'It's nearly there, Charlie. One more time.'

Another cylinder caught, then another. Smoke poured out of the exhaust, the engine accelerated, then it was roaring, even and strong. We all breathed.

Diesel stinks, and the stench sticks to you. We had nowhere to wash so had to live with it. The only food we had was three quarters of a loaf of bread, and we were hungry. The light was fading early with the cloud cover and the forest all around us.

'I think we're fairly safe here. Let's get some sleep and get going early tomorrow.'

The others both agreed. Robert said he'd sleep in the back under the tarpaulin. Being the gentleman, I said

Céleste should take the back row and I would try to get comfortable across the front seats, with the gear levers in between them.

'No, Charlie. You need sleep more than I do, you are driving. Also, I am smaller than you and will get comfortable more easily than you in the front. You take the back.'

'That's very good of you, but no. I'll manage in the front.'

'I insist. It is important you rest, I can sleep in the day while you drive.'

I gave in while still protesting. Why had she switched from being offhand to friendly all of a sudden?

How many hours had I been awake? Every time I attempted this simple calculation, my mind wandered onto some other irrelevant question, until sleep overcame me. I never worked it out.

Some time later – it was completely dark – movement in the cab hauled me up from the depths to semi-consciousness. Something was warm. A hand was on my cheek, another on my thigh. 'Charlie, I'm cold. Can I lie with you?'

That was ridiculous. The seats in the back were too narrow for two bodies. I was struggling to make sense, and grunted. She took that as a yes and lay full length, half on top of me and half on a few inches of seat. She wasn't cold.

'I'm sorry,' she whispered, her lips close to my ear. 'You rescued me, but I fought you. Truly we are on the same side and we want the same things. Please can we be friends?'

Really? We didn't want the same things back in Goma and Rumangabo. But that's not what I said. 'Of course. You were upset with everything that's happened and worried about your future. Your actions were understandable.'

What was she up to? Whatever it was, this wasn't a genuine apology. What was she going to gain from winning me over? I couldn't get the apes back for her, they would be safe in capable hands by this stage, and beyond her reach. There was nothing else I could do bar giving her a lift for the long drive to Nairobi. She might think of me as security, or someone who could look after her until she was safe. But that someone certainly wasn't me. If anything, it was what she could do for me by supplementing the information in the safe that was my hope. Without it, I had no use for her, but I wouldn't see her hurt, she wasn't the enemy.

She didn't answer, but her hand slithered between us to my crotch.

Decades ago, at the age of eighteen, in a tent at the foot of a mountain, a pretty girl named Cate latched on to me. There were ten of us in a group hiking through the Lake District. Some of us knew others, but mostly we were strangers. We paired off for the tents. Girls and boys who knew each other shared a tent, boys who knew each other also shared, and suddenly there was Cate and I left together as the odd couple. We shrugged and grinned. Late on the last night, Cate unzipped my sleeping bag and snuggled inside. Her hand went straight to my crotch and I got an instantaneous young man's reaction. That was a night I'll not forget.

In the morning as we were packing up, she kissed me. 'My lift's here. Thanks Andrew, it was lovely.'

I watched the car as it wound its way along the narrow lane and disappeared. I was feeling good. Well, I was until I found she'd stolen my wallet.

The experience of being conned when so young still rankled, and my reaction to Céleste's groping fingers at the apparent age of thirty-four was not so enthusiastic. 'Céleste, I have to sleep and this is not a good place. You're warm enough, it'll be best if you go back to the front.'

'When we are safe, Charlie. Sleep.'

I did.

THE OTHER TWO hardly looked fresh in the morning, and I felt the same way in spite of not having had a drink for two nights in a row. That had to be remedied soon for my sanity in this crazy situation. We'd eaten half of our bread the previous night, and we devoured the last of it as we packed up and checked around the site for forgotten items.

I looked at my phone to see the state of the battery and found it had locked onto a Ugandan network. We must have been closer to the border than we realised. As I put the phone away, it rang. Kirsten. I'd asked her not to call me except in an emergency, such as her or Lupus having an accident.

'Kirsten. Are you all right? What's the matter?'

'Andr … Charlie, I'm worried. I'm sure I've been followed for a few days now, and last night I had a silent phone call. Just loud, deep breathing. I hung up, of course, but an hour ago he phoned again. I've just put the phone down on him, now, again, only this time he spoke and told me to meet him later in the cemetery. He said he had something over me and it would be to my advantage to meet him.

'Charlie, it's possible it's someone from a past case of mine, but I don't think so. And this is more than stalking, I'm sure of it. It doesn't feel as if he's stalking me, I don't know why.'

An hour ago. That would be about three in the morning in the UK. 'You're probably right. This is more likely to be because of me rather than you having put someone behind bars. *Damn.*

'The first time these attempts started, before we met, NiPetco tried to persuade me by treating me well. Whoever is doing this, is using force. They failed to get at me through you on the last occasion, so they're trying again. But pharmaceutical companies have to maintain a squeaky-clean image to be reputable, which is why it's hard to believe that they would resort to strong-arm tactics and hostage-taking.

'It's possible it isn't actually the corporation that's doing this, it's someone else on their behalf. Will these bastards never stop?'

I walked away from the Unimog and the others, desperately trying to think. 'Okay, this is what you should do: go away, as far as possible – have you got a friend in the Outer Hebrides? I'm not joking, I've done this for years. Vanish off their radar. Buy yourself a pay-as-you-go phone and card and only use that number. If you have to use your usual phone, then only make outgoing calls and switch off between them. You can respond to messages at your discretion. Remember it's possible to locate a phone that's switched on irrespective of any calls, so never use that one when you're in your safe place. Keep Lupus with you at all times, he's better than a gun.'

'I understand. Actually, I've a cousin in Kirkwall, Orkney. I might go there. What about you? Where are you? What's going on? Are you going to come back?'

'Kirsten, if I could, I'd be on the next flight back to see you safe, but I'm in the very east of the Congo near Uganda, heading for Nairobi. It will take at least another nine hours to reach Entebbe Airport for an international flight, and our truck has been suffering from dirty fuel. You'll have to do this on your own for the moment, but I'll join you as soon as I can.'

'I'll call you as soon as I have a new phone. Take care, I want to see you back.'

'Be careful and make sure you're not followed, even to get the phone.' I hung up, my head in turmoil.

Robert had been watching me. 'Is everything okay?'

'Spot of bother at home, but nothing to worry about.'

'Then why make a face like a gorilla with too much in his brain?'

'Let's get going. Swiftness is of the essence. That's a quote.'

'Who? It's a good quote, sounds educated.'

'Never mind.' I needed an absence of conversation so I could think. Kirsten was bearing the brunt of some corporation's fight with me. She shouldn't be involved.

She shouldn't be scared, looking over her shoulder, even to a limited extent, as I had been. She certainly wasn't weak, but with her experience of childhood abuse and being kidnapped a few weeks ago, she was bound to be wary. She should not have to face these thugs on her own. But if I shelved my own plans it was likely that I would never see them fulfilled. Mertens would get away from me, Ajok would benefit, and many animals would suffer at their hands.

It was hard to accept it, but I had to do what I could for Kirsten ahead of anything else.

15

WE MADE GOOD time and were charging along the Masaka to Kampala road in light traffic. Before reaching the turn off to Entebbe, my phone rang – a UK number I didn't know.

'Hello, Charlie. Hey, I got it right first time. This is my new number and I'm on my way north. I'm sure no one's following me, but I'll double check using your tricks. I'm safe and there's no need for you to come home. I know you've important work you want to finish, so stay there and I'll call you from Orkney.'

'Are you sure? Use texts rather than call, there'll be a record if I can't answer you.'

'Okay, bye. Got to go, bye.' She hung up.

I stared at the phone for a moment – that was a bit abrupt for her. Perhaps she was holding up a queue for something.

Céleste was silent, staring out of the window, but Robert asked, 'What's happening? Is there a change of plan?'

I hadn't revealed that I had intended to leave them and was going to divert to Entebbe to find a flight to London. I think it was because I had hoped Kirsten would be safe before I committed to leaving. There was no point inviting conversation on something that did not concern these two. 'No,' I answered. 'A family matter at home.'

We reached Kampala, Uganda's capital eleven hours after starting the trip. The city was no different to others in the region, except the atmosphere seemed softer, more relaxed. Light motorbikes and scooters putt-putted their way past stalls of fruit and vegetables, tyre repair shops and cafés. Women carried brightly coloured, though grimy, plastic containers of water. Washing dried on strings between walls from which chunks of plaster peeled. The odd jalopy sat on its axles, the wheels stolen. The normality was reassuring after the drama of the last few days.

I found us rooms at a guest house I'd used before. They only had two available, so we agreed that Robert and I would share so Céleste could have her privacy. No words passed, but her expression said, 'You've spurned me.' Live in fear: everyone knows what that means.

In our room later, I had a text from Kirsten. I got up and went to the window to read it. *'All well. Night stop near John O'Groats. Too late for ferry tonight. Lupus is so good. Best K'* Excellent, the pressure was easing. Kirsten would be safe once she reached her cousin's house, unless she was careless and used her phone unnecessarily. With her being better placed, I'd be able to focus on the evidence which Céleste had said was in the safe as soon as we reached Nairobi. Nevertheless, I had to neutralise the threat to Kirsten, and get back to her as soon as possible.

Robert must have thought the message had come from the next room. He laughed at me. 'Hey, Charlie, you're missing out. That Céleste, she wants you. You must never turn down an offer like that. If you die tonight, you won't have been with a lady for weeks. Go for it, Charlie, I don't care.'

'Too bad. She's trying to trap me. I'm not sure what she wants – a safe passage to another life maybe. I'm not going to get involved.'

Robert raised his beer to me. 'Charlie, look at it this way: if she makes a prostitute of herself to get what she wants, you must take advantage and then walk away like she will.'

'Oh shut up, Robert, you're just stirring.'

'Okay, racist.'

We both laughed.

A SHOWER, A few well deserved beers, a meal and a night's sleep did the world of good. Back into the same dirty, smelly clothes, because that was all we had, we started out to Nairobi.

Kirsten sent a text as we cleared Kampala. I pulled over to read it. *'C, with Karen. All well. You stay safe. Lupus super excited on the ferry. Best, K'* I knew what she wanted to say was *'Love, K'* but felt she shouldn't. The assumption made me uncomfortable – it was my fault. My return said, *'Good. Be careful, limit your phone use and stay out of sight. Take care.'*

'What's so important? We need to keep going.'

I glanced across at Céleste but didn't bother with a reply. In the back, Robert gave a short laugh.

Fourteen hours later we reached Nanyuki where we dropped Robert, who was at the end of his leave. He couldn't help me in Nairobi anyway. Another four hours, and the Unimog, Céleste and I rolled into the capital.

Neither of us said much during that last leg. I was tired, and she slept a lot or looked away from me and out of her window. Only once did something liven up the trip.

The bus was visible when it came over the brow of the hill as we began our climb. It was going too fast. It bore down on us. Head on. On our side of the road. So much detail seen in a glimpse: old, faded blue, a yellow stripe, colourful decoration, a twisted chassis – the back wheels not in line with the front.

Céleste suddenly woke to the danger. '*Watch out,*' she yelled. 'What are you doing? *Watch out for the bus.*'

The bus swerved to its left, then abruptly back on to a collision course with us. I braked. There was nowhere to pull off. Go right? And if he pulled back to his side of the road at the last minute? I squeezed tight into the left verge.

Impossible to stop in time. The blue monster was fishtailing, the back swinging left to right. It thundered past leaving a glimpse of the driver wrestling with his steering wheel, his passengers a frantic sea of waving arms and screaming mouths.

A loud crack rang through the cab as the very back corner of the bus clipped the external mirror on Céleste's side. '*Aagh. Mon Dieu.*' She dived halfway across the cab towards me.

'Are you all right?'

She smacked her hand down on the dash. 'You're on the wrong side. *Imbecile*.'

'Céleste, this is Kenya, not the Congo. They drive on the left here. That idiot had lost control. It's time you woke up to reality. I know you're stressed and worried about your future, but don't take it out on me. I'm sick of it.'

She didn't answer but shrank into a foetal position, pulling her knees up, her heels on the seat, and sulked for an hour. I tried to cheer her up. I even told her she was looking attractive in spite of all she had been through. But apparently my refusal to spend the night with her was an insult which topped any good deeds I could try.

Eventually, she gave me a wan smile, her eyes tearful with dark rings beneath them that amplified the paleness of her drawn features. 'I'm sorry, Charlie. It's just because I am worried, as you said. Of course I don't think you're an imbecile. Not at all.' She reached a weak hand across the cab to touch my arm and immediately withdrew it.

'Understandable. The issue is forgotten.' At least the tension in the cab had eased somewhat. Without near-normal relations I was unlikely to get the information I needed from her. But how much of her act was genuine? She had an uncertain future ahead and, as far as I knew, limited resources to secure it. How much help did she think she could get from me? Maybe the answer to her problems lay in the safe.

To take my room in the Serova Stanley would not have been a wise move. If Idi Ajok was still staying there, the possibility of being spotted by one of his lackeys was high, and I wanted to meet the man on my terms and on my choice of when. Instead, I booked us two rooms at a B&B in Muthaiga near the Country Club. It's a pleasant area with a wood, tree-lined avenues, some upmarket hotels – a good part of the city.

We checked in, and in an attempt to ensure that our relations were back on a good footing, I suggested we have a drink.

'Oh yes, Charlie. I feel as if I haven't had a drink in years.'

So we did, while I found a locksmith and booked him for first thing the next morning. Then we shopped for fresh clothes before dinner, which involved two bottles of wine. We were getting on well, having relaxed for the first time since we'd met. But I had trapped myself, of course. It was clear Céleste assumed that after this lovely evening we were going to spend the night together and was getting romantic.

One-night stands have been rare in my life; I'm more in favour of longer-term but casual relationships in which both parties are more comfortable with an intimate friendship than a true love affair. There were a couple of single women in Nairobi who filled that role. One was a banker and the other a secretary at the British High Commission. Neither of them wanted anything more serious with me than having a fun time.

Céleste, however, was different. There was no doubt she had an agenda, and there was no doubt she intended to use me in some way to achieve her goal. If I rebuffed her for a third time she would certainly withhold any of the information I needed for a prosecution. On the other hand, I could follow Robert's advice and take advantage of the situation. She would tell me what I wanted to know, and would be more likely to help in other ways. I could walk away after one or two nights and leave her to get on with her life. I certainly wasn't going to let her hang on my coat-tails for any longer than necessary.

Robert had said she was prostituting herself to get what she wanted. The irony was, I was about to behave in the same way.

Céleste was asleep, her head resting on my shoulder. The weight kept me awake thinking of the safe. She had said it contained money and a list of contacts. The money was hers, of course; the contacts were for me, and if it had a record of transactions that would be perfect. Some of that information was going to be clear, she'd said, but she would supplement it with her own knowledge, giving me enough to have the criminals prosecuted.

Céleste was overly keen to get access to the safe. Yes, she needed the money, but there was something else in it that was of even greater importance to her.

MY HANGOVER THE next morning was mild, one of those that leaves you thick-headed and sluggish but without significant pain.

Satish, the locksmith, knocked on my door shortly after breakfast, bringing with him a faint odour of garlic and spices, which entered into conflict with the way I was feeling. He was a bubbly, overweight, middle-aged man, whom I had to help up onto the load bed of the Unimog.

The truck was parked under a jacaranda tree. With one or two exceptions clinging to life, its flowers had dropped into a purple, now turning brown, carpet across the ground, the season over. The shade was welcome, though, as the day was humid and warm under the early sun.

Satish brushed a few dead flowers away, adopted a cross-legged position in front of the safe and meditated on the lock. He glanced at the dent in the top half of the door made by one of the bullets for a couple of seconds but didn't comment.

Céleste joined us and stood over him. She fidgeted, worrying a loose thread on her T-shirt.

'Are you sure you can open this, Satish?'

He gave that slight head-wobble that Indians use. 'No problem, sir. I crack many safes. Some with locks like this, some with the combination, some with double locks. All honest purposes, of course. I am not a criminal, sir.'

'Please, I never suggested you were. But are all your customers honest, do you think?'

He laughed, teasing me. 'That is something you can answer better than me, sir.'

I grinned at him, but Céleste, beside me, was not amused. 'Come on. We don't have much time. Will this lock be easy?'

'This is very old safe. Antique, almost. The lock will be easy.' He buried his nose in his little folder of tools to hunt for the right implement. While he fiddled, he said, 'It is tall story that it's possible to shoot a safe open. That is Holly/Bollywood stuff. It might be possible, but most likely the lock will be damaged and never work. Also,' he grinned up at me, 'whoever aimed at this lock is very bad shot, if I may say so.' After a few minutes of tinkering, he turned the handle and the bolt slid back with a solid clunk.

'I'll open it.' Céleste leaned over Satish and gripped the handle. After he had scrambled out of her way looking slightly offended, she opened the door. She shot a glance at me, as if I was about to snatch the prize from her.

I handed some notes to Satish and thanked him. Maybe thirty seconds later, I turned to see Céleste stuffing wads of US dollars into the laundry bag from her room. 'It's mine. I inherit this company, so this is mine.'

'Technically, it's Jacques's money, but I don't care what you do with it.' I reached past her and picked up a small black velvet pouch from the shelf. She grabbed my wrist and glared at me. 'That's mine.'

'I only want to see.'

I tried to pull my arm away, but she clung on, digging her nails in and yanking at my sleeve. 'Give it to me. You have no right.'

'Relax, Céleste. I'm not going to steal it. Let go of my arm and I'll give it to you in a moment.'

She searched my face, mistrust and fear of being robbed written all over hers, but eventually released me. I undid the drawstring and felt inside. The first stone was a clear diamond about the size of the tip of her little finger. I held it up between us. Neither of us spoke. I put the stone back in the pouch, pulled the string tight and knotted it.

I held it out to her. 'This is more yours than mine. I'm only interested in the documents.'

As if I might change my mind at any moment, she snatched the diamonds away and took a deep breath. 'The papers are there. In them you'll find names and contact details. The transaction details are in the files.' She waved a hand at the filing cabinet. 'You can build a whole trail of the smuggling from putting the two sources of information together. I may be able to answer your questions, but you will have enough there.'

'Thanks. I——'

'I have things to do in the city. I'll be back tonight and will tell you what you need to know, if I can.'

'Fine. See you later. Don't spend all your money at once,' I quipped, but in her eyes there was nothing to joke about.

All her new-found wealth was in her laundry bag. With the diamonds, it was a considerable sum and extremely vulnerable. What was she going to do with it? She couldn't just walk into a jeweller's and sell the stones: they would have to go on the black market. Did she have the necessary contacts for that? It wasn't my concern but it was interesting. Céleste was a great deal deeper than she appeared on the surface.

Her mouth was pinched, her eyes flicked about, wary and fearful, but also defiant.

'Be careful, Céleste, and watch your back. Nairobi is also known as Nairobbery. Do you want me to come with you?'

'*Non.* It is not necessary.'

I was still sorting papers on the back of the Unimog when she left the building for a waiting taxi. She did not look my way.

SHE REAPPEARED JUST after six that evening, clutching a voluminous carpet bag, which was a marked improvement on the laundry bag. I was on my second Tusker on the verandah. She approached and stood over me. 'I am tired. I will not eat tonight. If you have any questions, they can wait for tomorrow.'

'No questions like that. But did you have a good afternoon? Would you like a drink?'

'No. I will go to my room.'

'See you in the morning, then.' I drained my glass. Staying in a B&B meant there was no evening meal, so I had to go out to find a restaurant, preferably one which served a devastating prawn vindaloo. Céleste was not to be trusted, so I made sure I held on to the keys to the Unimog.

The Bombay High was crowded, but the main man snapped orders and lesser men moved tables and chairs with great speed so I was tucked out of the way of larger parties. The air was thick with the smell of spices, cooking and incense. My mouth watered in anticipation, requiring another beer.

Idly nibbling poppadoms dosed with various sambals while I waited for the main dish, I could feel the tension of the last few days draining out of me. The hard part – meaning the violent, dangerous, dirty, sleep-deprived part – of my wildlife smuggling investigation was over. What remained was administrative and far less exciting. I thought about the evidence I had of Mertens's activities. I had removed all the papers from the safe and the filing cabinet and had spent my afternoon sifting through the documentation, photographing it and noting where deals were linked and with whom. It was going to take some time to build a complete picture of the man's activities from all that stuff. Once that was complete, though, I intended to take it to Interpol's Wildlife Enforcement Team, who, hopefully, would see that justice was done.

But that would have to wait. I had another mission to complete first.

The B&B's outside lights were on when I got back, but there was no sign of life from any of the windows. Céleste must have turned in.

The door to my room was not locked.

The folders and papers I'd left on the bed in neat piles were no longer there. All the evidence had gone.

Céleste did not answer my knocking. I tried her door handle – locked.

THE LOSS OF evidence was inconvenient but not disastrous, because I had photographed every document and list. But I had sorted the original files into categories, whereas there was no order to my photographs. I'd have to do it all again.

Who had done this? Céleste was first in the frame. But why, when she had willingly given me the evidence? Was it one of Mertens's men, sent to foil my efforts? Or Idi Ajok, to ease his way into the wildlife crime network? But how would he know where I was? Had Paul managed to follow us? He would want the information for the same reason as Idi.

Had we been followed, or had someone told the thief where I was? Céleste, for example. But again, why?

Céleste did not appear for breakfast. On the way back to my room, I knocked again. No answer. I tried the handle and the door opened, but the room was empty.

She had been there last night, because the door had been locked, the bed had been slept in and the bathroom used. But she had flown, leaving no trace and leaving me to pick up the bill.

I gave a mental shrug. She'd gone with a great deal of cash and a bag of uncut diamonds. She was financially independent at last after a long time under Eric's thumb. What she was going to do and how she was going to transform the diamonds into useable currency, I didn't know and didn't care. But good luck to her, even if she had reneged on me.

While I had been going through the evidence from the safe and files, I'd been keeping an eye out for any mention of Idi Ajok or Ajok Transport, but the man didn't appear in either the paperwork or the list of contacts. That wasn't conclusive proof that he wasn't involved in the wildlife trade, but it was likely he had not done business with Mertens. It was time to tackle Mr Ajok, not least because he owed me money.

THE SEROVA STANLEY Hotel receptionist gave me a wide smile. 'Welcome back, Mr Maxwell.'

'Thank you. Tell me, is Mr Ajok still in the Presidential Suite?'

'I can't divulge information about other guests, sir. Sorry.' Which meant that he was, because there was no harm in saying he had left the hotel.

I could not take the lift from my room to the Presidential Suite, so I went up the fire escape. The spyhole in Idi's door went dark as someone put their eye to it. The eye went away. I waited. The eye returned, then the person leaned back and the door opened.

The doorway was filled with the body of the guard. Hardly an inch of space was left between his shoulders and the door frame, or so it seemed. Six-foot me felt small. The guard said nothing, but indicated that I was to raise my arms. He frisked me, getting a bit too intrusive for my comfort, but objecting was not going to help. He beckoned and I followed him into an anteroom. He indicated a chair and thrust a thick finger at me, which I took to mean, *Sit*.

Nothing had changed in the suite since my last visit. It was as dim and claustrophobic as before, with the same stale odour of exhalations and bodies. Voices came from the lounge, Idi's deep and booming, and a quiet female who was indistinct over the noise of a television until it was silenced.

'The man is old and will die in a few months, maybe weeks,' Céleste said. There was a slight tremor in her words, which contrasted with the way she spoke to me.

With me, she had fought with someone who was not a threat; in that room she was scared and letting her opponent take her for timid. 'My husband is dead. Jacques is ninety-three and ineffective. I am or will be the owner of Nyiragongo. Therefore, if you want to have an interest in the company, you must negotiate with me.'

Idi's bright, broad smile and cold eyes were as easy to picture as his words were to hear. 'I know these things. What are you offering? What position do you think you could hold in the company when it is mine?'

Not *if* it is mine, but *when*.

'The company will be mine to manage. I will be the CEO, the person who makes the final decision on everything.' Céleste was no longer hesitant. It was as if she had rehearsed these demands and was now able to deliver them with confidence. 'If you want to put money into the business, I will welcome that, but I will make the decisions on how it will be used. And I will turn a profit for you.'

A long pause followed. I pictured Idi's pudgy face and the slits through which he stared across his enormous stomach at her. 'Céleste, you need to explain to me why you should have any powers at all. I am already in the process of taking over your company. My men have occupied your office and have control of the warehouse. Everything that used to belong to the Mertens family is now mine – everything. So, you own nothing. Perhaps you should ask yourself why you are here. In fact, it is best if you leave East Africa and Congo. These places are not safe for a white woman alone.'

Céleste was probably biting her lip and struggling to come to terms with her total downfall, for that was what was going to happen. Idi was not exaggerating his progress in taking over Nyiragongo. Except for the one thing he did not appear to know about.

Céleste was not out for the count, though. 'I am not going anywhere, Idi. You may think you have taken over my company, and I have no doubt you will add its trucks to your fleet and expand that side of the business with success. You will also continue the smuggling of wildlife, both live and body parts. That does not require any expertise, only knowledge. But the one reason you want Nyiragongo above other companies is because it has an air charter operation, and you think there is big money and prestige in that.'

Another pause. My image of Idi crushing one end of the couch and eyeing Céleste as something to be devoured returned.

She continued. 'You are wrong. First, the profit you can make running aircraft is very small. The expenses are vast: the insurance, the spare parts, salaries are not those of truck drivers, the training, and, if you don't pay for all that, the accident that follows. Aviation is extremely technical and you have to know what you're doing or you will go bankrupt very quickly. You, Idi, do not have that expertise, but I do. And there is another reason to let me run it: continuity. You should avoid the disruption caused by a sudden change of management and procedures. You will save money with continuity and satisfied employees.'

After yet another period of silence, Idi's voice dominated the room. 'There may be some truth in what you say, but the old man, Jack, is still there and he could be a thorn in my operation for five years if I let him. He has a lot of influence in Goma.'

'It's Jacques, not Jack. Get rid of him.'

'I may do that. Does that shock you?'

'No. He has killed many people, it is time he went.'

'So be it. I will think about this proposal of yours. I must speak to my man in Goma first, then I will tell you my decision. Go now.'

'One more thing, Idi. I know everything there is to know about Jacques's wildlife business. I know all the contacts, including the rebel commanders who have to be paid off to let the poaching take place. I know the prices asked for and paid, the poachers, the transport links to export the animals, everything. It will take you a long time to learn all that on your own.'

'I hear you. Go.'

Céleste had done well in standing up to Idi Ajok, gangster, thug, extortionist, and more than likely a multiple killer. To what degree did he respect her? Would he allow her to run his company on her terms? Or was he insulted by a woman telling him what to do, even if he knew she was right?

Céleste left the lounge for the main door. Her chin was up, her stride was firm, but she gasped as she saw me. She opened her mouth to say something, but shut it, looked away and turned for the door.

'Come, Charlie Maxwell.'

THE CURTAINS WERE closed but for a narrow gap through which a sign outside cast red flashing lights across the ceiling.

Was Idi photophobic? If he was, that might partially explain his bulk, assuming a reluctance to go out into the harsh sun to exercise. The man was sprawled on the couch like a massive blob of Play-Doh. Bulbous eyes had been a noticeable feature, but now they were almost covered by their lids. Idi was angry, which was not a surprise.

'You are a brave man, coming to see me, Charlie. Sit.'

The bodyguard had moved to stand behind me. At the instruction, he put his hands on my shoulders and forced me down into a chair. His overbearing presence behind me was uncomfortable.

'Really? Why? I came to report on the situation in Goma. A situation which won't make you happy.'

'Paul says you have betrayed me. You have acted outside our contract and stolen the apes and the safe with all the company cash and valuable files. You think you stole from Mertens, but I have bought Nyiragongo and all those things you stole are mine. I want them back.'

'Idi, you have been misled. When I took those things, I did it with Céleste, who owned them, and we escaped before Paul and his men occupied the company.'

'Don't try to confuse me with detail, I will not be confused. If you took them before Paul got there, or after, they are still part of Nyiragongo and therefore mine. Where is the safe now?'

'It's on the back of a truck where I'm staying, but there's nothing in it. We had to get a locksmith to open it. Eric Mertens must have taken the money, or maybe it was Paul before we got there.'

Idi's eyes narrowed even more at that revelation. They felt like two lasers focused on me, burning holes in my head. I gave him a brief and almost truthful account of what had happened, before spinning a tale to create chaos. Lying to a criminal is not a sin, is it?

'Paul is betraying you, Idi. He murdered Eric Mertens and was going to take over the company office, but we arrived before his men came to support him. We fought them off. We left the apes where they were and asked the National Park to take them. The Park called me later and said the apes had already been moved when they got there. There were no animals in the warehouse when they arrived with their truck and the vet. Only Paul could have taken them. At the ambush, I asked him if he was doing this for you or for himself. He said you are old, a has-been. You're not effective, he said, and it's time for someone strong to take over.'

The rolls of fat around Idi's neck quivered. 'You are lying. Paul is loyal. He knows I will pass on my interests to him.'

'Did you tell him to ambush us on the road to Uganda?'

'No.'

'Then he did it on his own, and we escaped because he and his men came under attack from someone else.'

'Who?'

'I don't know. Rebels maybe, or it could have been Mertens. When did you last speak to him?'

'It was yesterday. In the afternoon.'

'Tuesday. The ambush took place on Sunday. Why didn't he tell you about the apes and that his ambush had failed? He is setting this up in your name so that he can take over when it is running well.'

It was time to leave. I made to stand, but two massive hands blocked my shoulders from rising. Idi appeared to contemplating the manner of my death. 'Where are you going now, Charlie? What are you going to do?'

'I'm finished with this situation of yours. I was never asked to get involved in your fight with Mertens. It has nothing to do with me, and I want nothing else to do with it. I have a personal matter to attend to, then I shall go back to work in the reserve. But first, you owe me three thousand dollars.'

He grunted. 'That is true and you will have it. I always pay my debts.' Then he dropped his voice. It rasped. 'If your story is true, Paul is a dead man. But I will follow you, I will know where you are all the time. If you are lying to me I will have your hands and your feet cut off.'

He meant what he said, and it was chilling, but I shrugged. 'I have nothing to fear.'

He studied me for some time. 'I have a job for you. If you accept then all is forgiven, even if you have lied to me. Go to Goma and watch that woman, Céleste. You are an expert. You know how to manage aeroplanes. Make sure she knows what she is doing and is not cheating me.'

I shook my head. 'No, because to see what she does, to see how she manages the operation, organises flights and crew and training and spares and whether she isn't going to oversee an accident, will take a long time, months, and I don't have that luxury. Also, I told you I want nothing more to do with this business. I don't want to be involved with you or Mertens or Paul and your fights.' Which was not strictly true. I had a date with Jacques Mertens.

Idi said something to the goon behind me. The man released my shoulders and went into the next room. He came back with a small cotton bag and gave it to me.

'Three thousand dollars, as promised, Charlie. Remember, you will be watched, as I said.'

16

THE RESERVE OFFICE couldn't find Robert when I first phoned him. I left a message that I'd call back at six. In the meantime, I bought some more clothes and toiletries to replace those I'd had to leave behind in Goma. I was ready to leave for the Congo that day, but needed to speak to Robert first.

I brought him up to date with events in Nairobi, Céleste leaving, and Idi's threat. 'I'm going back to Goma for a couple of days.'

'What for, Charlie? You crazy. The place is a pool of crocodiles for you.'

'I have to speak to Jacques Mertens about something …'

'What? Whatever it is is not worth your life. There's Mertens and his thugs, and he's got agents all over the town. There's Paul who wants to kill you. And now you've got Idi and his gang watching you. If he hears you're talking to Mertens, you're dead.'

'I know all that, but I think I've stirred the pot enough to set Idi against Paul. If so, they may be so occupied, they'll forget about me.'

'Crazy. You can't be alone. I'll take a few days extra leave and come with you.'

'No, Robert. This is personal and does not involve you, must not involve you. You can do something for me, though. Get Jimmy to help me.'

'Mm. I can try, but I told him his debt was repaid. Will he be food for the crocodiles?'

'No. I'll keep him well out of it.'

Robert rang back two hours later and said Jimmy would help as long as he didn't have to fight anyone, or be caught, or go to prison.

THE NEXT MORNING, I was at Wilson Airport for my second legal trip into the DRC – legality had been cast aside for the last one.

I was taking a risk going back by air. I'd been seen by many people at the airport during the audit, and not only Nyaragongo's staff. To lessen the chance of being recognised, I had booked on a different carrier. I did consider going back by road, but it involved a twenty-four-hour drive over twelve hundred kilometres. It would take two days if I did it sensibly, and I couldn't afford that time. So once again I was having breakfast in the Aeroclub and watching the aircraft movements out on the parking area.

My knife shrieked on the plate as the rind separated from the bacon. Embarrassing, but no one seemed to notice. Then my phone pinged. It was Kirsten. *'All still well. No sign of baddies. Lupus loving the cold. I'm not. Best K.'* She had been sending a message a day, all short and sweet, which was good for me. Engaging in lengthy text conversations is distracting and a waste of time.

Two Cessna Caravans stood on the apron. One was from Congair, with whom I'd booked, and the other belonged to Nyiragongo. Once in the terminal, I would have to make sure I avoided the latter's pilot.

A handful of other people were eating as well. Passengers for Goma or somewhere else? A lone young woman sat at a table on the far side of the room. I noticed her, because I'm attracted to pretty women, although, with everything on my mind, I didn't credit her with more than a glance. It was enough to note her below-the-shoulder auburn hair, shimmering blue blouse and simple gold neckband, with nothing on her ring finger. A black jacket hung over her chair. She was too much the business executive to be going to a dump like Goma.

While I watched the activity outside, she was facing me, and I couldn't help but feel her gaze. Whenever I looked in her direction, she was studying her food or looking at her phone. Our eyes never met, but there was something about her features that was familiar.

At home, as my true self, Andrew Duncan, being under constant surveillance had become a part of my life. I had been followed by agents of NiPetco and another shadowy Big Pharma corporation that I had never identified. Enormous profits would reward them if they could get their paws on me to learn the secrets locked in my DNA. My senses came alive when one of them was close. My awareness kept me from their clutches almost every time. There, in the restaurant, I didn't imagine that the woman was spying for a pharmaceutical giant, but I knew she was watching me for some reason.

At the ticket desk, we passengers were informed that the Congair Caravan we could see outside was unserviceable and awaiting spare parts. Instead, we would be transported by Nyiragongo Air in an identical aeroplane. There was nothing odd about that. Such arrangements are often made at short notice amongst small carriers, so I wasn't suspicious. But what if I was recognised by either the pilot or one of the ground crew? If Jacques

Mertens was warned of my arrival, things could get very difficult.

An American tourist couple, three Africans and another two nuns (there were two on the previous flight; was this a pilgrim route?) were in the queue ahead of me. There was one seat spare. Or was there? The auburn-haired woman stood back against the far wall, talking on her phone. Was she coming to Goma too?

The pilot strolled up to the desk, whistling. What a relief, I'd never seen him before. He was middle-aged and portly, with a weathered complexion and a broad white smile – a complete contrast to the sour, recently deceased Eric Mertens.

'Bonjour, bonjour, bonjour.' He grinned at his expectant load and uttered a volume of rapid French in a loud voice, which had the nuns giggling. His eyes swept the queue, but they didn't dwell on me any more than on anyone else. Had there been the slightest hint of recognition, I would have pulled out and gone another day.

Boarding pass in hand, I followed the others to emigration and security, then into the waiting area. There was no sign of the interesting woman. What had she been doing in the airport when no other flights were departing at that time?

As the Caravan turned off the taxiway and onto the runway, a small executive jet, an early model Cessna Citation, was visible behind us.

WE LANDED IN Goma just after ten. The pilot stood at the foot of the steps and offered to help the passengers disembark, his broad white grin putting a positive spin on the morning. A mixed range of parked aircraft stretched from the end of the lava flow from the volcano's 2002 eruption to opposite the terminal. Closest were two executive jets: an old Hawker 125 and an equally old Cessna Citation. Was that the same aircraft that left Wilson after us? I hadn't taken note of the registration, but it would have arrived well before the Caravan, so it could have been. In the other direction, Nyiragongo's Caravan that I'd dumped among the scrapped aircraft had been taken away. Would Mertens have it inspected after its harsh adventure?

Most people would think nothing of the presence of private jets. They might wonder who had the money to travel around Central Africa in them and why they were important, but not much else, and their questions would be forgotten when the aircraft was out of sight. But when you've been under surveillance for months and your every activity has been monitored; when you've been abducted for medical experimentation and your loved one has been killed, then your radar sensitivity is set to maximum and is never switched off.

I checked into a hotel on the lake shore within a ten-minute walk of Mertens's house. Jimmy was supposed to meet me there some time after lunch. He turned up at three appearing half asleep. He had obviously tried to dress smartly since he was going into a hotel, but although his clothes were clean they hadn't seen an iron. He looked more out of place than he had done on my last visit, when he had a scruffy, soiled shirt with a hole in the sleeve and torn trousers.

We found a bench in a secluded spot in the hotel garden out of earshot of anyone. His English was non-existent and my French was limited – conversation was stilted, but somehow adequate.

Jimmy leaned forward, his elbows on his knees. 'Paul has been hiring more men. I think he has about ten now. He is preparing for a fight with Mertens. That's what I heard. That is what Paul has told his men.'

'What sort of men, Jimmy?'

'Poor men, they sleep on the streets, they have no home. Often they are drunk and fight each other. They live by stealing. Those men.'

'What about Mertens, how big is his force?'

'He has many, and he pays well for good men.' He laughed. 'I am one, but I don't want to fight. I think Paul will lose a battle with Mertens unless he becomes much stronger.'

'Maybe Paul is getting ready for a different fight. I met Idi Ajok in Nairobi. He is very angry with Paul. He knows that Paul betrayed him.'

Jimmy swayed back, his eyes wide. '*Eesh*. That Ajok, he is bad, that man. Everyone knows of him, and someone said he heard that Idi is coming here; but Paul has insisted he is fighting for Idi for the Frenchman's business. I was sure Paul was finding men for Idi's army to defeat Mertens. But if Idi is coming to punish Paul, Paul will use those men against his boss. It will be a big fight.'

'I reckon Paul hasn't told his men they will have to fight Idi because he's worried about their morale – they'll run away. I don't think Idi will come himself, or if he does, he'll stay safe. He's too fat to do anything physical. He will direct his men from his hotel.

'Jimmy, I'll tell you what I want from you. I want you to tell me everything you hear, even if you think it's not true. If you learn that Idi has come into the country, you tell me. If you learn he has diarrhoea after eating bush meat, you tell me. If he gets gonorrhoea, I want to know. You understand?'

Jimmy laughed and nodded.

'Same with Paul. Any trouble with his men or if he hires more, tell me. All right?'

Again he nodded, but this time it was more hesitant.

'Jimmy, I don't want you to put yourself in danger doing this for me. You must stay safe. Paul and Idi will not only fight over Jacques's company, but also who is going to be top dog. It will be a bloody fight, because if Paul loses he'll be a dead man.

'About your boss, Mertens: Jacques will also fight, but he will wait until Idi and Paul are weak from fighting each other. He might think he can stop Idi forever if he defeats him here, and maybe he has more men, fresh, fit men, than both the others together. You must please keep me informed. If I can do what I want to do successfully thanks to your information, I will double your money. But you must tell me the truth. Don't tell me what you think I want to hear, tell me the facts, and do what Robert says: don't become food for these crocodiles.'

Another factor that could complicate things was Céleste. She would be waiting for Idi's decision on her proposal to run the company, but Idi's priority would be to sort out the upcoming mess. Would Céleste come to Goma before the battle was decided? It would be very dangerous for her.

JIMMY BROUGHT ME news that evening and again the next morning. Over the two days he gradually slipped back into his comfort zone His clothing degenerated to his normal standard of trousers with a hole in the knee, a dirty white T-shirt and stained trainers, and his body odour gave a sour warning of his approach. His shabby presence aside, he did supply me with a mountain of information. The problem was trying to filter the truth from the improbable.

'Jimmy, how do you know all the things you're telling me are true? Who tells you these things?'

'My brothers. We work together and support each other. We work for men like Mertens, who is not a good man, so we don't trust him. We back each other up and tell everyone the latest news. That way we all know what's going on and can stay out of trouble.'

I knew that by 'brothers', Jimmy didn't necessarily mean family members. Calling friends and acquaintances family members is a common practice to engender support or sympathy.

According to Jimmy, by Saturday morning Paul's army had grown to fifteen strong. But, he claimed, they were getting drunk, arguing and falling asleep.

'What about Idi, Jimmy, has he got men here yet?'

'I didn't hear of this. But my friend says that Paul had an important phone call. When he took it, he walked away from the other men so they could not hear. When he came back he said he was told to go to Nairobi immediately. But my friend said Paul did nothing, he did not give any orders or prepare to leave, so I think he will not go.'

That was interesting, Idi ordering Paul back to Nairobi. It was most likely a test: if Paul went, he was loyal; if he ignored the order then it would back up what I had told Idi, that Paul was going to try and take over. Of course, if Paul went back, it would not be an acid test of his loyalty. He might try to usurp Idi in Kenya by killing him, but that would be difficult and a great risk. Idi's security was tight.

I could not rely on that: Paul might convince Idi of his loyalty, showing me up as a liar. To avoid my hands and feet being chopped off by some panga-wielding thug, I had to make certain that Paul did not go. How to do that?

If Paul wasn't physically present to lead his men, they would give up and run away. One possibility was for me to restrain him so he couldn't leave, which would be difficult. Or I could provide clandestine assistance to Jacques, which would mean Paul would have to be present to direct his attack. Whatever the answer was, it would dawn on me at some stage.

During Saturday afternoon, Jimmy gave my door a few urgent knocks. He was fidgeting, grinning with success and eager to come in. The little man was best met outside in the fresh air. I would never get rid of the pong if I let him in, so I stopped him in the doorway.

'A thing of great importance,' Jimmy said. 'Paul has blocked off all the entrances to Nyiragongo's office. Mertens's men are inside. Paul does not have enough men to attack the place, so I don't know what he's doing.

'Jimmy, can you get me a gun?'

'Sure. I know of some stolen from the UN. Bullets too. You got money – cash?'

I nodded, shut the door on him and went to get my dollars clear of his sight. 'A good one, Jimmy. Don't bring me a rusty thing that will blow up in my face. And don't bring it into the hotel, I'll meet you outside.'

THE SUN WAS dying. Its final arc above the horizon reflected as a golden spearhead off the waters of Lake Kivu. The spear pointed at me. Normally on a Saturday night at about this time I would be enjoying a beer and philosophising on what that meant, but with what lay in store in the hours ahead, alcohol was not a sensible option.

Things were building up to a battle in which some were going to die. There was no doubt of that. You give a gang of drunken men a machete each and they are going to chop each other up in this part of the world – over half a million were killed in the Rwandan genocide. My money was on Idi. He was more experienced, probably more ruthless and better armed than Paul. If Jimmy's description of the warriors was anywhere near the truth, Paul's ragtag bunch were going to be seen off very quickly by Idi's smaller, but professional, force. But this assessment excluded Jacques Mertens, who was a man who had killed for entertainment. It wasn't certain, of course, but Idi probably only killed out of necessity, albeit without feeling.

Earlier, Kirsten had sent me the day's text. *'Charlie. All well here. Karen tremendous. Great pub called the Bloodaxe. You'd like. Surprise the weather is good too windy. Love K.'* The tone was odd, as stilted as a child reporting to its parents from boarding school. There was no mention of Lupus, which she always did, knowing my affection for the dog, and lastly, there was her use of the word *love*. She knew to be cautious with her affection for me and had so far kept emotion out of the communication. She was a successful barrister, she shouldn't make mistakes like that – unless it wasn't a mistake. Was she becoming more fond of me in my absence?

Jimmy found me on the hotel verandah. Wide-eyed and with a serious, slightly scared expression, he would not stop moving. 'M'sieur Charlie, it has begun. Paul's men are close to the company office. They are trying to break the door and have also tried to get into the warehouse. If they get in, there will be looting. Paul is there, trying to control his men.'

'Did you bring the gun?'

'Yes. I hid it in the bushes. You want it here on the verandah?'

I stood. 'No, of course not. Show me.'

The weapon was a Chinese version of the AK47, what they called a Type 56, with a wooden butt and stock. The condition wasn't bad, a little rust showed, but it was oiled and the barrel gleamed on the inside. There were two fully loaded magazines with it and another box of ammo. What did Jimmy think I was taking on – a host of man-eating giants?

'Good man, Jimmy. What is Mertens doing about this siege of his office?'

'I don't know. The only thing I hear is orders being shouted inside.'

Strange. He must have been holding back until Paul's men were so drunk and tired they'd be overcome with no effort, or if Idi's men came, he could deal with them all at once. Jacques had been a soldier, he knew about conserving his assets, preserving their strength for the greater fight.

'And Idi?'

'There was no sign of his men when I left.'

So Paul had chosen to ignore Idi's order so far. I had to make sure it stayed that way, so it was time to complicate the mix.

'JIMMY, YOU DON'T have to, but will you help me?'

'I don't have a gun, and I don't want to fight.'

'You won't be fighting. I want you to make a noise here and there. You must not put yourself in the crocodile's mouth, understand? I'll double your pay.'

'*Okay*.' An instantaneous reply, the power of money.

I blacked my face, grinning at the thought of Robert's comments. Then we took a taxi to the industrial area. Somehow, I managed to hide the gun from the driver, helped by Jimmy, who held the man's attention through chatter from the moment we hailed the car. He sat in front and delivered a non-stop stream of comment without letting the driver get a word in.

The taxi dropped us off on the main airport road a block from Nyiragongo's office. As we got out, with Jimmy shielding me from the driver's view, the sound of banging against the doors of the warehouse reached us.

The attackers were shouting and chanting, with some laughter. Was this an attack or a party?

Jimmy had been ducking in and out of this area to gather information to pass to me ever since I'd come back to Goma. He knew the best way to approach the place, so I pushed him into the lead. Behind him I loaded and cocked the weapon. Jimmy twisted round and raised trembling hands. He was almost white with fear. I grinned at him. 'Not for you, Jimmy. Don't worry.'

We got closer. Heavy blows smashed at the steel door of the warehouse, the sound sharp, deep and timed with the chant. What the hell were they using, a sledgehammer? Metal screeched. Their efforts must have been succeeding, because the sporadic shouts gave way to a unified cheering.

The building was an alley away. We stopped on the corner. I gave Jimmy his instructions. He went off, and I moved closer to the warehouse.

The shebeen where Robert had been attacked was closed, the inner door shut. An awning extended out from the shack and into the alley, dropping down the sides and cutting the drinkers off from the neighbouring shops. Cheap plastic chairs and a wobbly table had yet to be wiped clean of spilt beer and scraps of food. Scrunched tissues and the odd bottle littered the ground.

A drunk lay face down on the earth, his dribble a small wet patch by his mouth.

Peering out from behind the awning, I could see the attackers. Five of them were huddled at the loading-bay door. One had a crowbar, all had pangas. Another five were trying to batter the office entrance to death by hitting it with a small hammer. If I knew anything about Mertens, they needed a stick of dynamite to crack that handle. Paul called out from my left. The man had a tendency to voice his presence yet not be at the front of the action. He wasn't going to usurp Idi like that.

Close under the side of the awning, I took careful aim. The crack of the shot was loud. So was the clang of the bullet smacking into the metal door between two heads. As a group, the men jumped. Two cowered at ground level, three snatched looks left and right, searching for the source.

Over to my right, Jimmy shouted something. I moved three shacks down in his direction, to where I was opposite the office door. These men had heard the shot, but it wasn't at them. They'd also heard the shout. They were sitting ducks, bewildered. I could pick them off with ease, but I wasn't there to kill anyone. My next round hit the door at head level. Down to the ground they went.

Jimmy ran past me and shouted again from the other side of the shebeen. I fired a round close to the cowering group and moved again. Four different firing points, and Jimmy yelling from several locations, should have created an image of a greater force than only one gun.

The group by the loading bay were crouching at the foot of the door. Loud whispers as they argued on what to do. They needed help, so I gave them another round.

They ran. I sent a bullet after them. Jimmy shouted something. Paul was louder, trying to get his men to hold their positions, probably. The band at the office door were summoning the courage to move. A single shot helped them to decide.

Paul yelled again, giving me a pretty good idea where he was. I switched the fire selector down one click from 'safe' to 'automatic', pointed it in his direction and gave him a burst. Three rounds went off before the bloody thing jammed. *Hell*. I didn't have time to muck about clearing it. Instead of chucking it behind the shack, I held on to it because it could be used to threaten someone.

Paul had been silenced by my burst of fire, and his troops appeared to have run away. What did he think of this? His little army had been decimated, and by whom? Had Mertens counter-attacked? Had Idi stepped in? In which case he, Paul, was in a very sorry position. What would he do now? Had he left to unite his men and try again? Maybe he was going to try to engage me, although he didn't know that I was the culprit. It was time to leave.

Jimmy was grinning. He'd played his part and survived without a scratch. And he'd made some extra money. 'They ran away, they ran away.' He laughed and slapped his thigh, then got serious. 'I have news. My friend found me a few minutes ago. I don't know if this is true, because my friend doesn't know Idi Ajok, but he says a private plane landed two hours ago and a very fat man got off, as well as some other men. He thinks about six of them. They all had the same type of bag. He said they were fighting men. He said he was frightened of them and kept out of the way.'

'Where did they go?'

'Some house on the lake. I don't know which one.'

If Idi knew that Paul had tried to break into Mertens's office, surely he would have his men take control as soon as possible, while Paul was disorganised and before he could consolidate? And what was Paul doing? He'd lost the element of surprise over Idi, and he had an inferior force, which might just have disbanded altogether. And Jacques – was he waiting for the two raiders to annihilate each other, before taking out the winner? That would be sensible. I needed to choose the optimum moment to tackle Jacques, and that would be when the others were most occupied.

Suddenly I realised where Paul had gone, and that he was going to ruin my plan.

17

MERTENS'S HOUSE WAS one of several exclusive mansions on the northern end of Lake Kivu. The property was protected by a six-foot wall topped with four strands of electric fence, but not on the lake side. This was a surprising oversight from someone who thought of himself as an experienced legionnaire, knowledgeable about all things military. To me, it was the obvious route in for some thief wanting to burgle the place …

The shore was not a beach, but the end of an old lava flow from Mount Nyiragongo. Uneven with crevices and waist-high lumps, it was a slow, steep clamber in the dark and probably why Mertens thought it too difficult a barrier for would-be thieves.

On the other hand, with the old man being a serial killer, a psychopath, he may have deliberately left the lake route onto his property unprotected. Anyone bold enough to approach in the full glare of the security lighting would satisfy Mertens's blood lust – death by dog, perhaps. And he would get away with it.

In its jammed state, the assault rifle was no longer any use. I almost chucked it into the lake before working my way up the lava slope. But to confront a killer like Mertens without a weapon in my hands would be a stupid thing to do. So, when I found a tiny flat spot to rest the parts on, I set about trying to free the thing. It wasn't an easy fix, and I failed. The gun was now an empty threat. Rather than carry the useless thing, I slung it over my back and freed both hands for the scramble. The sling buckle squeaked as I moved.

Climbing the lava was a matter of finding rock to stand on and not stepping into a hole when holes and shadows were indistinguishable. Finally, scraped shins and painful feet later, I reached a point where my head was just above the level of the swimming pool.

The security lights were so bright, I couldn't look towards them for long. Individual blades of grass, bushes, flowers and shrubs in front of the house were lit up as if in sunshine. Anything moving in that area would easily be spotted from the lounge. By shielding my eyes from the glare, though, it was possible to make out details on the verandah and see through the open glass doors into the lounge. Jacques Mertens was in a chair talking to someone out of view. I was too far away to hear the conversation or even to recognise facial expressions, but something about the man, the way he moved his head, the sharp slap his hand gave the chair arm, not once but three times, told me his mood.

If I stood and he looked outside he would see me, so, keeping low and, out of the direct light, I crossed to the side of the grounds where his view was blocked by one of the brick pillars supporting the verandah roof. Using the blind spot this pillar gave me, I moved along its length towards the open door.

Who was Mertens talking to? Before surprising him, I needed a sense of the conversation. Given the current circumstances it had to be about the takeover attempts of his company. I risked one quick glance round the pillar. Mertens's eyes were narrowed, his thin lips set in a flat line. All that was visible of the other man was his black hand, which jerked emphatically as he spoke. It was in French, of course, but the timbre was unmistakeable – Paul.

This was not a surprise. Unable to win the physical war, Paul had to pressurise the owner of Nyiragongo himself. Were there any legal hoops he was going to have to jump through to complete the takeover? Would a corrupt authority sign off the change of ownership irrespective of whether Mertens agreed or not? Or did Paul have a card to play that would force Jacques to sign away his company? This was the DRC; recognised business practice was not necessarily applicable.

I was standing side-on to the pillar, minimising my profile. I turned to peer around the other side of the column. It made little difference, but I saw Paul take a few steps to his left leaving his back towards me and blocking my view of Mertens. Paul's right arm dangled at his side. In that hand was a gun. It wasn't pointing at Jacques, there was no need. Mertens could neither move quickly nor fight back from a chair before the gun was raised.

This situation would be best handled in silence, and my squeaking weapon would give me away. I unslung it and put it down on the lawn. The old man had left his walking stick propped against the inside of the glass door. As a weapon it was too light to damage a strong man, but it would do. I crouched behind Paul, reached for the stick and tried not to breathe. Mertens saw me; his expression didn't change, but his eyes flicked to me and back to his adversary in a second. With the stick in my hand, and careful to avoid my clothes rustling, I stood and stepped back. The space was confined, the height limited, with no room for a full swing. Even in that short strike, the stick swished. Paul reacted. But he had no time. It was as if he hadn't moved at all, and his wrist took the full force.

Was the crack only the sound of the blow, or did Paul's radius break? The gun clattered to the tiles. He screamed and spun round. Stiff fingers, jabbed into his Adam's apple, had him choking. He dropped to his knees.

Jacques nodded and stood. '*Merci*,' was all he said.

I handed him his stick. 'You have some ties, or some rope, to secure this man?'

'It is not necessary.'

Paul's breath came in harsh, painful rasps. He wasn't going to be a problem for a few minutes.

Leaning on his stick, Mertens limped round Paul and bent to pick up the gun. Ejecting the magazine, he cocked the weapon, captured the round ejected from the chamber and fed it back into the magazine. His movements were precise and careful. 'Czech CZ75 – good, reliable, well made.'

What was he going to do? He had followed best practice as any professional soldier would when taking hold of a new weapon. There was nothing unusual in that, and he hadn't replaced the magazine. He turned as if going back to his chair.

Paul, on his knees, was head down to the floor and cradling his arm. His pained cries alternated between wails and lower-pitched howls – a bit over the top for a broken arm. Children make less noise. Jacques moved to the man's front. With harsh jabs of his stick Jacques poked Paul until he knelt upright. Casually, Mertens hooked the handle of his stick over his left arm. It swung loosely as, with smooth, rapid movements, he inserted the magazine and cocked the weapon. '*Look at me.*'

Paul's eyes went wide.

'*No,*' I shouted.

Jacques put the shot exactly between Paul's eyes. His head jerked back. His body swayed and toppled. Matter spattered on the tiles. Blood spread.

'What did you do that for?'

He shrugged. 'To remove a problem. 'E was telling me to sign my company over to 'im, or he would take it by force. Now it's not possible.'

The pool of blood was expanding. I stepped back to avoid it reaching my shoes. I looked up and into the muzzle of the CZ75. It was rock-steady in those ninety-three-year-old hands.

'You killed Eric.'

'No, Jacques, I didn't, but I'm certain Paul did. I was inside the warehouse when someone attacked Eric. I was taking photos for evidence. When I came out, Céleste was there, but I'm sure it was not her. Then I saw Paul. He stood to gain everything by getting rid of Eric, weakening your forces.'

Mertens nodded his understanding. 'Then justice is done.' He let the gun drop to his side, took the stick off his arm and leaned on it.

The CZ75 has an external hammer. If the hammer cannot strike the firing pin, the gun is useless. As Mertens turned his back on me and limped to his chair, I reached down and grabbed the weapon, slipping my finger between the hammer and the firing pin. He fought – incredibly strong for someone his age. But not strong enough. I ripped the pistol from his grasp.

MERTENS, PANTING FROM the scuffle, sank into his chair and leaned on his stick. Hollow-cheeked, thin lips turned down, I swear he saw me more as prey than someone he hated. After all, he was a practiced murderer. With his breath regained, he propped his stick up against the arm and gave a two-note whistle. In a moment, with the clicking of claws on tiles, his two dogs appeared. They looked at him, then at me. I tensed. Getting no signal from the old man, they both sniffed at the hand that had held the gun. They sat as he stroked their heads, their amber eyes focused on me. 'What do you want?'

There was no point in wasting words, it was also a waste of time. 'I don't know why, but you were in England in 1944.'

'So?'

'You killed a number of women in 1944 and '45. You are a serial killer.'

Mertens was not the sort of person to be easily shocked, but his eyes widened and his brows shot up for a second. He gave a short harsh laugh. 'That is stupid. 'Ow can you say such a thing? What are you, some kind of police?'

'You smothered a prostitute with a pillow in August 1944. Her name was Sybil. There were at least eight other girls killed around that time in various parts of England, all by asphyxiation. You killed them all.'

'You are ridiculous. How can you know this? Why do you think it was me, and why think these whores were all killed by the same person.'

'I saw you kill Sybil. I was ten years old and hiding under the bed.'

'*Ha*,' he scoffed. 'You were ten in 1944? That is ridiculous, you are only in your thirties now.'

'You wore dark grey socks with a yellow stripe and, most importantly, the birthmark on your right ankle is so distinctive it is conclusive proof. Also, how did you know the other women were prostitutes?'

Mertens swallowed. His voice lowered and his words came slowly. 'I assumed from the way you spoke. I don't know, of course. In any case, this is nonsense. You have made it up after seeing my birthmark. It is not possible for you to have been alive in '44.'

'I'm going to tell you something I've only told two other people. I have been hounded by the big pharmaceutical companies for the secret my body holds. I cannot age. I stopped ageing at thirty-four back, in 1968, after a serious accident. Something changed in my genetic makeup and the pharma giants want to know what that is so they can replicate it and make huge profits. I have been abducted and I've been hunted for a long time, and my girlfriend was murdered in their attempts to win me over for experimentation.

'I know what a disaster it would be for the world if my genetic secret was applied throughout the population, so I'm determined to keep it a secret. My real name is not Charlie Maxwell, either.'

'This is nonsense, *bêtises.*'

'Sybil was my true friend when I was ten, and then you came along and killed her for no apparent reason. You took the person who was a sister, a friend, even a mother to me. I loved her. You didn't know her. Why did you do that?'

As I said that I caught a faint whiff of a delicate fragrance.

'Nonsense. If this big secret is to remain a big secret, why are you telling me about it?'

'Because you are not going to live to tell anyone else.'

Something caught the dogs' attention. Their noses were aligned slightly to my right. Jacques's eyes flicked off mine for a split second, just as they had done when he saw me behind Paul.

I DIVED TO my left, rolled on the floor and levelled the gun at the woman behind me. She was slow, her own weapon wavering as it tried to follow my moving target.

A low whine and a growl came from two aggressive dogs. I was seriously outnumbered here. If that damn weapon hadn't jammed, I'd have sufficient firepower to even these odds. The last thing I wanted to do was shoot the animals, but if they were going to kill me …

The woman was a problem, she was another person who knew my secret. To kill a serial murderer was one thing, to kill a stranger whose only fault was her knowledge of my condition was another.

Mertens cleared his throat. 'Let me introduce my daughter, Marine.'

'Marine. It's good to put a name to a familiar face.' The family resemblance was immediately clear once it had been pointed out. The pale, almost white, hair; the washed-out blue eyes, the pinched features. They were there in Jacques, had been in Eric, and were there too in Marine. If I'd been more suspicious earlier, I'd have realised there was another antagonist in the mix.

'We've met across tables before. The Thorn Tree ten days ago and yesterday at Wilson. You were wearing a wig. It suited you. What brings you here, Marine?'

At first glance, her eyes were as cold as her father's. They turned her otherwise attractive features into a cruel visage, but they lacked the steel in his. 'My brother was murdered. I am here to support my father. They say you did it.'

I pointed to the mess of Paul on the floor. 'I didn't. He did, so you can put your gun down.'

'*Non.* I hear what you say. I will not let you kill my father.' She raised the automatic and aimed at me. She was struggling to hold the weapon still with one hand round the grip and the other over the top of the pistol.

'Marine, you're not going to shoot me. You are not like your father. He enjoys killing, but you are too nervous to pull that trigger. But, if I sense that you pluck up the courage and are about to do it, I shall shoot you first.' What I didn't say was that she didn't have a clue about automatic pistols and that if she continued to hold the gun with one hand over the top, over the slide so it couldn't come back, she was going to do herself an injury – her problem.

But Jacques had noticed. All I understood from his rapid French was the last few words: 'Shoot him now.' She changed her grip, but wasn't going to shoot, I was convinced of that. Even so, in her nervous state she could accidentally pull the trigger. The contrast was stark: my gun levelled at her head, a rock-steady threat, her gun wavering and quivering, a weak and almost harmless gesture. I took a step forward. She cracked, sobbed and let her arm drop.

I was going to kill her father. If pushed, I would have to shoot her. Even so, I was in a precarious position. Those dogs were worth a whole troop of special forces as far as I was concerned. One word from Jacques and I'd be lucky to survive.

'Jacques, you could have ordered those dogs to attack Paul. You could have ordered them to attack me. Why haven't you used them?'

He gave me what he classed as a smile. 'The dogs are my final weapon. You know they are dangerous. It is amusing to see 'ow you be'ave. It is amusing to see Marine. She is scared of you, she wants me to order the dogs, but I 'old them back, she worries. You are frightened of them. That is as it should be. It is like watching a play. I can see the emotions and the calculations of the players. But they are not acting, their reactions are real. It is amusing.'

That he found this life-threatening situation amusing ('intriguing' would be a better word) was not a surprise, taking his age and his inclination to kill into account. But did he not care about his daughter's life?

'Put your gun on the table and move this way, Marine. Jacques, if those dogs move, I will shoot your daughter, so keep them under control.' I took a couple of steps to put Marine between me and Jacques – or more specifically, the dogs.

I stepped up close behind her and put a hand on her left shoulder. It shook under my fingers. I pressed the CZ's muzzle into her neck. Her body quivered on the brink of collapse. 'Jacques, open the doors and order those dogs outside. If you don't, or you order them at me, I shall kill Marine.'

One would expect hatred to be in Mertens's eyes, but all I saw was calculation. I wasn't worthy of feelings on his part, but how to overcome me, how to win one of the last battles of his life, was. He didn't panic, he maintained a complete absence of emotion as his daughter trembled.

He stretched to reach the remote control. It seemed that he did have some feelings, family feelings at least. A man like that, a criminal, a killer who would take lives purely for his own satisfaction, a human with no regard for anything other than his own gratification, a man with no heart, had some heart after all.

Caesar and Brutus stood at Jacques's command. His eyes were on me. I swivelled Marine so he could clearly see the gun at her neck. Her legs trembled against mine.

'*Dehors*,' Mertens snapped. The dogs moved as one to the verandah.

'Close the doors, Jacques, and throw the remote to me.'

He tossed it in my direction. It landed short, halfway between us and within range of his stick.

'Marine, pick that up and hand it to me, then go and sit down over there.'

With no gun to her neck and an extra bit of distance between us, Marine seemed to gain an illusion of safety. She took a chair on the far side of the room and managed to scrape herself at least partially together. A dark cloud of shame hung over her, palpable from where I was. She had failed in front of her father: she had been unable to summon his strength in a time of crisis, she couldn't shoot and had given in too easily. Her voice quavered. 'What are you going to do now?'

There's no pleasure to be had from torturing the innocent, and the range of answers would not be pleasant for her. The dogs were no longer a threat, Mertens was too old to leap at me from his chair in a hurry, and Marine was temporarily, at least, an emotional wreck. It was safe to let the tension drain away and think. Her pistol was a Browning Hi-Power, another good, reliable weapon which took the same 9mm ammunition as the CZ. I made sure it was cocked and ready with the safety on, and tucked it under my belt.

Jacques had not moved, nor had he stopped watching me. I looked at Marine. 'In 1944 your father would have been hanged for the murder of at least one young woman. We've moved on from those times, but I was going to carry out that postponed death sentence. However, you interrupted, and I don't want to kill an innocent person, which I would have to do to protect myself. On top of that, I have just given away the secret of my condition, the repercussions of which I believe are hugely important for the future of mankind. People have died because of this knowledge, and the information cannot be allowed to get out. It's a dilemma. So, in answer to your question, I'm not sure yet.'

Mertens had been slipping down in his chair. Apart from his cold stare, he was remarkably calm. Was it because he was so old that the prospect of imminent death didn't concern him? 'If what you say is true, that you cannot age, then that means you cannot die of natural causes? Is that correct?'

'I assume so. No one has determined that.'

'Can you die from injury?'

'It hasn't been tested.'

Mertens smirked, obviously keen on finding that answer himself.

18

MY BACK WAS to the glass doors to the garden. Mertens's narrow eyes, from the sockets of his skull, were fixed and unrelenting, tracking my every move as a cat hunts a mouse. That is, until a human distracts it. And one did. Unlocking their hold on my face, his focus flicked to something behind me. When he had seen Marine his visual distraction had taken less than a second. Now, his gaze was steady on the garden.

Was he diverting my attention from him? I didn't turn. 'What is it?'

'There are men out there.'

Two steps left and I was behind the curtain. Marine, eyes clamped shut and head down, her hands clenched together, the knuckles white, seemed to shrink in her seat.

'Don't worry. They cannot see in, the glass is one-way and bulletproof,' Mertens said and wormed himself higher in the chair. 'Twenty-five millimetres thickness with a polycarbonate sandwich. It will stop an AK47.'

'If they don't shoot too many rounds into the same spot,' I said. 'How many? Who are they?'

'Two by the pool, maybe more. Who? I am not certain, but they will find it very difficult to get in. This house has *meutrières*, places where you can shoot at intruders and they are not able to shoot back. Like those narrow openings in an old castle.'

This was eyebrow-raising. 'We call them arrowslits. You built the house as a fortress?'

He shrugged. ''Ere, in my business, the possibility of attack by rivals is always present. I 'ave to defend my-self.'

Door chimes sounded from the front of the house. Marine jumped; she was not her father's daughter. Mertens and I both knew it would be stupid to answer. If the door were to be opened a crack, the men outside would force their way in. If this place was built as a fort, then the front door would only open to explosives. The chimes rang again, and again.

Out beyond the verandah, the dogs barked, the sound muffled behind the thick glass. The answer was a burst of automatic gunfire. Poor animals.

Something smashed at the front door; an axe, a sledgehammer? Whatever it was, it had no effect. Mertens sat in his chair in apparent calm while his daughter trembled in the corner. As well she might: if the intruders got in, her future would be very unpleasant. I too was scared. When these men kill, a simple clean bullet is not enough. The panga is a favourite weapon.

'Who are these men? His?' I pointed at Paul, whose pool of blood had mostly congealed around his head. 'Although, he had as many as fifteen, more than appear to be outside. I think they're more likely to be Idi Ajok's people. They are much more professional than the drunks and scum Paul recruited.'

'I think Ajok. I 'ave been waiting for this for some time. I knew it would come one day. I can deal with it, but you 'ave taken my gun.'

If I gave Mertens his gun back, he might shoot me. But then he would be facing the intruders on his own, Marine being a quivering wreck. If I kept the weapon, it would be up to me alone to defend the house, and I hadn't a clue what the secrets of its defences were.

Another blow to the front door echoed through the house, then another. Regular smashes, a few seconds between them, told of a sledgehammer. If they could keep up this pounding, they would eventually break the door down.

I ejected the magazine from the CZ75 and made the gun safe. That particular magazine could hold twenty rounds. I flicked them out and counted some back in. It was important to know how many bullets Mertens would have.

'Have you more ammunition in the house?'

'In the cupboard – over there.' He pointed.

'Marine, we need your help, please.'

The woman had curled up in her chair. She didn't move, she wasn't listening. She had shut out the events as if by ignoring them they would melt away. I took a step towards her, but Mertens's voice was a whip-crack. '*Marine!*' She started and turned her head to face him, slowly lowering her legs to the floor. He blasted her with a volume of rapid French, leaving her looking sheepish. She crossed to the cupboard and took out two boxes of ammunition. Head down, and with eyes that would not meet mine, she handed the boxes to me.

'Jacques, you know the best way to defend this house. You've obviously given it a great deal of thought – tell me.'

'This part of the 'ouse can be made separate from the bedrooms, where you escaped. The only way they can enter this section is through the front door and these doors. The ceiling over the whole 'ouse is concrete to prevent entrance from the roof. But above these glass doors, on top of the concrete, is a place you can shoot the attackers outside through the *meutrières,* your arrow-slits, in the floor. The same over the front door, but there you can also shoot from the side at intruders through thin holes. The problem is there are two doors. We have two guns, one for each door, but only one of you. If you want to stop these people you must give me back a gun.'

'I will give it to Marine. I don't trust you not to shoot me while I'm defending you.' I glanced at her, wondering if she could summon the will to fire at another human.

She couldn't help but hear us discussing her. I was embarrassed for her, but Jacques had no such feelings. His voice was rich with contempt. 'Marine will not shoot. She does not have my soldier's DNA. She is the same as her mother – a pacifist.'

I turned to her. 'Will you shoot at these men to stop them? You know what will happen to you if they get in, don't you? 'She stood, head bowed, her shoulders shaking gently, but didn't answer me.

The hammering at the front door continued.

I handed the CZ to Jacques, holding on to it as I spoke. 'We deal with the immediate threat first, and settle our own problem later – agreed?'

His empty, pale eyes did not blink. This man thought nothing of life, he would kill before breakfast and again during a sumptuous meal. He would kill in a crowd, in a church, in his own bed. If a psychopath has a particular look to him, Jacques Mertens had it in bucketloads. 'Agreed. Soldier's honour?'

'Soldier's honour,' I confirmed, although I'd never heard of it. I didn't trust the ninety-three-year-old further than he could dribble.

THE POP, POP, popping from the pool area was overridden by the sharp smacking of bullets on the verandah doors. Within seconds they were peppered with rosettes of wounded glass, spider cracks radiating out from the points of impact.

The glass held, but how many rounds would it withstand? The men came closer. Because the doors were composed of one-way glass, they could see nothing, but their features contorted as they attempted to. One of them had a sledgehammer. Even though the bullets had not penetrated the doors, they had weakened them and a sledgehammer might now break through. That had to be stopped.

The heavy hammering at the front door did not let up. Mertens rose unsteadily to his feet and pointed out to the garden. 'You go up above that door. It is a difficult route for me. Marine will show you the way. I am going to the front. We need to show these idiots it is stupid to try and break in 'ere.'

Marine beckoned me to the curtains on the side of the glass frontage and held them back. A steep spiral of steps disappeared above the ceiling, so narrow I had to force my shoulder inwards and hold my weapon above my head. The darkness of the loft closed in. A hint of light shone upwards on the far side, presumably through arrowslits above the porch outside the front door.

I crawled across the concrete slab on my belly to the arrowslit at the edge, under the slope of the roof. Above the glass frontage, the opening was easy to see as the verandah lights shone up through it, illuminating the drifting cloud of dust I'd disturbed.

The slit was perfectly positioned. Looking down, I had a clear, although narrow, view of the outside of the doors and four men, all armed with AK47 assault rifles.

I had no desire to kill anyone. In any case, it's often of more value to injure than to kill, because it ties up more of the enemy's resources in rescue and care.

One man had a sledgehammer in his left hand and his AK slung over the other shoulder. Putting down his gun, he stepped forward to strike. He swung the hammer back and up. At the top of its arc, I put a shot into his shoulder. He screamed and fell to his knees, clutching his arm. The hammer thumped onto the tiles. The other men leapt back, rifles up, swivelling left and right, blindly searching where my shot came from. I put another round into another shoulder. The target spun away. Only his feet remained in my sight. Should I shatter his foot?

Two shots came from inside the house – aimed shots, not double-taps. That meant two rounds less in Jacques's arsenal.

Hammer man had crawled away, groaning. Cries of *'Maman, Maman'* came from out of view. Two out of four were down, and the others were no longer in sight. There wasn't any more I could do up there in the loft.

From the lounge, I got a brief view of two men leaning to the side and clutching their shoulders as they staggered away from the verandah lights for the safety of the dark. One had left his AK47 on the floor. The temptation was great.

Marine was staring at me from the corner. Frightened silly, she was almost useless. It was no good asking her for help: she could be paralysed with fear at a critical moment, or unintentionally do something idiotic.

Jacques fired again – two more rounds out of his magazine.

The remote control for the glass doors was not visible at first glance. I couldn't waste time searching for it, so manual operation would have to do. The lock operated easily. Crouching down, I slid the door open just enough to squeeze through. The AK lay on the tiles about four metres away. Beyond it, a dead dog. A run, a snatch and a run back as two wild rounds smacked into another part of the window.

The gap in the one-way glass frontage was less than shoulder width. Marine was watching me. I could see her mind working. She saw an opportunity, made a decision and took a step. She reached for the handle.

Bitch. I dived full length, got my left hand in the gap. She slammed the door against my fingers. It hurt. I almost pulled back at the pain, but getting inside was the only way not to be a sitting duck. More bullets thwacked into the glass at waist height but off to my right – useless idiot. I wrenched at the door. Marine yanked back, over and over in total panic. I could see her feet slipping on the tiles, limiting her efforts. Likewise, I was lying on the ground with no purchase of my own. My fingers screamed at me, but the gap widened. A bullet zipped through the opening and hit the far wall. The shooter was getting better. Another round went through the gap.

Marine cried out and fell back. I dived in. A third bullet hit the door a second before I got it closed.

Marine sat on the floor, her fingers in her mouth, quivering and staring at me with tear-brimmed eyes. Blood spread through her shirt sleeve on her upper arm.

'That wasn't very nice of you.'

She didn't answer. Clearly, I was a monster come to annihilate her and her father. She was half right about that.

'Let me see that.'

She shrank away, shaking her head.

I took her quivering arm and pulled up her sleeve. 'It's only a flesh wound. Probably hurts more than it's worth. I'll dress it for you.'

She shook her head even more violently and, still sitting, tried to back further away, which wasn't possible. She'd tried to get me killed, so I didn't have much sympathy. Still, she wasn't much of a threat.

Her father was another matter. Had he finished with the men at the front door? If so, he had only one round left, because I'd only reloaded his magazine with five. As an ex professional soldier, he would naturally conserve his ammunition, so five rounds would be all he'd need in a secure defensive position to force the intruders back from the front porch. Whereas I had retrieved a fully automatic weapon with two magazines, taped back to back for swift reloading. One was full with thirty rounds, the other was part used.

But, at the end of the day, it might only take one well-placed shot to kill me.

DIFFICULT CHOICES. SHOULD I hunt through this unfamiliar house for him, or let him come to me? Now that the threat at the front door had passed, his only option was to find and kill me before I carried out my promise.

This was a game of cat and mouse. The question was, which one of us was which?

I'm not the hero of a Western movie, so the concept of using two guns at the same time was out of the question, especially since one of them required two hands. The AK had more rounds and was a bigger threat, but I didn't know its previous owner, who might well have left the weapon lying in the mud while he chatted up the whores in the local shebeen. The Browning pistol would be more reliable, and more handy in the confined space of the house. I removed the magazines from the AK and took them up to the loft out of immediate reach. The weapon itself, I left as a useless ornament on the table.

Had Mertens checked the bullets remaining in his CZ? If he was careless, he was in for a surprise. If he knew he only had one round, what was he going to do? He would have to use stealth and his knowledge of the house to get the better of me. Although incredible for his age, it was not on his side. His movements were slow and stiff, and how good was his eyesight?

The last shots were fired about ten minutes ago, but he had not come into the lounge. Was he waiting for me to walk into his ambush? Remaining in the lounge was not an option: it was too exposed, with nowhere to hide. Fighting in buildings is a horrible thing. The enemy can be through the next door, round the corner, just inches away, waiting for you to show yourself.

Mertens was not in the hall. The arrowslit he had used was level with the front door and gave a good field of fire covering visitors on the outside. Two bodies lay sprawled across the steps. But where had Jacques gone? The only way out was to the lounge, and he hadn't been there.

In searching the space for a clue, I glanced at the ceiling. Something wasn't right. A break in the uniformity of flat concrete made me look again. There was another slit that faced down and covered anyone who had come in through the door. Pasted over it was some white material which almost hid it from casual observation.

I leaped out of the way. A shot blasted into the hall. The crack bounced off the walls and set my ears ringing.

The bullet smacked into the floor next to my foot. That was close.

To the side was a curtain similar to that in the lounge, and behind it was another short spiral staircase. It drew me. But was it to a satisfactory conclusion in my lifelong hunt for Sybil's murderer, or was it to my own death?

I climbed until my eyes reached floor level and stopped, waiting for them to gradually adjust to the gloom. As on the other side of the house, the only light came up through the arrowslit above the hall. It wasn't much, but it was enough to make out the shape of a body lying on the floor.

'You've no more bullets, Mertens.'

Four rounds snapped in my direction. His aim was low, the bullets ricocheted off the floor and zipped away to hit the roof. Chips of concrete hit my forehead. In the confined space the noise was deafening. Could he see detail? Admittedly, only the top of my head was visible to him, but we were close, yet he'd failed to hit me.

He laughed, his voice grating. 'Marine gave me a new box.'

I could make him out clearly by then. This was not the way I wanted to do this. He had smothered Sybil and used various methods to asphyxiate the other girls. I wanted to hold a cushion to his face so he could feel what it was like for her. To feel what it was like for her straining for air, becoming weaker and weaker, her lungs in agony as her legs thrashed the mattress in desperation. To do that I would have to get him out of the loft and down into the lounge. That was too difficult to do without being shot. Unless he was incapacitated first.

It only needed a single shot. His body jerked with the impact. It wasn't possible in the gloom to see where I'd hit him, but I had, judging by the grunts and suppressed sounds of pain he made. These were not cries for help. This old man was tough, and I wasn't going to take any chances. Watching him for signs of turning and aiming at me, I climbed up to ceiling level. He was feeling with his right hand for the CZ, which lay beside him. I brushed it out of his reach with my foot, picked it up and made it safe before tucking it into my belt.

'Right, let's get you downstairs to check the damage.' Dragging him by the ankles to the top of the staircase was perhaps not explicitly covered by the Geneva Convention on the protection of the wounded. It was, though, the best way to move him since height was restricted under the slope of the roof. Descending four steps, I managed to slide him onto my shoulder and carry him into the lounge.

Marine had gone back to her chair in the corner. She looked apprehensive and miserable, but summoned the will to move and see her father on the couch. His normally tanned features had paled, and a dribble of blood escaped his thin lips. There was no softening of his eyes, though; they were pale, flint-like and as murderous as ever.

'You have killed him.'

'Not yet.'

Mertens's breathing was shallow and rapid as he struggled to get air. Marine knelt on the floor and put her arms up to hug him. He coughed, spattering her shirt with bloody spittle. More blood was spilling out of his mouth. She began to undo his shirt buttons, although what she thought she could do by looking at the wound I couldn't imagine, and he brushed her away.

'Jacques, you are dying. Your body is craving oxygen just like Sybil and the other women you killed. Now you know what it was like for them as they fought for the air you deprived them of. Perhaps now you understand how helpless they felt as their lungs hurt and their muscles got weaker and they were no longer able to fight the strong man pinning them down. For no reason, Jacques, for no reason. That is why I'm content to watch you struggle to stay alive, knowing you won't. Why don't you admit to your daughter that you killed Sybil and the other girls. Why don't you admit to the pleasure you felt in snuffing out the lives of others. Come on, Jacques, it's the least you can do to make up for your sickness.'

Marine leaned over her father. 'Is it true? Did you do what he says you did? I will forgive you, but you must tell me the truth.'

I waited. Although his birthmark alone was sufficient evidence for me, supported by his criminal activities, his treatment of animals and his whole cold-blooded demeanour, there was a tiny element of doubt within me which would only be assuaged by his confession.

Mertens had another coughing fit. More blood escaped his mouth. It was not going to be long before he died.

'*Papa?*'

His eyes tracked slowly round to me, stopped, then moved back to Marine. It might have been my imagination, but they softened. He nodded, coughed a final time and was still.

MARINE'S HEAD LAY on her father's chest. Her shoulders shook, but she made no sound.

I helped myself to a beer. The cold, refreshing liquid washed the dust and some of the bad taste from my mouth. I drank it too quickly and opened another. Part of the reason, I told myself, was that I didn't want to disturb Marine's grieving too soon. Outside, tiny ripples on the pool's surface told of a faint breeze. Otherwise the garden was quiet. Had they gone, and if so, for how long?

'Are you going to kill me now?' Marine asked.

'Why would I do that?'

'You're a psychopath.'

'No, but your father was. I have no compunction in killing a killer.'

'You killed those men outside.'

'No, I didn't. I shot them both in the shoulder to make them useless, but if they die – too bad.'

'I know your secret. I know you will kill to protect it – you said so. So why don't you kill me now?'

'I won't kill you, because you're innocent. Killing people is not something I do. But I beg you to keep my secret. I believe the consequences of it falling into the hands of a pharmaceutical giant will be horrendous for humanity. If you care about the planet, about the environment, then keep silent – please.'

Something changed in her. The grieving daughter's tear-stained face took on a harder, calculating look. She'd seen a way to get back at me. 'You killed my father.'

'It was almost the other way around. He was trying to kill me.'

'You killed him. I am going to have revenge. Not good for you, but I work for CUZ Pharmaceuticals. It is not a big drug company, maybe you never heard of it, but it does important work. For a long time there have been rumours in the industry that a man that doesn't age exists, but no one has found him. So, you are that man, and I have found you. My little company will profit greatly when your secret is learned. Suddenly we will be one of the big players.' Her voice was rising all the time. 'We will hunt you down. I will see to it. We will cut you into pieces to find your precious secret. *I can't wait to see you cut to pieces,*' she screamed at me, tears of hysteria running down her cheeks.

'That's a refreshing approach, Marine. At last one of you lot are telling the truth. Up to now they all tried to sweet-talk me into cooperation, offered me exorbitant sums of money so they can cut me open or fix me up with a string of gorgeous girls for as long as they let me live. I've been hunted for decades, Marine. I was hoping to stop running from your industry, but if you tell, my life will not change. It won't change for the better, but it won't get any worse, either.'

19

THE AK47 STILL lay undisturbed and harmless without any ammunition on the table. I'd put the magazines out of sight up in the loft. They too had not moved, proving that Marine had not tried to sabotage my actions. She watched me check the weapon. I worked the cocking action a few times in an uneven fashion.

'This thing is stiff and hasn't been oiled,' I said. 'I hope it doesn't jam if I need to use it.'

She didn't respond.

'At least the magazines work freely.' I slung the gun over my shoulder and looked at the miserable woman in front of me.

'Marine, I'm going to leave now. I need to get out of here. This fight for your father's company has nothing to do with me. You and his workers must battle it out with Idi Ajok yourselves. If I had control, I would shut down both Ajok's outfit and Nyiragongo, both of which are criminal. Whatever happens, I hope you stay unharmed.'

She glared at me but didn't say a word.

'This house is no longer safe. I think you should go to a hotel for a while. If you leave with me, I'll escort you to the one down the road.'

'No, I will stay here with my father.'

'You cannot help him anymore. You cannot defend this house on your own. At least for tonight, stay in the hotel. Sleep if you can, and tomorrow you can sort out what to do next.'

'I told you, I am going to stay here with my father. *Now go.*'

'All right. I'm going, but I need to prepare first.'

'Get out of this house.'

There was no point in further argument. I reloaded the Browning from the box of ammunition on the table and tucked it under my belt at the back. 'Make sure you lock the door behind me.'

A loud series of clicks. The electronic locks on the front door had retracted.

Marine's eyes widened. In desperation, she looked at me, her enemy, for help. I unslung the AK and cocked it as I moved to the side of the room. Who the hell could unlock the door? Only someone with a key or another remote control.

The door clicked shut and the locks slid back into place. Trainers squeaked across the tiled floor. A determined stride. I raised the AK.

Marine was on her knees by the sofa and facing the doorway.

'What are you doing here? Where is your father?' Céleste snapped.

The two women stared at each other. One, tearful and immobile in her misery, and the other with a new-found confidence, a woman who sought to dominate. There was obviously no love lost between them.

'What's the matter with you? Where is your father, Marine? I want to speak to him.'

'He's behind the sofa next to you,' I said, still pointing the AK at her.

Céleste whipped round. 'Wha— what are you doing here?'

'I had a score to settle with Jacques. See for yourself.'

She stepped forward. Marine was still kneeling at her father's side.

'Is he dead?'

'Yes.'

'Did you do it?'

I lowered the weapon. 'It was a firefight. He lost.'

'Good. It makes my life simpler. I thought I was going to have difficulty with him. I'm here to take control of the company. It is mine now, Marine. It is best if you go back to your job in France.'

Marine clambered to her feet, still standing over her father. 'How can you say that? Naturally this company is mine. My father left it to me.'

'No, Eric was running it, and as his wife, I get to own it. Besides, you know nothing about it. You have no experience of aircraft, of transport, of the wildlife trade – you know nothing and would very quickly wreck the company.'

'This is ridiculous. My father founded this company. It is a Mertens company. You cannot have it unless I am dead.' Marine paled suddenly as the implications of what she'd said dawned on her.

Céleste gave her a humourless smile. 'Yes, Marine. That. Is. True. However, there is no need to worry. You only have to face the facts and go back to France.'

'No—'

'*Listen to me you stupid, useless Mertens bitch.* If you think I'm going to give up my right after years of being beaten by your sick brother and laughed at by your psychopathic father, you are very, very wrong. You have done nothing to deserve this company. Your family is evil. Maybe not you, because you are weak, but your men were evil, and the best thing to happen in this awful world was for them to die.'

'No—'

'*Don't interrupt me*. You need to understand what is going to happen, then perhaps you will see sense. The men who attacked this house were Idi Ajok's men. I made an agreement with Idi and I led them here, but unfortunately ...' She glanced at me and smirked. 'I forgot to tell them of the secret defences of the house, and it was easy for you to defeat them. With them out of the way I have no one watching me for a while and can consolidate my position.

'Idi is very powerful. He will take this and many other companies in the region. He is like mafia. He is a god-father. You cannot fight him. However, I have convinced him to let me own and run the company and to pay him a percentage of the income. It is not the best deal for me, but it is better than losing everything. He understands I have expertise that he doesn't. If you have control without the expertise, he will kill you and steal everything. With me running it, Nyiragongo will contin-ue, and under Idi's protection there will be peace.'

Marine collapsed to her knees beside her father again. The fight had gone out of her. She looked up at me as if I could magic up a solution.

I couldn't and, what's more I had no intention of trying. 'None of this has anything to do with me. I am going to leave you two to settle your differences without me. Céleste, are any of Idi's men still out there?'

She took time answering, no doubt considering whether to help me or tell me lies that would get me into trouble. Perhaps she was grateful for what help I had previously given her, because she sounded honest. 'Most are dead. Two were hit in the shoulder, but they went to hospital. There is another man who didn't assault the house, but stayed a distance away. I don't know any more about him.'

'Thank you. Marine, you are best getting out. Céleste is right, you should go back to France and forget all this.

'Céleste, you need to understand that I am going to do my best to stop the trade in animals by all participants, that's Nyiragongo and Ajok in this case. I have enough evidence to have Nyiragongo charged with animal trafficking and diamond smuggling. Wheels turn slowly, but eventually Nyiragongo will be shut down and anyone involved will be charged. If you are still here, you will go to prison. Idi Ajok may well escape prosecution, because mafia bosses have many ways and means to get off, but smaller fry, like you, he will sacrifice for his own ends. It will be easy, because you will be the official owner. I shall be submitting all my evidence to

Interpol's Wildlife Enforcement Team who will assist the local authorities.'

Marine stood. Her attractive face was contorted into a mask of hatred. 'Get out of this house. Go back to Nairobi or wherever you come from. I am going to expose you. You can run and hide, but we will find you. I promise. You killed him and you will suffer. I will see you again – on the operating table.'

'A little melodramatic, Marine. I'll put it down to stress.'

There was no point in putting off the inevitable. It was time to face whatever dangers lurked in the streets. A press of the button retracted the front door bolts. They still worked smoothly after the battering they'd had, which was amazing. The house wasn't impregnable, but it was hard to conquer.

I opened the door a crack. There was no sign of human life. There was little sound of anything. It was too late for cicadas, but a dog barked somewhere, setting off a few minutes of canine conversation across town. A vehicle honked, an engine revved, and dim strains of primitive music could be heard.

The guardhouse door was open. The man himself was sprawled over his desk, lifeless and bloodless judging by the amount of the stuff on the floor. I didn't stop to inspect, it being of no interest to me. The CCTV was frozen on an image of the front gates. One was off its hinges, leaving a gaping hole in the defences.

Moving into the bushes at the side of the gates, I un-slung the AK47, cocked it and fired a short volley towards the house. Then, with the Browning I fired three rounds into the garden, where there would be no sound of impact. Another volley from the AK, making sure some hit the front door, was answered by two more 9mm rounds, then a final burst of automatic fire.

If Marine had heard that exchange, and she should have done, she would hopefully conclude that my AK had jammed and I'd had to resort to the Browning and just lost the gun fight. No one came to investigate. The odd gun battle at night between gangs was not uncommon in Goma.

I had left the two women to either reach an agreement (doubtful) or for one to emerge as the winner (and probably as the only one alive). Each wanted the other out of the way. Marine was consumed by her misery, and was unpredictable. She wouldn't kill, even in her current mental state, but she would easily take her revenge in some remote fashion, like reporting me to her company. What would she do about Céleste if she wouldn't kill her? How would she win control of Nyiragongo? And if, by some slim chance, she did win, would she continue trafficking wildlife? At this time she was confused, depressed, miserable, weak and easy to defeat. She was not a cruel person, however.

Céleste, on the other hand, was not the beaten waif I had first seen her to be. Probably as a result of Eric's treatment of her, she was much harder. In spite of my convincing Jacques that she had not killed Eric, that might not have been the case at all, and I had blamed Paul because he was convenient. She was quite capable of murder. If Marine stood in her way, her chances of survival were slim.

20

WHEN I OPENED the door of my room at the Serova Stanley, it was five o'clock on Monday afternoon. The flight from Goma to Nairobi on Sunday had landed mid-morning so, with most of the day ahead of me, I drove up to the reserve near Nanyuki to find Robert.

I brought him up to date with all the material I had and left him with a signed statement. He then knew as much as I did and, if anything happened to me, he would have all the information and evidence to help prosecute the traffickers. We sank a few beers that night in celebration of our progress and had a few laughs.

After shrugging off a mild headache I made a leisurely start and took the trip back to Nairobi, knowing that was probably the last time I'd see my friend, for I was not likely to go back again. I'd also been coming to terms with what I felt about Jacques Mertens's death. I thought of all the years I'd spent following innocent men, watching them and taking ridiculous steps to examine their ankles. It was a struggle to realise that seventy-five years of search was over and the bastard was dead – and I had killed him. For Sybil, at last. I felt not a shred of remorse.

This life of running, hiding and using false identities was both wearing and created a sense of impermanence. And, with the pharmaceuticals on my tail again, and now with Kirsten in their headlights as a lever to get to me, my, maybe our, future was uncertain.

Kirsten was not a person to be forgotten, but with the distraction of the violent activity over the weekend I hadn't realised that there had been no daily texts from her. In my room, I checked my phone. The last text I'd seen was the one on Friday evening which I'd thought strange. The next one had come through on the drive back, which meant she'd missed Saturday and Sunday. It was similar: there was no mention of Lupus, and it ended with *Love K*. I couldn't work it out, but I needed to satisfy my raging thirst.

Rather than raid the minibar, I went down to the Thorn Tree. It was always good to watch the antics of naïve tourists, local hard drinkers, businesspeople after work, and socialites. It wasn't as much fun as it used to be in the '60s, but it was still good entertainment.

The waiter delivered my beer. I took a large swallow and asked him to bring another. As I looked up, the elderly woman two tables away caught my eye. She gave me a wicked smile and got unsteadily to her feet. If she'd been drinking, she might become loud, and I didn't want to draw attention.

No, not her again. I didn't need this. *Please*. What was her name: Allison? Or was it Annette? I'd known her in the army, decades ago. Her husband was a Signals Officer, Mike Trench. She must have been in her late seventies. Fair and now grey-haired, her skin, heavily wrinkled, had not responded well to the dehydrating air at Nairobi's altitude and the African sun.

'Andrew, dear. We meet again. It's so nice to see you looking so healthy. I wish I knew how you do it – keep your age. It's amazing.'

What was amazing was how she equated the young image she remembered with a person who, fifty years later, she was unlikely to recognise. We first met in the '60s, then, again, at this very spot, thirty-seven years ago. She must have harboured her first memory of me and, perhaps wishfully, failed to account for the passing of years. Had she been that struck on me? I never had that impression.

'Look, you're a very sweet lady, but I told you last time, ages ago, that my name is not Andrew, it's Charlie. Charlie Maxwell. I must be Andrew's spitting image for you to be so insistent, but I promise you I'm not who you think I am. Here, look at my passport.'

Her scrawny hand with its pronounced veins and parchment-like skin trembled slightly as she took the document. She fumbled for her glasses. 'Cursed thing, getting old. Everything falls apart or droops or sags, and we have to resort to these damn things to see. Annette's my name, in case you forgot.' She flicked through the pages. 'Travelled a lot, haven't you?' She raised an eyebrow and looked keenly at me. 'Born in '85. That's not right, can't be. Last time I saw you here was before that, wasn't it?'

Damn. This was the trouble with running into old acquaintances. She was right, we'd met in '82 and my 'renewed' passport had my current claimed birth date. Mistake – I should never have shown it to her. I put a consoling hand on her arm. 'Annette, you're confused, I'm afraid. We met only two years ago, certainly not before I was born.'

'So how old are you now? I can't be bothered to employ my mental arithmetic. It's a strain at this age.'

'Thirty-four,' I said and held out my hand for the passport. 'Do you believe me now?'

'I don't know. There's something not right. Anyway, let's not worry about it. Shouldn't we have a drink?'

Across the far side of the café was a face that looked familiar, but I couldn't place it. Narrow, high cheekbones, pale eyes, a Slavic nose, thin lips – they tinkled a bell, but not enough to confirm an identity The man took his dark glasses off the top of his head and put them on the table. He picked up his phone and studied it as any person would do, except that it was angled unnaturally high for that purpose, and it was pointing at me. If it wasn't for the hair … Jakub Kowalski with a dark brown wig. Marine had been as good as her word. She must have already alerted her company, CUZ Pharmaceuticals. I'd always wondered who he worked for.

'I'll have another Pimms, please,' Annette said. It suddenly occurred to me that she might only be on the take for a few free drinks and had no idea who I was at all. No: I knew her, and she certainly knew me. I gave a mental shrug and waved at a waiter.

Kowalski stood, tall, slim but strong. He pocketed his phone and weaved his way between the tables to ours.

'Andrew, fancy seeing you here. What are you doing in Kenya?'

I put a quizzical look on my face. 'I'm sorry. I think you have the wrong person.' Beside me, I could sense

Annette's triumph that someone else knew me as Andrew.

Kowalski bared his teeth with the intention of a smile. 'Oh come on, Andrew. You have to drop this pretence.'

Don't agree, Annette. Please don't agree with him.

She looked up at Kowalski. 'Young man, I've know Charlie here for twenty years. I can assure you his name's not Andrew. You're mistaken.'

'I'm sorry to disturb you.' Kowalski gave me a not-so-subtle wink and turned away.

'That was good of you,' I said. 'I know you're still convinced I'm Andrew. What made you decide to lie for me?'

She gave a slight titter. 'I didn't like the look of him, and you're buying me a drink.'

I bought her three. While working her way rapidly through the second one, she studied the table in front of her and said, 'Charlie, can you help me out?'

'In what way?'

'My husband and I came here after he left the army. He got a job managing a farm. He was brought up on a farm, so he knew a great deal about it. We had a wonderful time until he died. Mike was good on the farm, but he was awful with money, and I've been left with very little. It's too expensive to move back to England. Friends here help me out in kind a bit, but it's not enough.' Annette looked me in the eye. 'I'm getting awfully short and honestly don't know what to do.'

This I didn't need. Prior to Alex's death, I was not stinking rich, but was comfortably off. Since she died, I was supposed to be extremely wealthy, but I didn't yet know what attributes, positive or negative, were attached to the inheritance, let alone the tax involved. I could afford to give Annette a token sum, but that could be a one-way trip to disaster. It could lead to some sort of relationship to which she would cling, and I would find myself with a dependent that I wouldn't have the heart to dump.

The trouble was that as my true self, Captain Andrew Duncan, when Mike was based in the same camp as me, Annette and I had come close to a one-night stand, even though we were both married. It was a drunken error which began with a close and sexy dance. Fortunately, we both came to our senses and backed away from taking it further. Saffron, my wife, had a rare sense of humour failure for couple of days, and my memory of her hurt still influenced me.

Annette was giving me an intense look. 'What do you think … Andrew?'

Her switching from addressing me as Charlie to using Andrew was not a mistake, nor was it subtle.

I met her challenging stare. 'Annette, I like you. Genuinely, I do, and I would like to help you out, but threatening to expose me as someone else is not conducive to a successful result for you. Also, the threat wouldn't work, because I really am not this Andrew. You would probably cause me a little inconvenience for a while if you go ahead, but I'd get over it, and you would have gained nothing.'

'That was a slip of the tongue. I'm sorry you saw something different in it, Charlie.'

'I'll give you a one-off gift, but it will be one-off. If you're not frivolous with it, it should last you a while. After this afternoon, you will never see me again, and you will have no way of contacting me. Stay there, I'll be back in a few minutes.'

She was still sitting at the table when I returned, apparently lost in thought. Was she depressed at what she imagined was a poor result of her begging? Or was she wondering how much I was going to give her?

I handed her the money bag that Idi had given me.

'Thank you, Andr— Charlie.' She started to spread back the rim of the bag.

'No. Don't open that now, Annette, do it in private later. I'm going back to the DRC – Goma. I need to carry on my work there. You won't see me again.' Pushing my chair back into the table, I smiled at her. 'Don't spend that all at once. And good luck, Annette. I mean that.'

It felt wrong to leave her like that. In a different era, long ago, we'd got on well, been friends and, if we hadn't both been married, might have been lovers. But now, decades later, things had changed, and as people we had changed. I was experienced and much more cynical. She was in her seventies, no longer appealing and now forced to live on the charity of her friends. How and what I could give was limited because I was always on the run as a freak of nature. Not her fault, and not mine.

My thoughts were interrupted by the second text of the day from Kirsten. *'All well here'* – again, just like the last three messages, and again Lupus was not mentioned. But *'When you coming home?'* was added this time, plus, *'Love you'*, which was somehow a lot more personal than, *Love, K.* Either worry over the future and my absence were having an effect on her, or something else was wrong. Kirsten was a very controlled person, and these messages were out of character.

If all really was well back in Orkney, then it was good news, because it gave me the freedom and time to act where I was, in Kenya. Something had to be done about Jakub Kowalski and his company, CUZ Pharmaceuticals.

ANNETTE WAS CLUTCHING the bag to her chest when I was at the door, as if savouring it. She must have been dying to look inside, but was perhaps too scared to, in case it turned out to be a paltry sum. She looked up as Kowalski pulled back a chair and sat down beside her. That gave me something to grin about – he was going to learn something completely false in the next few minutes.

At the door, watching me, was Idi's bodyguard, manservant or whatever. I took the opportunity to give him a challenging glare. He wasn't going to flatten me with one hand where we stood, in front of all the people, even though he could do.

As far I knew, Idi himself was still in Goma, directing the seizure of Nyiragongo, or monitoring Céleste's progress on that. How long would it take the monster in front of me to alert his boss and get an order to act? I needed to disappear, get out of the hotel and out of Nairobi, and quickly.

The only reasonably safe place for me was back in the reserve. But I had just come from there, it was late, and the thought of a four-hour drive at night with the possibility of stray cattle or other animals on the road was off-putting.

Not only that, but submitting my report to the WWF was both essential and urgent and could only be done the next morning before someone stopped me. The person I spoke to had to be senior, someone who carried responsibility, someone tenacious who knew all the strings to be pulled to see an investigation through in full knowledge of the dangers of opposing organised crime – Idi Ajok and others. That person had to take it further – to Interpol, because this involved another country.

The hotel was a dangerous place for me to be, though, with Ajok's man based in the Presidential Suite. In my room I bundled my things together and stuffed them into my rucksack. The Browning, tucked into my belt, was hard on my spine and weighed heavy on my trousers. The Aeroclub confirmed they had a room available for the night. I was almost ready to check out.

The best way to stop someone trying to chop off my hands and feet (if that was what he really meant) was to rid myself of the threat before they snuck up behind me.

Outside the Presidential Suite, I looked up at the CCTV camera and gave it a friendly grin. As the lock turned, I took the Browning out of my belt. The door opened a crack. I rammed it forward, brought the gun up and drove it into the man's forehead. His eyes crossed focusing on the barrel. I don't think anyone had threatened this chap before. Because of his size, he had always been the bully, the enforcer. It's amazing how a gun pressed to your head can change your outlook on life.

Behind me, the door clicked closed.

'Turn around.'

He hesitated.

The gun was still pushed into his forehead. *'Turn round. Get down on your knees.'*

I felt a shiver run through him. As his head turned away, I kept the muzzle pressed against it – from his forehead to his temple then his ear, then slowly round to the back. His fear fed back to me through the quiver of the weapon.

It was not my intention to fire the gun. The noise, even up here on the top floor, would invite curiosity. I checked that the safety catch was on, reversed the Browning and smashed it down onto his skull. He dropped.

There was no doubt that this chap was going to come round with a headache and a serious thirst for revenge. He had to be put out of action. Killing him would be stupid, because I might well be caught before leaving the country. In any case, I had no desire to kill anyone else after my revenge on Jacques had been satisfied.

A possible accidental discharge of a shot had to be eliminated, so I gave the safety catch a double-check.

The man's grizzly-bear paw extended from a wrist crowded with elephant hair and bead bracelets. Banana fingers were difficult to spread out, but I got the right hand flat on the floor and knelt on it. Even if he wasn't conscious, his instinctive reaction to what was coming might result in him pulling his hand away.

I brought the butt of the gun down on his fingers, one by one. Two of them actually crunched. Then I started on the left. Ugly behaviour which wasn't a pleasure, but I was fighting for my life, and this brute would repair eventually.

With Idi's enforcer rendered useless for a few weeks with no workable fingers, it was likely that I was safe for a few hours. It would take some time for the man to contact Idi when he couldn't even press the keys on a phone, and then his boss would have to find another pawn with which to exact his vengeance. Maybe he could do it quickly, but it would still be time lost to him and time gained for me to get away.

AT THE AEROCLUB after a good night's sleep, I dawdled over breakfast while waiting for offices in the city to open. My future was uncertain, to say the least. CUZ Pharmaceuticals was after me, although hopefully Kowalski had taken the bait and left to find me in Goma. The greatest danger came from the most ruthless gangster in the region – Idi Ajok. I was going to ruin his business. In return, he was going to kill me. I had to get out of his reach immediately.

The options were few: I could lie low in the reserve with Robert for a while, but Idi would still find me, probably sooner rather than later; I could fly back to London that night if seats were available, but although I would have escaped Ajok, I would expose myself to the pharmaceutical giants hunting me once I landed; I could also go to the reserve for a couple of days and from there, while still unseen, go to Entebbe in Uganda to catch a London flight.

It was getting too complicated. I phoned the airline.

The visit to the WWF took three hours. By the time I'd found the right person to talk to, explained the sensitivity of the issue, the dangers involved and the criminals behind the trafficking, all supported by my evidence, including photographs of the apes and the warehouse where they had been held, it was time for lunch.

It was bright outside, so I put on my sunglasses. A smear made me take them off again and rub it away. As I put them back on, a man stepped out of a red car on the other side of the road and waved.

MY PULSE RACED, my ears pounded. A vision of this man's blood spilling out over the pavement flashed into my imagination. *I have had enough of this.*

I crossed the street without looking. Tyres screeched, a horn blared. *So fucking what?*

'Andrew, so good to see you again.'

My hand was beyond my control. It seized Kowalski by the collar and rammed him backwards, stretched him over the bonnet. He tried to kick back at me, but missed. His hands went round mine, but I clenched my fingers round his Adam's apple as if to rip it out. His breathing rasped.

'*I am getting very tired of seeing you, Kowalski.*' The quiver in my own voice was clear. 'This is the last time you will follow me. I am *not* going to do what you want. Do. You. Understand?'

Some sort of strained acknowledgement was grunted. I pulled the Browning from my belt and held it at belly level. He was shaking. No one was watching us.

'Look down.'

He did. His eyes widened. 'No. No. Please. Listen to me, Andrew, hear me out—'

'You are perilously close to sealing your fate, Jakub. Make no mistake, I will use this gun if you don't do as I say. Unlock your boot.'

He fumbled with the electronic key until he found the right button, his nervous eyes on me the whole time. Pleading, blinking. The boot lid rose.

'Give me the key. Give me your phone. Get in.'

'But—'

'*Get in.*'

He manoeuvred his long frame into the boot, curling into a foetal position. My anger was easing, but even so I slammed the lid shut with unnecessary force. He needed to know the depth of my rage.

The ping of a message stopped me. *'Have Every concern about Lupus your Pooch he getting worse. K.'* What on earth was she talking about? Then I read the capital letters and went cold.

The boot lid sprang open as I pressed the button and with Kowalski pushing it up, but he quickly pulled back his leg when I rammed the Browning into his temple. 'I don't have any time for CUZ Pharmaceuticals, Jakub, but I don't think even they are going to stoop so far out of normal legal bounds as to kidnap innocent people to achieve their aim. You're not employed by CUZ are you?'

His bottom lip was quivering. He shook his head.

'You're a bounty hunter, aren't you? It's illegal, did you know that? How much are they paying you?'

'No, a bounty hunter catches criminals. All I'm trying to do is to get you to see reason.'

'Then why is my friend asking for help? What have you done?' I pushed the gun harder into his temple. It must have hurt. I hope it hurt. His eyes were closed, the lids fluttering. Drool wetted the carpet. 'Jakub, you are going to call off your men now. You phone them and tell them to leave her alone and to get away from her. *Do you understand me?*'

'Y … Yes.'

'When you've told them, I will call her and confirm. If they have not gone, then I'll kill you. Is that clear? Do you understand that I will *not* do what you want, and I'm prepared for murder to make sure I stay free? Here's your phone – *do it.*'

He dialled the number with uncertain fingers. A rapid conversation followed in a Slavic language. He gave his phone back to me. I slammed the boot lid down again. His scream might have come from his fingers. I didn't care.

It was mid-afternoon, so with time to waste I drove around without any purpose other than making Kowalski's life miserable.

After a while, I dialled Kirsten's number, a little suspicious as to who might answer – no one. No answer the second time either. My pulse was rising. Once again I pulled over. 'What did you tell your men?'

'Exactly as you told me, to let her go and to leave her alone.'

'Then why is there no answer when I call? Has she got her phone?'

'She must have, she's always had it. How else could she text you?'

Matters were getting out of my control. What the hell had happened to Kirsten after the HELP message? No phone contact; no knowledge of exactly where she was; no knowledge of who her cousin was, so there was no one I could call; and I was four and a half thousand miles away. I *had* to get back to the UK that night.

All this frustration did was increase my anger with Kowalski. It was time to take him to Wilson Airport. There were too many hours to wait until it got dark, but only two until most people stopped work for the day. The trouble with aviation is that regular times mean nothing. Aircraft return at all hours and people have to wait for them to administer passengers, maintain the machines, complete paperwork and more. I had to stay out of sight until it was dark, which would be about six thirty. But I couldn't leave it until too late, I had a flight to catch.

On the way to Wilson I called out, 'Can you hear me?'

A muffled reply must have meant yes. 'Don't shout for help, don't kick the car. Lie still.'

'Yes.'

The gate leading onto the air side at Wilson was manned by a disinterested individual who was listening to what sounded like a football match. I flashed my expired pass to Goma Airport across his vision. He nodded and held his tiny radio up to his ear. Something positive occurred: tinny cheering came from the speaker, and the guard danced a few steps with a huge grin on his face. He gave me a thumbs up, but he didn't move the barrier. After staring at my signals with a blank expression for a minute, he finally got the message and lifted the boom.

The slow, cautious drive down to the western end of the airport went unchallenged. On the grass were the usual dead monuments to African aviation – dirty corroding hulks of aircraft stained by dust and rain and mould. Some with engines, some without, some with parts removed, flat tyres, collapsed undercarriages, hatch doors swinging in the breeze, windows broken – wrecks.

Why did all these wrecks look so sad? There must be many reasons they no longer flew, why they no longer made pilots happy and passengers grateful, but in Africa it was highly likely that the company had run out of money. It's a tough business and not for those who only seek the prestige of owning an airline.

An Embraer 120, a thirty-passenger commuter aeroplane, sat on the grass with no engines and a collapsed left landing gear. The baggage compartment was accessed by a vertical rising door on the left side aft of the main cabin. It wasn't fastened and hung loose and ajar.

Kowalski had difficulty getting out of the car's boot, having been in there for so long. 'I have to go to the toilet,' he claimed.

It was probably true so, with the gun in full view I let him pee under the wing. I pointed to the aircraft. 'Get in there.'

'But—'

'*Get in there.*' He clambered up the high sill. The space was much bigger than the car boot – he could even move around. All I wanted was for him not to be found for seven hours. 'Don't argue with me, Kowalski. You've pursued me for months now, getting in my way, intruding on my pleasure time, desperate to involve me in CUZ Pharmaceutical's immoral investigation. I've had enough. How much will you get for capturing me? Is it a lump sum or is it profit sharing? Whatever – it stops – you've failed.

'I'm going back to Goma. I've unfinished business there. I want to have a discussion with your friend Marine Mertens.' There was no harm in creating a little alarm in the enemy camp.

I didn't know if it was possible to open the compartment from the inside, but I wasn't going to take a chance. Having latched it and enclosed him in the dark, I wedged a plank of wood between the door and the ground.

'If you make a lot of noise in the morning, I'm sure someone will hear you. From now on, stay away from me. And if any harm has come to Ms Pearman, I will hunt you down. I have recent experience of doing that successfully.'

21

I MADE IT to Jomo Kenyatta International Airport well in time for my flight. Checking in was straightforward, but that was to be expected. Passport control was a concern, though. While my Andrew Duncan identity and documents were genuine and fault-free, they were no guarantee that Ajok wouldn't find a way to exact his revenge.

'*Jambo.*' I greeted the bored looking official with a couple of gold bars on his shoulder and pushed my passport through the window of his cubicle. Without acknowledging me, the man carried on pressing a few keys, noted something with his pen and then, without looking where his hand was going, slid the passport off the counter and down onto his desk. He studied it for a few moments and looked up at me. Back down to the passport, back at me. He turned away and studied something I couldn't see below the counter.

'Is there a problem?'

He didn't answer, but pushed his chair back and stood with some effort, as if he'd been sitting too long or was seriously overweight, which he was. Clutching my passport, he waddled out, leaving me standing at his window, ignorant of why I wasn't being processed.

I turned to the queue behind me and gave a helpless shrug. An impatient woman scowled; a seasoned traveller gave me an understanding grin. Five minutes passed. People at the back of the queue left to find another. The worst thing I could do was to draw attention to myself by creating a scene.

Had Ajok found a way to stop me? Had he distributed my picture to his network of thugs, who had informed the immigration officers? After years of dodging those hunting me for my body, my paranoia was never far from the surface and was now in danger of taking control. I had to steady myself and act like a normal person.

The official re-entered his cubicle; another man with more gold bars on his epaulettes stood behind him and looked at me.

'What's the problem, please?'

A short conversation in Swahili took place, then the senior man left. My passport was stamped with unnecessary force and tossed across the counter, where I caught it before it fell.

After a whisky in the lounge, I relaxed and had another. The gangster could still stop me. If he could pull strings, if some petty authoritarian was in his pocket, he might be able to get the flight turned back and have me arrested. I wouldn't be safe until the aircraft had left Kenyan airspace. No, that was too far-fetched, even if it was possible. I tried to call Kirsten to tell her I was on my way home, but there was no answer.

On board, the cabin attendant, a seasoned, middle-aged lady asked, 'Orange juice or champagne, Mr Duncan?'

I grinned at her. 'What do you think?'

She laughed, placed a coaster on my shelf and put the fizz on it. 'I'll be back with more later.'

As the aircraft doors were closed, I relaxed a step. As we reached the runway, I breathed a little easier, and easier still as we left the ground. An hour into the flight I'd had enough to drink and slept for five hours, not even disturbed by the thought of someone interfering in my life from the moment I landed at Heathrow. After all, Kowalski might have managed to get out of his baggage bay and send out a warning. Would there be a reception committee waiting for me at the airport?

There was no normal reason for entry to the UK at Heathrow to be a problem. The e-gates were not working so I joined the regular queue. Behind the row of cubicles in which Border Force officials checked passports stood three men. One of them was looking up at something above the desks. Was it a screen, its back to the queue? The other two were watching the people leaving the passport gates. Were they studying the crowd, looking for someone in particular?

I kept my head down just in case. As I left the gate, tucking my passport into my pocket, the three men stepped forward, determined, forceful. No point in running, not there.

'Excuse me, sir.'

The North African man beside me stopped, frozen to the spot. Whatever he was guilty of, he knew the game was up.

22

NO SEATS WERE available on the first flight to Orkney. I caught the second, though, which arrived mid-afternoon. The sun had already set that far north and by the time I'd hired a car it was almost dark. The trip up gave me an opportunity to consider my options. I had to find Karen, Kirsten's cousin. I knew she lived in Kirkwall and was looking after Lupus, but I didn't even know her surname. If she had reported Kirsten missing, then the police would know her address. Any normal person would go to the police and ask, but I was not normal. They would want me to identify myself before giving information on the whereabouts of a missing woman. Considering I had once been suspected of Alex's murder, they were unlikely to help. And in order to protect my future, I had other reasons not to be seen by the police or anyone I knew, so it would be stupid to approach them.

My best option was to put an ad in the local papers and ask at the pub Kirsten had mentioned, the Bloodaxe. My hotel told me it was within walking distance – surprise: everything was within walking distance in that wee town.

The odd spatter of icy rain stung my cheeks. Festive lights strung across the streets swung with erratic violence in the howling wind. A large Christmas tree outside the cathedral was lit with waving blue and silver lights. A gentle oscillation of brightly lit masts showed that every fishing boat and leisure vessel in the harbour was decorated for the season. High spirits abounded. I felt out of it, being so serious.

The Bloodaxe was a warm, welcoming and crowded bar. I ordered a Skull Splitter ale, because it sounded appropriate. The barman was busy, but during a lull I asked about Karen. 'I don't know what she looks like, or what her name is, but she has been in here with my friend, who's a short, pretty redhead called Kirsten. The only way I can find her is through Karen, but I don't know where she lives.'

There was so much chatter about violence against women at the time, which probably accounted for the suspicion that was written all over his face. 'Redheads are common around here. Why're you looking?'

'Kirsten has my dog with her. I've been away, and now I'm back I want to take him home. I've been trying to call her but the number's unavailable.'

A customer at the far end of the bar rapped on the counter. The barman poured two pints and came back. 'What kind of dog?'

'He's a Malinois – looks like a German shepherd.'

'Yeah, they've been in here with the dog. Beautiful animal. Wait, I'll ask Morag if she knows this Karen and where she lives.'

Morag was the owner. She had a no-nonsense air about her and had probably thrown plenty of men out into the street on her own. I told my story again.

'Karen reported Kirsten missing three days ago,' Morag said.

'She's officially missing?'

She nodded.

'Look, I'll understand if you won't tell me where to find Karen, but will you tell her, Andrew is here and wants to meet. I want to find Kirsten.'

'Aye. You'd best wait. If she's home, I know she'll come straight here.' Morag disappeared A few minutes later, she stuck her head round the corner and gave me a thumbs-up.

I KEPT AN eye on the door and wondered if it was wise to have another Skull Splitter. It was good, very strong and definitely hangover material. There wasn't much coming and going through the entrance. Those inside had no intention of leaving and those outside were on their way somewhere else. A resonant tenor began to sing at the far end of the room to a chorus of cheers and boos.

A woman in a pink beanie stuck her head round the door and went out again. Another, with a red beanie, was pulled in. Lupus saw me almost immediately and took off. Drinkers scattered, beer was spilt, Karen nearly lost her feet. Lupus was up on my chest. A brave lad thought I was being attacked and grabbed his collar.

'It's all right, leave him, he's mine.'

'You must be Andrew.'

'And you must be Karen. Lupus has a way with welcomes and introductions.'

We found a table. I felt like Karen looked: tired, worried and at a loss as to what to do.

'She always took Lupus with her wherever she went,' Karen said. 'But this time she just went to get wine and milk and left him behind as he's not allowed in the shop. It's not far, maybe two hundred yards down the street from my house.'

I told her of Kirsten's odd messages. 'I think someone else was sending them, but she must have had her phone at some stage, because of the HELP message. All right, you've reported her missing. What else has happened?'

'The police have put out an appeal for witnesses. They've done house-to-house visits and had a helicopter up every day, covering all the islands. They've checked the ferries to make sure they didn't leave. The local and the Scottish press have reported it. I sense they want to turn it into a big issue. It's horrible, but I suppose it has to be done to find her.' Karen stared at me, looking for help. At that stage, I had nothing to give her.

OUTSIDE THE PUB, a young woman, a fur-lined hood shielding her from the wind yet still pink-cheeked, stepped in front of us. 'Karen, good evening. I'm Melanie from the Orkney Crier. How are you getting along? Will you consent to an exclusive interview? It will boost the publicity and might trigger some memories.'

'Sorry, not tonight. Contact me tomorrow.'

'What about you, sir? Mr, er …? Would you like to add any information that we could publish?'

At least this woman from a small-town paper was respectful, unlike those hyenas who had pestered me after Alex's murder. 'Oh, I'm just a friend, here for moral support. I'm completely ignorant about the case.'

This had to happen, of course – media attention putting my future in doubt. The worst part was they would want to put a face to words. Surreptitious pictures would be taken, and if mine was circulated nationally, any privacy would be shot to hell. My intention to remain incognito would only work if I stayed out of sight. Kirsten had to come first, though, ahead of my needs.

THERE WAS NO doubt Kowalski was behind Kirsten's disappearance. I had witnessed him telling his goons to leave her alone – or had I? His instructions had been in a Slavic language, Polish, Czech, Russian maybe? I couldn't tell the difference. He could have said anything to them.

I was making coffee the next morning: Wednesday the eleventh of December and four days since I had last heard from Kirsten. Karen answered the door and let someone in. They were talking in the hall. Police, by the sound of it, giving words of reassurance. She offered them coffee. 'Andrew's making it as we speak.'

Damn. I had found no way to tell her that I wanted to remain as anonymous as possible without encouraging questions. Now she was exposing me to the police.

'Morning, sir. I'm Sergeant Ross and this is Constable Ross – no relation. What's your connection in this terrible event?'

Same answer as last night. 'I'm just a friend, here to see what I can do to help and give moral support.' But I was torn. Should I tell them about the foreigners? In this small community, locals might well have noticed them, and therefore the search area could be minimised. But if I did, how would I explain how I knew they weren't British? I would have to lie, and that would put me on the brink of a very slippery slope.

They left armed with my name and address. In a few minutes of good-natured conversation, my plan to vanish had evaporated.

23

'WE NEED EGGS, milk and wine,' Karen said, her head almost buried in the fridge. 'We've got to have enough for Kirsten when she's back.'

I was putting on my boots. Shouldn't that 'when' be 'if'? 'I'll go past the corner shop.'

'Lupus isn't allowed in there.'

'I know. He'll be fine waiting outside.'

My walk was short and frustrating for my dog. But time not spent looking for Kirsten seemed wasted. Even so, I had to get out of the house, take a little exercise and think. Outside the shop, I told Lupus to wait and went in. Up and down the short aisles, and gathering the stuff I was told we needed, I reached the till, third in the queue.

In front of me was an old lady leaning on a stick. She had a carton of eggs and a solitary bread roll in her basket – not much money there. A great hulking figure of a man in a long black coat and a black flat cap was paying. When he reached the door, he turned side on to me. Then he glanced back and saw me looking at him. He knew me, and I knew him.

I dropped my basket and ran. Flinging his shopping across the floor, he was through the door and off down the road, his coat splaying as he ran.

'Lupus. *Fass.*'

The dog streaked ahead of me. The man risked a turn of the head, saw me, saw Lupus, and panicked. A car parked at the curb started. Grey vapour belched from its exhaust into the bitter air. The passenger door swung open. The man dived in, the vehicle already moving. His leg was still outside. His hand scrabbled for the handle to close the door. Lupus leaped. A scream of pain. The car swung out into the traffic. A screech of brakes and the crunch of colliding metal came from further back in the queue.

Lupus had the man's ankle. The car edged forward in the slow-moving traffic, dragging Lupus with it. I shouted at him, but he clung on. He was going to be hurt. I screamed at him, but when that animal has his prey, he won't let go until his handler takes over.

The car stopped. I caught up and hauled the man out of his seat. He was ashen and whimpering. Lupus's lips were curled, his long teeth sunk into the ankle. Beside me the car revved and took off into the traffic again – so much for loyalty.

'Sit, Lupus.'

He let go and sat back, panting and pleased with himself.

The man was on his back on the rain-soaked pavement. He'd lost the cap that had covered his close-cropped head. He was breathing hard, looking at the dog. I was on one side of him, Lupus on the other. People gathered round us, but at a respectful distance, wary of the animal.

'Where is she?'

'Who? Who you speak?'

'Lupus.' I pointed to a spot next to the man's shoulder. Lupus sat closer and stared into the man's eyes, drool dripping onto the black coat.

A deep voice from the crowd with an accent so heavy I could barely understand said, 'Wha's he doon? Ye canna treat a man like tha'.'

Several murmurs of agreement came from anonymous rubber-neckers. I shouted them down with, 'This man and another abducted that woman everyone is searching for.' The inside pocket of the man's coat revealed his passport. He put his hand out to stop me. Lupus bared his teeth. His hand dropped.

I flicked through the document. 'Russian,' I told the crowd.

A police siren wailed down the street. This had to be over before they arrived.

'Where is she? You tell me before the police get here or my friend here will take a chunk out of your face.'

'Okay, okay. Please, your dog go back.'

'He'll go back when you've told me where she is. The police are almost here.'

'Okay. Please, I great danger.'

'You're right you are – Lupus.'

Growl.

'*Niet*, no. Please. She in house in street.'

'What number? How far? Which side?'

'Five-six. I no know street.'

The siren stopped. A blue light continued to flash over the scene. It reflected off windows, sent slivers in random directions, turned raindrops into glittering, coloured shards and stabbed at trees.

Sergeant Ross broke through the onlookers. His namesake peered over his shoulder. He looked down on my group: the Russian on his back, torso on the pavement, legs in the road with Lupus staring down at him, and me squatting on my heels. 'Mister Duncan. That is an interesting way of conducting an interview.'

'It's effective, and no one's laid a hand on him,' I claimed, bending the truth a little. I handed Ross the Russian's passport. 'According to Comrade Semyonov here, Ms Pearman is in number fifty-six but he doesn't know which road. He's hurt his ankle and it will need medical attention, but not urgently. Perhaps he should show us the house before you take him away.'

Sergeant Ross bent down beside Lupus and flicked through the pages of the man's passport. He and the dog ignored each other. 'So, Mr, er … Semyonov. You say the woman is in number fifty-six? Did you put her there?'

He seemed willing, perhaps too willing, to cooperate. When he said he was in great danger, what kind of threat was he under? 'Sorry. I no understand.'

'Sergeant, I think it's your accent he doesn't understand. May I try?'

Ross gave me an odd look as if I was being rude. 'Aye.'

I repeated the question.

'*Da.* With Yuri,' Semyonov answered.

'Where is this house?'

'I no know. Always Yuri drive. I no know. Can walk.'

'This road, left off this road, or right?'

'Constable Ross. Arrest this man on suspicion of abduction, then put him in the car. Call the station and get them to make a list of all houses in the local area numbered fifty-six.'

'Sarge.'

'Excuse me, laddie.' A small rosy-cheeked and elderly lady in a tweed skirt had her hand up. 'Excuse me. There be a fifty-six across the way from me, but it's been empty these last few months Nice couple, they went away to Australia. Why would they want to go there? It'd be too hot for me. I've seen no movement in the house. Mind you, I don't spend my time watching the neighbours.'

Someone gave a jeering laugh.

SERGEANT ROSS, CONSTABLE Ross and prisoner Semyonov left in the police car. I wanted to go with them, but the sergeant wouldn't have Lupus in the vehicle. We ran behind, Lupus part towing me and therefore upping my pace. The car made a difficult passage through the traffic, even with its blue light and siren, so we were never far behind.

I lost it, though, and only found it again when the flash of blue struck from a side street. More officers had arrived and were preparing to break open the door.

Semyonov appeared keen on proving his good credentials and offered the police his key.

The place was empty. Sergeant Ross told me they'd found signs of occupation: food in the kitchen, dirty plates and cutlery, three beds had been slept in and three toothbrushes were in the bathroom. Semyonov confirmed that he and Yuri had stayed there guarding Kirsten. He was insistent that they had not harmed her in any way.

But now she had gone, and there was no sign of Yuri either. So the balloon of hope had expanded only to be pricked as we were on the brink of finding her. I sat on the garden wall and stroked Lupus. He was damp from the rain, and I was as flat as that balloon with the thought that we could be further from finding her at that moment than ever before.

I PLODDED BACK to Karen's house with no enthusiasm at all. We were back to square one. The only consolation was that we knew she was on the island and that it was an island – no one could leave by ferry or air without the police knowing. It would therefore only be a matter of time before someone in this small community spotted something that would lead to us finding her.

In Nairobi, Kowalski had told his men to release Kirsten, or so he had assured me. So what was puzzling was why his man, Yuri, had taken her abduction upon himself. Once caught, Semyonov had decided to save as much of his skin as he could by showing some enthusiasm in assisting the police, but his mate Yuri had taken Kirsten away, to achieve what? Was he going to demand a ransom? Was he going to offer her safety in return for me giving myself up as if playing Kowalski's game? Or was Kowalski still controlling things and hadn't given up after all? Whatever reward CUZ Pharmaceuticals had offered the man for my capture, it had to be substantial, because he had spent a lot of money on this, so far for no result.

I didn't have a key. Karen's doorbell bonged deep in the house, an ominous knell to my ear. A curtain parted briefly upstairs. Attitude – it's all about attitude. Doom in my outlook, yet Lupus's tail kept thumping at my leg.

Karen stood above me on the step. 'You've been a while. Didn't you get the wine after all?'

'Oh hell. So much has happened I clean forgot why I went out. I'll go back and get some. I need it.'

'Let Lupus stay and get six bottles while you're at it.'

Ten minutes later, I was back. The front door was unlatched and opened with a push. Nothing stirred, not even Lupus.

A cold shiver ran through my veins. A spectre of the past took my mind: Alex's hand dripped blood off the top step of the stairs; Lupus, critically wounded, lay on the floor at the foot; blood was everywhere. I blinked, and there was nothing.

I put the bottles on the floor without a clink. Adrenalin surged, arming me for anything. The lounge door, the nearest one, was ajar. I listened. Nothing. As the door opened further, the view gradually expanded. Lupus lay with his chin on the carpet, watching me. Karen sat on the couch behind him, and next to her was Kirsten, grinning her head off.

Then she was up. Her arms went round me and pulled me into her.

'Andrew, Charlie, whoever you are, you're safe,' she said into my shoulder.

'You … are you all right, unhurt?'

'I'm well – tired, but well.'

I returned her hug. It felt good to do that, and my reserve slipped a little. She looked up into my face, a question written in her eyes. Suddenly her doubt was thrown aside and she kissed me. That felt good too. I gave in. Karen cleared her throat and left the room. We stayed that way for an age, and it would have gone on longer if Lupus hadn't pushed his nose in between us.

'Sorry to make you wait, I was in the shower when you came back with Lupus. What's been going on? At one point I feared the worst.'

'I could say the same to you. First things first. Let's have a drink and I'll tell you my side.'

I did: I told her almost everything, only holding back on how Jacques was killed. I made that out to be more an accident than murder. Which was true in a way. After all, my goal was to smother the man so he would feel the way his victims had felt as they were starved of oxygen. Instead, I shot him, with no intention to kill, but he died from the wound – tough.

The two men had ambushed Kirsten as she came out of the shop and had bundled her into a car. 'They were much too strong for me and smelt of alcohol and garlic. *Yuk*. I was blindfolded and held tight. They didn't hurt me. I think the smaller one was inclined to be violent, but the big one treated me well. I don't think he was happy doing what they were doing. I was kept in a back room in the house, upstairs. The window was jammed shut so there was no way I could shout or signal to any-one for help. They took my phone.'

'I guessed. Some text messages from your number didn't look like you wrote them.'

'Well, I got the phone back briefly and sent that help message. But they caught me and removed the SIM card. I'm not sure when, because I've been drugged and don't know how much time has passed, but they had an important phone call. The big one came to me later and said they were going to let me go. He gave me some food and I passed out. I suppose they wanted to buy some time to escape before I did. Anyway, I came round and heard nothing. My door was not locked, so I crept downstairs. I didn't see them again, so I walked back here, avoiding the main road in case they were on it. I was a couple of streets away when I heard the police sirens.'

I told her how Lupus had stopped Semyonov.

'I'm sorry he was hurt. He really tried to be kind, in a rough sort of way.'

'How did they find you here? Were you followed? Did you use your normal phone at all?'

'I don't know. I'm confident I wasn't followed, but then I'm not an expert, so maybe … I did use my phone once. Stupid of me, I wasn't thinking. I suppose it was that. Sorry, it's caused a lot of trouble for you – for everyone.' She stroked Lupus for a while. 'What identity did you use to get back into the UK?'

'Andrew's. It's my only valid ID. Only Kowalski knows that Charlie and I are the same person and he's not going to divulge it – there's no point. There's a low chance that someone will work out that some fraud has taken place in this deception. Remember that Charlie Maxwell was invented for Kenya. He emerged in the country and stayed in East Africa. He was never here, he's unknown here. No one at his work knows where he is. If they check the airlines they won't find him. And, with a bit of luck, Marine Mertens believes Charlie's dead and says so. I'm sure she never knew my real name. She only talked about a mysterious, fixed-age man to me – as Charlie.

'Andrew Duncan, who no one in the region knows anything about, will be killed. There is no connection between the two. Charlie is unknown here, and Andrew is unknown there, as far as I'm aware.'

'What do you mean, "Andrew will be killed?" I don't like the sound of that.'

'When I left Goma, there were riots against MO-NUSCO, the UN force. There was fighting between rival gangs, and both terrorist and rebels fought battles with the Congolese army. Andrew got caught up in it all. Only CUZ Pharmaceuticals knows Andrew was there, because I told Kowalski I was going back. They aren't going to tell anyone about me, because I'm their closely guarded secret. Andrew being dead is the only way I can think of to halt their interest in me.'

'That feels terrible.' Her eyes on mine, she paused. 'Hang on – if Andrew died in the DRC, then how do we explain that he entered the country today?'

'That could prove to be a problem, I agree, but it would be a hell of a coincidence for a Border Force official to read about the death and remember that he'd checked my arrival yesterday, especially if that news is only published next week.

'I do need to put the minds of those at the reserve at rest, though. My friend Robert will be worried and will start asking questions soon. I'll let him know I'm alive and back in the UK for personal reasons – family crisis, great-grandpa died – or something, and that I won't be going back, sadly. Please give my regards to all, etcetera.'

Kirsten laughed. 'Your great-grandpa would be dust by now.'

'Hopefully no one makes the connection between Charlie in the DRC and Charlie in Kenya, and the knowledge stays there and doesn't find its way here. Only CUZ may be looking. No one else will be interested.'

'What about the police?'

'I'll have to sell my house and move away from the area, because if DCI Payne recognises me, the game will be up. More than that, people know you and I are connected – we've often been seen together. If Andrew, who is supposed to be dead, is spotted coming and going from your house, someone's going to ask awkward questions.'

Kirsten nodded, her disappointment obvious.

'So, may I ask you to liaise with the estate agent for the sale? I'll sign a predated letter authorising you to act on my behalf.'

'Of course. I'll do everything you need: put your house on the market, publish obituaries, and put death notices in the national papers and station toilets, if you want.' She laughed. 'By the time I'm finished, you'll be surprised to learn what a hero Andrew was – someone who lost his life in the defence of wildlife. How are you going to prosecute those traffickers?'

'I've given the WWF everything they need to interest Interpol's Wildlife Enforcement Team. Robert has a copy of all the evidence, and he's keen to take it forward. I'm disappointed, of course, because I want to fight the cause, but I must stay out of sight.'

OBITUARY

THE DAY'S COPIES of the Times, the Telegraph and the Guardian, three sensible papers irrespective of their political stance, did not cover Covid-19, because the disease had apparently only been discovered in China a few days before. A few weeks later, of course, it occupied a place on all front pages. Tucked inside in their allocated space, though, all the papers carried the same obituary, albeit with different headings.

'Man who could not die is killed.'

'Andrew Duncan passed away earlier this month in Goma in the east of the Democratic Republic of the Congo (DRC) during a battle between rival gangs.

Born on 15th January 1934, he joined the British Army in 1953 and served in the Malayan Emergency and in the Radfan Campaign (Yemen). He became an army helicopter pilot and suffered a serious accident in Malaya in 1968. His injuries were extensive and almost fatal. At the time he was thirty-four years old.

He was well known amongst a very small group of people, almost all of whom are connected to the pharmaceutical industry, for his theoretically impossible condition. Andrew Duncan never aged following that accident. He remained as fit and alert as he had been in 1968 aged thirty-four.

As soon as he realised his inability to age, Andrew determined to keep it a secret. His condition meant that he could not die of natural causes. He foresaw dire consequences for humanity and the planet if it could be replicated. He believed, as do many serious thinkers, that the root cause of our environmental crisis is over-population. Humans have outpaced all other forms of animal life. The effect is disproportionate, and any action that would help to increase global population would be both irresponsible and destructive.

Somehow, his secret became known. From that moment, Andrew was pursued by at least one giant pharmaceutical company, and was even abducted in order for them to investigate his condition. He escaped the fate of an experimental animal (as he put it) and, realising he could not fight those hunting him without broadcasting his secret to the world and making the situation worse, decided to fight for just causes.

Having almost reached the end of his natural life at the age of eighty-five and feeling he had nothing to lose, he would take extreme risks in his chosen battles.

Earlier this year, Andrew went to help shut down the appalling trafficking of wildlife in the eastern DRC, particularly that of the great apes. He gathered evidence to convict the perpetrators and was going to present it to an international body to prosecute the gangs. Unfortunately, he became embroiled in a fight between two gangs in Goma and was killed in a gun battle some time in the last week.'

***

Before You Go

Thank you for reading ***Running Forever***. Hopefully you enjoyed it. If you did and have a moment to spare, writing a short review on your favourite site will be greatly appreciated. Authors depend on reader opinions in order to produce enjoyable works. Reviews help authors to further their careers.

To find out more about the author and his works please visit: https://www.helifish.co.uk where you have the option to subscribe to his mailing list.

You can also find him on Facebook: http://www.facebook.com/casole74

Also by C.A. Sole

Thirty-Four – The first Andrew Duncan story. Andrew is a unique specimen, and the secret in his DNA could change humanity. Big Pharma sees massive profits from learning his closely guarded secret.

Andrew is framed for a gruesome murder. There are two suspects in his eyes: the giant corporation and a gang of child traffickers. Is there a connection between these two? He must find out to prove his innocence and employs barrister Kirsten Pearman to defend him. But her determination to destroy the gang goes beyond the professional – why?

As Andrew tries to dodge the tentacles of the pharmaceutical giant and avoid the police, he finds two abused children. He's torn between rescuing them or leaving them to their fate in order to bring down the entire gang of traffickers. All the while, with the help of his dog, he has to find a traditional, trained assassin before the man finds him.

\#

In ***Scott's Choice,*** Cuthbert Jonathan Scott is a young man with a dominant adventurous spirit. He grew up being indoctrinated by his father into an approach to life that was completely at odds with his nature: take no risks, caution in everything, settle down while young, save your money, on and on. A random event results in a decisive moment. He is torn between two options: following his father's teaching or being himself.

Two personae emerge. One, Jonathan, begins a life following his natural instincts. His spirit of adventure predominates. His choice has consequences which bring several life-threatening events but also great rewards.

Jonathan's alter ego, Cuff, is the brainwashed youth who tries to adopt the more cautious approach. But his nature conflicts with this and leads him on a dangerous path to escape the mundane existence which was the consequence of his choice. It seems he cannot avoid risk. Indeed, danger appears to seek him out.

Two independent stories develop in *Scott's Choice*. The tales are linked only by his friends and enemies, who continue to influence and react to events in Cuff's life in one way, and in Jonathan's life in another. However, certain events are common to both and fixed in the calendar.

Nature's Justice is the first sequel to *Scott's Choice*. It traces Jonathan's life as he and Gudrun experience a horrific event in Southern Africa. Witnesses to the killing of a rhino and the sighting of the person responsible for the trade in horns, they are chased and hounded over a thousand kilometres from the Kruger Park through South Africa and Botswana to the Victoria Falls.

The Pilot is the second sequel to *Scott's Choice*. Cuff Scott tries to follow a career to become an airline pilot, but his attempts to lead a stable and prosperous life are ruined by events.

At the flying school where he instructs, he becomes aware of someone smuggling illegal immigrants into the country by night. That's not his only problem. One of his students is being stalked by an increasingly dangerous man, and she thinks it's him.

It seems that trouble seeks him out and brings his inherent instinct for adventure to the fore. He is forced to question whether he's really the persona he's trying to be.

#

*A **Fitting Revenge*** is a thriller about extraordinary events that happen to ordinary people.

Your friends are in deep trouble. What if you take a step too far in avenging them?

In rural southern England, Alastair is helping his close friend to avoid a punishing divorce from Sandra. But Sandra is ruthless, and determined to win.

As Alastair is drawn into a situation which he battles to control, the love binding him and Juliet is ripped apart. With the common goal of rescuing their friend, they strive to work together, but the tension between them only widens the rift as Alastair faces the ruination of his life.

Fighting his way out of the turmoil, Alastair stretches reason to exact a terrible revenge for the extortion and assault that has affected his friends. In doing so, he discovers a side to himself which he never knew existed.

Revenge must be taken, but is Alastair's 'eye for an eye' concept too extreme? Will Juliet remain a love lost?

The Author

Colin Sole writes thrillers. They're different, with abstract concepts: your friend's wife is a misandrist inclined to violence; your inability to age is dangerous not wonderful; and what if you'd made a difference choice for your future?

Colin's experience in the army and as a helicopter pilot and aviation safety consultant has taken him all over the world. Hence his books include travel to exotic destinations of which he has first-hand knowledge.

He likes dogs and horses – they're honest.

There is far too much of the less-trodden world left to see.

To find out more about C.A. Sole's works and future projects, please visit: https://www.helifish.co.uk

www.ingramcontent.com/pod-product-compliance
Lightning Source LLC
Chambersburg PA
CBHW020645120726
47906CB00001B/135